"What!" He looked up, making out a shadowy figure faintly outlined against the far-off light still burning in his office. It seemed to be bent over, perhaps headed down, he couldn't tell. "Is that you, Elenice? I'm down here, in case you don't know it, and you went and turned off the light." He continued his upward trek, the wall-anchored banisters straining audibly with his every effort.

When he had gone another six steps and still received no reply, he said, "Did you hear me? Do you want me to trip and break my goddamn neck?"

The silent figure was still.

The funeral director cursed under his breath. When he was within two steps of the landing, the figure struck out with one sudden, jerking movement.

Leo Frame felt his lower teeth sink deep into the foreroof of his mouth as the foot caught him squarely under his chin, sending him reeling backward down the staircase. A splash of color flooded his brain, his scream swallowed up behind the clenched jaw as his mouth filled with blood.

GRAVE UNDERTAKING

GRAVE
UNDERTAKING

James R. McCahery

KNIGHTSBRIDGE PUBLISHING COMPANY

NEW YORK

For Ray and Linda
who never lost faith in me

Published in the United States by
Knightsbridge Publishing Company
255 East 49th Street
New York, New York 10017

ISBN: 1-877961-68-X

10 9 8 7 6 5 4 3 2 1
First Edition

Chapter One

Leo Frame bounced down the narrow, carpeted staircase, his sweaty hands clinging like leeches to the wooden banisters mounted to the walls on either side of him. His blubbery frame sent up a painful creak on each step. Once at the bottom, he paused, as he often did, to admire his handiwork in the spacious room before him. Leo Frame was proud of his Selection Room. Not just this one, of course, but those in his four other funeral homes in the state as well, not to mention those that would be in the six soon-to-be-opened chapels out of state.

The indirect lighting around the upper portion of the white, flocked walls reflected off the pure-white, tiled ceiling, giving the windowless room its cool brightness. A series of small floodlights positioned with painstaking care on overhead tracks bathed the individual open caskets below in a tasteful assortment of pastels, each suited to its subject. It had taken him a long time and a great deal of trial and error—not to mention money—before he settled on the present décor, lighting, and arrangement of merchandise. Each casket, as he was more than eager to point out to his colleagues, had its own sixty square feet of space, thus allowing for proper viewing and ultimate appreciation prior to purchase. While he no longer hid away his "cheaper" models behind closed doors, their inferior workmanship and low-grade rayon linings stood out now like sore thumbs, placed, as they were, in the proper lighting alongside the richer, expensive, metal models with their velvet linings and luxurious satins in white or pastel, each set on a thick carpet of corresponding color.

It still irked him, however, to have to admit that in spite of all his loving care, there was still the occasional client—was he correct in feeling they were becoming more common?—who would have been perfectly satisfied to send off his loved one in a flimsy, six-piece, nailed-together, pine box—or even a shroud—if it meant saving a few precious dollars. Well, even a concerned funeral director could do only so much; breeding was a thing apart. All in all, though, the dying business, as he jokingly liked to call it in private, had afforded him a very comfortable living over the years. And this was only the beginning. After all, he was only fifty-seven, and had recently begun expanding out of state, putting the Frame Funeral Home on the national scene. He would have to latch on to something clever like McDonald's golden arches, of course, something eye-catching that would become synonymous with the Frame name. It was a prospect that would take a great deal of thought.

Satisfied now that everything was in order for the night, he stretched a chubby hand behind him along the wall to the right of the staircase until it reached the dimmer knob, which he pressed with a pair of thick, stubby fingers, dousing the indirect lighting. Then, dropping his fingers to the eight switches below it, he flicked off the track lights, leaving only the dim light at the head of the stairwell.

He turned, grasped the handrails again, and pulled himself back up the staircase. Halfway up, he halted as a shadow fell across his path. Then, the light beyond went out as well.

"Shit!" He looked up, making out a shadowy figure faintly outlined against the far-off light still burning in his office. It seemed to be bent over, perhaps headed down, he couldn't tell. "Is that you, Elenice? I'm down here, in case you don't know it, and you went and turned off the light." He continued his upward trek, the wall-anchored banisters straining audibly with his every effort.

When he had gone another six steps and still received no reply, he said, "Did you hear me? Do you want me to trip and break my goddamn neck?"

The silent figure was still.

The funeral director cursed under his breath. When he was within two steps of the landing, the figure struck out with one sudden, jerking movement.

Leo Frame felt his lower teeth sink deep into the foreroof of his mouth as the foot caught him squarely under his dewlapped chin, sending him reeling backward down the staircase. A splash of color flooded his brain, his scream swallowed up behind the clenched jaw as his mouthed filled with blood.

Chapter Two

Lavina London shook open her thin copy of the morning *Record*, and having moistened a long, slender, middle finger against the tip of her tongue, paged through the upper corners of the paper to the Obituary section. Not that she expected to find old Mr. Shaw's death listed already that Monday morning (the poor man had only passed away last evening after supper), scanning the obituaries was just part of her daily routine. There were some who might have thought—even if they didn't come right out and say it—that it was because of her age (not that seventy-one was so old nowadays), but it wasn't; it was a habit, pure and simple, one that she'd acquired long ago from her mother—rest her soul—and had never relinquished.

She pushed aside the white, plastic bottle of AARP vitamins on the wood-grained-Formica tabletop and opened the paper, smoothing it out with her hands.

She propped her clear-plastic-framed reading glasses on the tip of her nose and let her eyes wander over the notices. First, the more substantial items scattered over the left-hand page—always the left-hand page; she wondered why that was—then, when she saw no names she recognized, down the regular alphabetized columns.

When she was satisfied that there was no one listed that she knew, even remotely, she flipped the paper closed, neatly patted in the protruding pages, folded it back in half, and got up from the table. She then padded over to the stove against the right-hand wall and shut off the low flame under the glass coffeepot.

She brought the pot over to the table, filled her heavy, clear-glass mug almost to the brim, and then set the pot down on a crocheted pot holder that had been her mother's. The heavenly blue morning glories, she noted sadly, were now gray with age, much like her own hair that she had once, several years back, foolishly tried to camouflage with the help of Miss Clairol.

Seated again, she raised the cup to her lips without the slightest tremor of the hand—some half her age, she knew, would even have found it necessary to use both hands—and took a careful sip of the steaming liquid. Although it was taking her longer than she had hoped, she was growing accustomed to drinking her coffee black and unadulterated, ever since Hamilton —Dr. Hamilton Dane, that is—had insisted on her avoiding all forms of sugar until her triglyceride level dropped back to within the realm of normalcy. Six hundred was a bit high for anyone, never mind "a woman in her seventies." She had almost given him a tongue-lashing for that bit of unnecessary exaggeration, but had finally settled for what she liked to consider her withering scowl.

With her left hand she tugged her yellow, knit sweater around her wide shoulders against the early-morning chill. Mid-May in the Catskills, after all, was not quite the same thing as it was in New York City. She got up again and, taking her mug along with her, went over to the doorway leading into the living room where she moved up the little plastic wheel on the Honeywell wall thermostat until she heard the furnace start up in the basement under the rear of the house.

Then she headed across the blue-and-white linoleum to the kitchen sink and looked out the small, closed window above it toward the side yard and the lake off to the right. Masses of red and white tulips bowed gently in the lake breeze in the natural-rock flower bed that Kenneth had constructed way back when the house was still merely a summer haven from their sweltering Manhattan apartment. He had put it in, as far as she could recall, soon after he built the house itself. Tracey wasn't even a teenager at the time. Ken had long since redesigned the house, enlarging it, adding their upstairs bedroom that looked out over the lake, and converting it for winter use. Lavina heaved a sigh as the memory of the years flew across the front of her mind. Poring over her old photo albums, seeing how things had changed over the years, was a nostalgic trip she never tired of taking. She was one of the few original residents still on Hemlock Lake, she, and maybe the O'Kirks in the house down the road next to her own piece of property.

It had not been easy for her after Ken died, but a

lot had happened in the intervening six years to keep her mind and body occupied. Somehow, she never felt alone or lonely in the house, however remote her New York-based daughter and son-in-law insisted she was from what they termed "civilization." Well, she'd had her share of New York and the "civilization" it afforded, and while she had loved it at the time, that time was long since gone, if not forgotten —as were so many other wonderful people and things. And while one could enjoy remembering, it was only the present that held any true meaning in life.

Lavina lifted off her glasses, took another sip of coffee, and then set the mug on the windowsill. She squinted beyond the lawn and cultivated area of her property, beyond her still-wooded plot that separated her house from the O'Kirks', and through the thinned-out pines and hemlocks. She could make out Winifred O'Kirk puttering around in her own rear yard near a stand of wild rhododendrons heavy with soon-to-burst white buds. She knew it was Winnie by the bright lavender sweater. She lifted her eyes to the recessed clock above the window. Almost ten past seven. While she regretted the fact now, she had promised to accompany Winnie to the funeral home this morning to make arrangements for her father's wake—Winnie's father, that is, old Mr. Shaw. Although they had been unable to find any actual records to substantiate the fact, it was generally believed that Peter Shaw had been ninety-seven. It was also said that he had practically run the nursing home up in Monticello, bossing staff and patients alike. Having known him when he was younger—her own age, as a matter of fact—Lavina could well believe it. Well, no one could say he hadn't lived a full life, however unproductive.

There was little movement on the lake itself now, except for the occasional bobbing of rowboats and sailing craft secured to docks around the shore. The early-morning sun reflected off the clean, white sand down at the beach end of the lake. Lavina was forever grateful that the lake community had banned the use of outboard motors. She remembered proudly having spearheaded the movement the first time the threat had cropped up; she was president of the community council at the time. A few of the younger members hadn't taken too kindly to her vehement harangues against their proposal, but then most of them were only summer residents and had long since moved on. It was a shame her antihunting campaign hadn't been as successful—not that she had completely given up in that area.

An unexpected movement across the lake brought Lavina's attention to a glorious, dawn-colored heron that was just taking wing, heading skyward. And while she couldn't actually hear it, she could imagine the thuderous flapping of the great wings, a sound she had come to know and love. The present-day lake was a far cry from what it had been when they first built here, after it had just been dug out. She could recall how unsightly it looked every spring before the snows melted upstream, sending down icy waters, enabling it to rise to its banks. Stumps and logs protruded everywhere around the shoreline in those days, and it was all but impossible to go rowing without the oars becoming weighed down and entangled in masses of sodden muck and weeds. But progress here as else-where had its drawbacks, so that the herons were becoming fewer and fewer as the marshy areas on the far side of the lake gradually disappeared. Over the years, the artificial lake had been cleared and deepened so that now it looked as good as any other God-made lake in Sullivan County—or anywhere else, for that matter.

She stifled a yawn and turned to look to the left toward the road that encircled the lake, separating the parcels of land on either side, all of which had been long since sold by the original developer. It, too, had undergone a change over the years. What was now blacktop had once been caked dirt, muddy and puddly in early spring, choke-dusty in summer—not to mention completely impassable under winter's cloak of ice and snow. Now, at least, the plows could get through. That, for Lavina, was civilization enough. Kenneth, fortunately, had lived long enough to see the progress and had been able to sit back and enjoy the fruits of his own labours—not that he really ever sat back for long; for him, finishing one project was merely the sign that it was time to undertake something new. And while the workaholic in him had often irked a younger Lavina, she was grateful now for the wonderful legacy and memories he had left her. She smiled at the thought, wrapped her hands around the still hot mug, lifted it to her lips, and took a deep swallow.

The phone rang just as she was crackling open the cellophane wrapper around a loaf of soft rye. She slipped a slice of the bread in the toaster on the kitchen counter and went over to answer the phone on the wall next to the thermostat. "Hello?"

"Lavina? Sean."

"Good morning, Sean. If you're looking for your wife, she's out in your yard. She hasn't run away with the milkman."

"More's the pity. As a matter of fact, she asked me to call. She's here whipping up a batch of her homemade frozen Aunt Jemima's Pancakes for breakfast."

"Ha, ha. Very funny," Lavina heard her friend comment in the background.

"Said she figured on leaving here about eight-thirty," Sean went on.

"Why so early? The funeral parlor doesn't open before nine or nine-thirty, does it?" Lavina stretched the coiled telephone cord across the doorway to the living room and peered through the window in the toaster just to make sure her rye toast wasn't getting too dark.

"Who knows?" Sean said. "I don't question Red here anymore once she gets an idea into that head of hers." He was referring, of course, to Winnie's walnut-red dye-job, a valiant effort to preserve to the last what had once been her crowning glory. Lavina had to admit—albeit somewhat grudgingly—that the sixty-eight-year-old woman could still have passed for fifty—well, fifty-eight, anyway.

"Does she still want me along?" Lavina asked, mentally crossing her fingers.

"Yes. And since she's taking our car, she says for you to come over here when you're ready." Well, so much for vain hopes.

"Aren't you coming along, Sean?" She moved back across to the refrigerator, yanked it open with her free hand, and slid out the butter dish from its compartment in the door, which she then swung shut with an agile hip. Back at the kitchen counter, she set the dish down alongside her paper plate.

"No. I'm to stay here by the phone—her orders, mind you, Lavina—and take any calls that might come about Pete's death—"

"Well, you never know who might try to reach us," an insistent Winnie broke in in the background. "Somebody should be here."

"She kept me up half the night drawing up a list of things that have to be done."

Lavina laughed. "You almost sound surprised." She pulled open the cutlery drawer under the counter and took out a knife, then pushed the drawer closed again. Without waiting for the toaster to do its thing, she coaxed up the handle on the right-hand side and lifted out the piece of toast.

"You're right. I guess I shouldn't be at this stage in the game."

With the receiver cradled under her chin, Lavina quickly spread a small portion of butter across the bread, then lifted the plate and mug and brought them over to the table where she set them down. "You know, Sean," she said after a brief hesitation —more to get herself settled than anything else— "Winnie should really have her minister along with her rather than me. Just to make sure they don't try to sell her something she doesn't need. You know how some of them can be—like car salesmen, for heaven's sake. 'Dismal traders' my father used to call the lot of them. An exaggeration, I'm sure; most of them are probably as honest as the next person, but still . . . Do you know this Frame Funeral Home, by the way, Sean? As you probably remember, Ken was

waked down in the City, so I've never had any dealings with any of the parlors up this way." She took a
small bite of the toast, then, before washing it down,
quickly added, "I do know the wife, though, somewhat, come to think of it. Elice, I think her name is.
Something like that. A little on the . . . well, that's
neither here nor there. What was I saying, anyway?"

"You asked about the minister and about Frame."
Lavina could tell by his slurred words that he was
lighting a cigarette. "You'll have to ask Win about
the minister yourself. As far as Frame goes, well, I
met the fellow only two or three times—without the
wife, by the way. At the Elks, I think it was. A bit
taken with himself, I thought. Seemed more interested in making himself seen than anything else—for
business reasons, I suppose. Not that I can blame
him, of course. Business is business, no matter what it
is." Sean gave a little chuckle. "What sort he is in his
business dealings, though, I've no idea. Wait, here's
Herself now with my breakfast, motioning for the
phone. Hold on. . . ." Lavina could hear the pleasant
banter on the other end before Winifred O'Kirk managed to wrangle the phone away from her husband.

"Lavina?" she said at last as if not quite sure.
"I heard the two of you. What's all this about the
minister?"

"Winnie, I only said that I thought your minister is
the one who should be going with you to make the
funeral arrangements. Just so they don't try to put
anything over on you."

"Really, Lavina! You'd think I was a child the way
the two of you go on sometimes. And even if I wanted
Reverend Quirk along, he's up in Liberty and won't
be back until sometime tonight."

"I'm sure I could get Father Cernac to come along," Lavina said. "They'd think twice about trying anything if they saw a collar."

"You make it all sound like a case of vampires and crucifixes, Lavina. You should have more trust in people. But as long as you're so worried about it, you can play watchdog for me yourself. That leery eye of yours is as good as a religious collar any day. And besides, Leo Frame has a fine reputation, from what I've heard."

Lavina sighed. She had more than made her own bed, and now Winnie was artfully tucking her in. "And what and where did you hear about his reputation?" she asked as a last resort.

"Elenice was telling me about him only a few weeks ago. He's even planning on opening chapels—that's what she called them, anyway—out of state. He already has four or five parlors here in New York State alone. Did you know that?"

Yes. That much she knew. "Elenice? You don't mean his wife, do you?"

"Yes."

"A fine reference, if I ever heard one."

"There you go again."

"All right, all right. Forget I said anything. What do you want your watchdog to do?"

"Well, you know. You can advise me and whatnot. Let me know if you agree with any suggestions Mr. Frame might make. On prices, services, things like that. Just pretend you're Reverend Quirk or your Father whatsisname."

"Cernac."

"Right."

"I will, if that's what you want, Winnie. But I

really don't like interfering in personal matters, even when I'm asked.''

Lavina was sure she detected an intake of breath on the other end of the line. "Since when, Lavina? Since when?''

After she hung up, she finished her piece of cold toast and replenished her half-empty mug from the coffeepot on the table. She could tell it was nearly cold from the looks of it, so she rose again, and taking the mug over to the microwave on the counter opposite the toaster, stuck it in, setting the oven for two minutes. Then, taking the cassette she's brought out from her bedroom earlier, she slid it into the radio-cassette player she kept on the little kitchen desk she used for her household accounts, and returned to the microwave to wait for the buzzer to signal the end of the countdown.

Uh-uh-uh! Don't touch that dial! Listen to . . . Blonnnnndie!

She had always liked Arthur Lake, even though *Blondie* was one of the radio shows she'd never had an opportunity to act in back in the days when she was a successful and—she had to admit to herself— fairly famous radio actress. She had been twenty when she first started out. That was back in 1937. Her career in what is now called old-time radio spanned the Golden Age and beyond, eighteen years full-time on both coasts, up until 1955 when she went into what she liked to consider semiretirement, the year before Tracey had started high school. Her last performance as a full-time actress had been on *The Lux Radio Theatre*, the same year that had seen the end of the program as well. There had been a number of appearances even after that, up until 1960; she never could refuse her agent, and was still in demand, even then. And, of course, there had been television. She shuddered at the thought, even now. She'd never forget her first TV appearance; it was a *Studio One*— though, for the life of her, the story line had escaped her completely. The sight of the cameras and the knowledge that she'd somehow be seen in homes across the nation had almost frightened her to death. And while she had gone on to do a number of later roles—nothing, though, like her radio parts—she never did quite get used to the medium. Radio, on the other hand, had been something of a lark. There, only the voice mattered, and that, for Lavina at least, had never posed a problem. Even as a child, she had loved to mimic—frequently to her regret when she overstepped the line and ended up with a red bottom for her cleverness. "Nice little girls don't do things like that, Vinni," her mother never tired of telling her by way of explanation—*after* the paddling, that is. Even when it was her father who had the onerous task of carrying out the punishment. Funny, she thought now, how the nickname had never caught on outside her home; her parents had succeeded in their constant insistence that she be addressed by her full name. And so it had been all her life. Or until Kenneth had resurrected the "Vin" part of it, that is. But even then, it had been only between the two of them.

The triple buzz signaled the end of the brief microwave cycle, and she opened the door and lifted out the mug, returning with it to the table. Then, realizing that she had already lost the thread of the program she was supposed to be listening to, she moved back to the desk, stopped the tape, and rewound it. Her mind just wasn't on comedy this morning, for some reason. Perhaps it was the thought of the impending visit to the funeral parlor. *Parlor!* There she was, dating herself again. She chided herself out loud and sat down again. If she couldn't remember to use funeral *home* instead of funeral *parlor*, she was sure as shootin' bound to let *undertaker* slip out as well. The thought made her wince even more. It wasn't that she didn't know any better; she did. It was just a question of "habits of a lifetime" again; the bad ones were as tenacious as the good ones. Sometimes, even more so. It was hardly worth her while keeping abreast of the American idiom of the eighties through William Safire's column and books if she forgot to apply what she learned in her everyday dealings. Forgetting while hidden away in the mountains in Boulder, New York, was one thing; appearing provincial in public was something else.

Unconsciously sipping her coffee, she ran a steady hand through her short-cropped, steel-colored hair, styled in what she still called a feather cut. She began to wonder how Winnie had come to know Elenice Frame so well that they'd ended up discussing the woman's husband. Through her church, perhaps? The idea seemed unlikely. Elenice Frame didn't quite seem the churchgoing type, somehow. Oops, there she was again judging without knowing the facts—if, indeed, there were any to know. Not unless you can call reading a person's eyes knowing facts—as she thought she had read Elenice Frame's eyes that afternoon they had met at the Lambert garage sale. She smiled now as she recalled the sheer, childlike delight she had experienced that day after just barely beating the woman to the purchase of an obviously valuable six-piece, antique-brass fireplace set that was now sitting on the hearth in her living room. There was something in those roving, green eyes that day all right, something that seemed to say more than words ever could whenever those eyes fell on a presentable male. That day, she remembered specifically, they had drunk in her son-in-law, Damian. Had she misread the look? Well, maybe . . . Damian, at any rate, claimed she had when she teased him about it later that evening. But, then, he had also turned a lovely shade that nearly matched the brick red fireplace in front of which he was setting up her latest find. That, in itself, told her he was of much the same mind as herself, regardless of what he said.

Chapter Three

Young Marty Knappe had worked up a sweat long before it was time for his coffee break. He cursed now under his breath as he struggled alone to stack the thick-plastic bags of peat and sphagnum moss behind the nursery greenhouse. It was one hell of a way to start the work week.

"Are those young azaleas and 'dendrons all balled and burlaped?" he heard behind his broad, shirtless, glistening back from the direction of the building that adjoined the greenhouse and housed the florist shop. He'd like to ball and burlap her some day, Marty thought, smiling at the unintentional pun.

"Yes, Miss Barth," he fairly shouted, turning his wiry, blond head and catching a glimpse of her across the yard standing in the doorway of the white, concrete building. She was wearing a maroon, velvet pants suit, for God's sake, and here he was sweating like the proverbial bull.

"Are they out front? I didn't notice," she said as he crossed the dirt yard to join her.

"Most of them, yeah. George and I tackled them earlier, right after we got in." He had told George she'd be on their backs if they hadn't finished the job.

"Where's George now?"

"Potting in the greenhouse." Another of her jobs that couldn't wait.

"Good." She looked over his shoulder toward the bags of moss, dismissing them with a heavily ringed right hand. "Leave those go for a while. We have a number of funeral orders that have to be taken care of before this afternoon, so I'll need your help. Besides, you can do with the practice."

"For Frame's or up to Monticello?" the boy asked, grabbing the wooden frame of the screen door his boss held open for him, and then following her into the cool, floral-scented interior. The air was sheer heaven by comparison to the outdoors. He wondered briefly whether it had begun to warm up early or whether he was just overheated from all the muscle work.

"Frame's," Annis Barth said, stopping and turning around when she reached the center of the large shop with its two, long, windowed refrigeration units set in the walls on either side of the open work area. A five-by-eight foot black linoleum-topped worktable ran down the room from front to back. Two similar, but smaller, tables stood on the far side of each of the refrigerators, with mirrored tiles running up the walls behind them. The entrance to the greenhouse was in the rear on the left, opposite a walk-in refrigeration room.

"Go and dry yourself off and put something on

before you catch pneumonia in here," Annis Barth scolded, pulling open a wide drawer in the center table. She lifted out two pairs of bright-red-handled shears, a small knife, a handful of eighteen-gauge wire in twelve-inch lengths, and a large spool of strong, green thread. "I can't afford to have you out sick on me at a time like this."

Her concern was nothing short of edifying. How he continued to put up with her, Marty never knew; why was something else. What had started out as a part-time job three years ago during his Junior year in high school had eventually turned into a sort of modern-day apprenticeship, like the ones back in the Middle Ages he remembered reading about in World History. And while he often felt like a downright serf to this dyed-blond lady of the manor, he could hardly deny that it was a damned good opportunity to learn the ins and outs of a very profitable trade. Better, certainly, than anything he saw ahead in the already glutted computer field so many of his friends had gone on to get their degrees in. So, he'd made up his mind to grin and bear her daily shit—no matter how much it hurt to swallow his masculine pride—until such a time as he was ready to strike out on his own. The one big problem, of course, was the money he'd need to buy into a business.

He had wondered more than once whether or not Annis Barth had anyone to leave her business to, but was never able to find out. She certainly wasn't young anymore, that was for sure; he figured she had to be at least forty. Whenever he brought up the question of family or a husband, she somehow always managed to channel the conversation into shallow waters. Either that, or she barked out an order for something she suddenly decided had to be done yesterday. Her peculiar insistence on being referred to as *Miss* Barth —not even Ms.—was another unsolved puzzle he was determined to unravel.

Without a word, Marty went back to the bathroom beyond the refrigeration room, down the dark, windowless corridor cluttered with stacks of wicker baskets, fern stands, design foundations, packages of bamboo stakes, urns, heavy wire, and wood easels. When he returned a few minutes later, he was wearing a faded, yellow muscle shirt. His already tanning face was fresh and his tight, blond ringlets were wet where he had splashed his face with cold water.

"I should have told you to bring a couple of medium baskets and a few Styrofoam frames back with you," Annis Barth said, unabashed. "You want to go get them?" Neither a sorry nor a please. Not that Marty really expected either. It wasn't even a question, for that matter.

Without a word, he did as he was directed, and returned with three white baskets dangling from one muscular arm and two spray frames gripped under the other.

"These aren't for Judge Cioffi, are they?" he asked, easing the frames onto the table.

"Yes, why?" Miss Barth asked, lifting a cobweb off one of the frames and letting it waft to the floor.

"I thought his obit said 'In lieu of. . . .' " He mouthed the words slowly, careful to give the *lieu* a French pronunciation, wrong as he knew it was.

"You think I read obituaries to prospective customers?" Annis Barth asked, looking up and emphasizing her point with a flourish of one of the pairs of shears. "Especially asinine ones that could eventually end up putting me and every other florist in this country out of business. Funerals are our bread and butter.'' She jabbed the shears now in Marty's direction, causing him to pull back his chest with a jerk. ''Today, it's 'Please omit flowers'; tomorrow, it will be ''Please omit mortician'—and the assholes will be too dumb to know what hit them. It's about time they woke up—the bunch of them—and realized the direction the funeral business is headed in, before it's too late. For starters, they *all* have to get together and support the florist. This is something we have to fight together . . . and don't you forget it!''

In a way, Marty felt proud that she included him in her imagined battle, as silly as he thought the whole thing was. He knew the situation was a sore point with her, though, as it was with many florists nowadays, and one that had caused quite a bit of friction between her and Leo Frame, for one. The funeral director, he knew, couldn't care less if he ever saw a flower in his establishments; he had as much as told Annis so to her face—and more than once, too. And while, as a prospective florist, Marty couldn't actually ignore the problem, he had no intention of letting it give him an ulcer, either. By the time he was established, for heaven's sake, it might well be resolved. Why project? He had enough real problems now without creating a few unnecessary ones.

He did enjoy the present storm his question had stirred up, though—which is why he had asked it in the first place. It was one of the few ways he had of getting back at the woman, though he was a bit surprised she never caught on to him. If she ever did, she might well terminate their feudal relationship—and then where would he be? He'd have to be extra cautious if he intended to keep it up, which, of course, he did.

"Is there anything else you need?" he asked, ignoring the harangue now.

"Not from the back, no. Just the flowers." Without depositing the shears on the work table, she raised her hands to her hips and stood staring at him, with one toe tapping away on the rubber mats beneath her. "Do you plan on hanging on to those baskets all morning? Put the damn things down, for God's sake."

Marty looked down at the baskets that were still dangling from his left arm and felt the blood rush to his face. "Yes, ma'am," he said, letting the baskets slide down his arm, careful to grab them before they toppled over, earning him another uncalled-for rebuke. He placed them in a row at the foot of the table, then sauntered over to the refrigerator in the right wall. He remained standing in front of one of the two sliding glass doors, his left hand on the handle. When he felt his short nails digging into his palm, he eased his grip.

He watched Annis Barth at the table as she fished a few slips of white paper out of the pocket of her velvet jacket, which she then removed, hanging it around the back of the tall swivel stool at her side. Her flamboyant, home-dyed, yellow hair was brushed back over her ears and held in place on each side with a bobby pin. She bent over to decipher the writing on the slips, and Marty could see that the part at the top of her head was crooked and off center. He could also detect the dirty-blond roots under the fluorescent lighting she had turned on. The slashes she called lips stood out clearly under metallic-blue lip gloss, and looked almost cracked. The green eyes behind what he knew were contacts had seemed a little bloodshot when he'd seen them earlier. While he'd never actually seen her drunk, there were many times when he was sure he detected the smell of alcohol on her breath.

"Let's see now," Annis Barth suddenly said, choosing one of the slips of paper from the pile and shoving the others in a plastic catchall attached to the side of the table. She held the slip out in front of her. "White anything," she read, "Sixty-dollar piece. NO gladiolas." Marty remembered the order; he'd taken it himself that morning right after he opened up. The phone had been ringing even before he reached the door. "Get out a couple dozen white carnations, the same in glads, some buttons, and baby's breath. Your choice of greens." She was testing him again on the foliage.

Marty just shook his head as he slid back the door, emitting a cool blast of air. He shook the carnations out of their vase one by one. "Glads, did you say?" he asked over his right shoulder without turning around, just to make sure he'd heard correctly, though he was sure he had.

"You heard it," she said, as if reading his mind. "And make sure they're the most open ones."

The oldest ones, you mean, Marty thought, shaking his head again in disgust. Would he get to be like that after he had his own business? He sure as hell hoped not. He strode over to the work table to the left of the refrigeration unit and, with his free hand, lifted out two of the metal pails stacked underneath. He deposited the assortment of flowers in one and then returned with the pails to the still open refrigerator door where he set them down quietly on the linoleum-tiled floor. Then he dug out some asparagus fern and a bunch of laurel branches from their individual receptacles and transferred them to the empty pail.

"I heard old Mr. Shaw died last night up at the home," he said, suddenly realizing that the news hadn't been mentioned by either of them.

"Who, pray tell, is old Mr. Shaw?" Annis Barth asked.

Marty slid the refrigerator door closed and returned with the pails to the table where he set them down alongside the two wicker baskets still on the floor. Annis Barth was pressing a block of Oasis onto the pinholder she'd anchored with clay to the bottom of the third basket, now on the table. "You know," he said. "The O'Kirks over on Hemlock Lake. Mrs. O'Kirk's father."

"Sean O'Kirk's father-in-law?"

Brilliant deduction. "Yeah. You know them, don't you?"

Annis Barth shrugged without looking up. "Slightly. Where's he going to be laid out?" She hesitated. "I mean, there will be a viewing of the body, won't there?" Without waiting for an answer, she added, "Yes, of course there will. Sean O'Kirk's Irish. That's like asking if the man drinks, for heaven's sake."

Marty shrugged, and when he saw that she hadn't seen him, added, "I don't know. I haven't heard." He paused for a few seconds and then said, "I don't think Mrs. O'Kirk is Irish, though, Miss Barth, and it's her father." He made a bite at his lower lip and somehow managed to keep a straight face.

"Start on one of those sprays in there," Annis Barth said, ignoring him and nodding in the direction of the catchall. She then stood back and turned the basket on the work table from right to left and back again, looking for its best side. Since she hadn't mentioned anything about the laurel leaves and the fern, Marty figured she must have been satisfied. Well, you can't lose them all.

Chapter Four

Lavina London sat forward on the long, three-cushion, brown-leather sofa in the overly ornate office of the Frame Funeral Home watching Winifred O'Kirk pacing up and down in front of her, the woman's pink sandals sinking into the spongy wall-to-wall, dark-olive carpeting.

"Sit down, Winnie, will you. You're making me nervous."

"*I'm* making you nervous? After what happened down there?" Winifred O'Kirk snapped at her friend, momentarily halting in her tracks and pointing off vaguely into the bowels of the earth. "You've got to have nerves of steel to sit there like you're doing."

"I thought you were so cool-headed?" Lavina said with a smile that her friend missed because her back was toward her again.

"I am, Lavina, I am!" She turned to confront her friend again and stopped with her back to the closed office door. Compared with Lavina's five feet nine, Winifred O'Kirk was a shrimp—not that her friend ever actually called her such—at an inch short of five feet. Petite, though, she was not, because the two women were basically the same weight. The distribution of the excess pounds in Winnie's case somehow always gave her the appearance of waddling, Lavina thought, especially when she was moving away from you. As Lavina watched her resume the incessant pacing, she wondered whether a carefully controlled walking schedule might not be helpful. She'd have to remember to ask Dr. Dane.

"You certainly don't look it, Winnie," she said, settling the canary-yellow cardigan around her shoulders.

"Come on, Lavina! This isn't your normal, everyday, run-of-the-mill accident, you know."

"Don't be redundant, Winnie. It wasn't an accident at all. You heard what Tod said. The man was obviously murdered." She was referring, of course, to Leo Frame whose body now reposed—that was the word the funeral director would have preferred, certainly—downstairs in his own Selection Room, in his most magnificent—and certainly most expensive—solid bronze casket. Somehow, though, Lavina had found the soft, pink satin incongruous. It, and the pastel lighting, didn't quite suit the man's semirotund figure—not to mention his blood-spattered, heavily stubbled face. No matter how hard she tried, she still couldn't quite shake the image of the huge, dummy-like eyes staring off unblinking into the floodlight overhead. The whole scene had reminded her of an old *Suspense* script about an accident victim in a deathlike, catatonic state, rigid yet somehow conscious, stretched out on a laboratory table awaiting the embalmer's knife. "Dead Ernest," she believed it was called, and she'd never forgotten how, at the last minute, they discovered that the man was still alive. Thinking about it, she had wanted to bend over the display casket to see if she could detect any life-saving sign of breath in Leo Frame's body, but of course she didn't.

She and Winnie had arrived at the funeral home shortly before nine, in spite of Lavina's urging that they wait until at least nine-thirty. The immaculate, glossy-white front doors were still locked and they had to ring—bong, actually—several times before one of the doors was opened by a man who turned out to be Leo Frame's assistant. Jeffrey Marcus was in his mid-thirties, of average height, and had what looked under the Brooks Brothers suit jacket to be highly developed shoulders and arms. He had a handsome face that became more handsome, Lavina thought, as he smiled. What they used to call a winning smile. A euphemism, no doubt, for sex appeal—itself probably a euphemism, even though Lavina could remember how she and her crowd used to hide behind the less shocking "S.A." when they were teenagers. The lips themselves were thick and sensual, and the dimples a feature that had always given Lavina a case of goose flesh. Another euphemism! Lord, how their language fought to deny human nature! His light brown hair was soft and thick and looked as if it had been recently—that morning even—washed and blow-dried.

"I'm afraid Mr. Frame hasn't come down yet," he said in response to Winnie's explanation for their early visit. "I'm his assistant, Jeffrey Marcus." He closed the door behind them and directed them into the same office in which the two of them now waited for Sheriff Tod Arthur to return.

"Can you help us or do we have to wait for Mr. Frame?" Lavina asked, taking the initiative when Winnie said nothing.

"Oh, I'll be glad to be of service. Please have a seat." He motioned toward the sturdy, leather-upholstered chairs on either side and in front of the wide mahogany desk that stood before a plant-filled bay window Lavina had noticed from the outside. As he proceeded around the desk, he said, "Mr. Shaw arrived last evening from the nursing home." He hitched up his trousers at the knees and sat down in the high-backed swivel chair after the two women were seated. "My sympathies, Mrs. Kirk."

"O'Kirk," Lavina corrected for her friend.

"Right. I'm sorry. Mrs. O'Kirk."

"Thank you," Winnie finally managed, cuddling her foot-long handbag to her Maidenformed bosom. "Will you be able to wake him tonight, do you think?"

"If you wish, Mrs. O'Kirk," Jeffrey Marcus said. "Tonight or tomorrow afternoon. Mr. Shaw can be ready." In what seemed to Lavina like a deliberate attempt to avoid the word "deceased," he made it sound as if the old man were still alive and kicking. It came across more phony than anything else.

"What are the hours?" Winnie asked. "For the wake, I mean."

"Visitation is between two and five, and seven and ten." It seemed to Lavina that the word "wake" was a thing of the past, too, which was too bad. In spite of its original meaning, it still seemed a more honest and descriptive word than any of its modern replacements—visitation, visiting, viewing. But here again the funeral industry seemed to want to maintain the appearance of life rather than death, fiction rather than fact. For whom? That it was more for its own profit in the long run than for the families, relatives, and friends of "the loved one"—bless you, Evelyn Waugh—Lavina had no doubt. Well, it was their game no matter how you looked at it, so you had to follow the rules.

"I think I'd like it to start tonight," Winnie said. "Then go through tomorrow, with the funeral on Wednesday morning. I'll have to get in touch with Reverend Quirk, of course, to make sure that's all right."

"We'll take care of that, Mrs. O'Kirk," Jeffrey Marcus said, fingering a sword-shaped letter opener on the blotter before him. On his manicured nails, Lavina noticed, was clear polish. "What you'll want to do now, however, is select the casket." He rose even as he spoke and started back around the desk, rebuttoning his jacket. "The Selection Room is downstairs."

"Yes," Winnie said, rising to join him, "I suppose we should get that out of the way."

"Your friend can stay here in the office if she likes. There are plenty of magazines there on—"

"Oh, no, no, Mr. Marcus. Lavina—Mrs. London, I mean—is my moral support. I want her to come along." Winnie gave the man a faint smile and then glowered in Lavina's direction for confirmation. Lavina was sorely tempted to seek out one of the magazines and tell her to go on, but didn't quite have the heart. Instead, she merely nodded and joined them.

"As you wish, Mrs. O'Kirk," Marcus said without further discussion. "If you'll just come this way." He preceded the two women out through the doorway and across the large foyer, with its highly polished Duncan Phyfe tables, to a closed door near the rear of the building. He pulled it open and switched on a light at the head of the staircase, lighting the stairwell, and again preceded them, this time down to the Selection Room.

It was there, even before they had a chance to examine and compare the casket models on display, that they discovered the body of Leo Frame. The reason for that being the closed lid on one of the caskets—a case of the dog in the night, because it should have been open. Jeffrey Marcus had seemed more puzzled than annoyed by the fact, and had gone over to raise the lid after he flicked on a series of white and pastel lights that made the windowless basement room spring to life like a movie-theater candy counter. Lavina and Winnie had walked across the room after him and were at his side when he lifted back the heavy, pink-lined, bronze lid. "Jesus Christ!" was all he said. No niceties of language that time, certainly, though it probably could have been worse, Lavina thought later when she looked back on the incident. Winnie had let out a little screech and had turned and grabbed onto Lavina's cardigan, briefly burying her head in the taller woman's shoulder. In so doing, she had snapped off the pearl button that held the sweater in place over Lavina's shoulders, and had sent it flying. Lavina herself, as far as she could recall, had just stared down at the man lying in the lavish casket, had swallowed hard several times and had then recalled her *Suspense* episode.

When Jeffrey Marcus regained his composure, he hurriedly tried to shoo them back across the room and up the staircase. Lavina was having no part of that, however, until she first had a chance to retrieve her button. She remembered clutching at her throat where it should have been, and hoping it hadn't fallen into the casket with the dead man. It was when she stepped back to search for it in the shadows of the caskets and *prie-dieux* that she noticed the telltale stains on the white linoleum that stretched out like an ocean between the thick islands of carpet under the individual caskets. When she finally spotted it embedded in the rug where they had been standing, and picked it up, she rejoined an impatient Marcus at the foot of the stairs. She and Winnie preceded him up to the ground floor.

Back in the office, the assistant funeral director telephoned the state police and then left them, closing the door behind him. They must have been there a good twenty minutes before Ted Arthur arrived with two of his troopers. Their somber, gray uniforms couldn't have been more appropriate. When they arrived, the sheriff was shown into the office where he briefly acknowledged the women's presence and then went off downstairs, after asking them to wait.

Lavina and Ken had known Sheriff Arthur for a number of years—certainly long before he had become sheriff. In spite of the difference in their ages, they had gone out with him and his wife on several occasions, though neither couple had ever actually entertained the other in their own homes. Since Ken's death, she had seen less and less of them. As a matter of fact, this was the first time she had seen Tod since Christmas when he'd dropped off a couple of home-made wreaths and a huge fruitcake.

It was another twenty minutes before he returned to the office where Lavina had finally gotten Winnie to join her on the sofa. When the door opened, Lavina noticed an appreciable addition to his force out in the foyer. Whether they were coming or going, she couldn't tell, because they seemed to be doing both at the same time.

Sheriff Arthur left the door open and sauntered over to stand above them in front of the sofa. Lavina had to strain her neck to look up into the strong face of the six-foot-four figure. His thick, sinewy neck attested his earlier swimming career. "Mr. Marcus tells me your father passed away last night, Winnie. Sorry to hear it. Are you up to talking about this unfortunate business?" He motioned backwards with his head toward the foyer. He was still wearing his trooper's hat, its brim parallel with the deep lines that formed now across his wide brow. Lavina was con-vinced he was too proud to display his balding pate more than he had to. Not that she blamed him; the man was barely fifty, if memory served her correctly.

"I'm fine, Tod," Winnie said, toying with the rub-ber band that held her reddened hair back off her face in a carefree knot. "I'm more upset by this thing downstairs than anything else. After all, my father was an old man—ninety-seven, as far as we've been able to ascertain. His death came as no great surprise."

"Even so . . .," Arthur said hesitantly. "He was still in the nursing home, wasn't he?"

"Yes. Wayland, up in Monticello. He didn't recognize any of us anymore, of course. Not in the last three or four years, I guess. He had Old Timer's disease—or so it seemed."

This was the first time Lavina had ever heard her friend use the malapropism and it struck her as so funny that, in spite of the circumstances and surroundings, she started to laugh. "*Alzheimer's*, Winnie. Alzheimer's disease. Not Old Timer's." She laughed again and looked back up to catch a glimpse of the sheriff wiping a large hand across his mouth in an obvious attempt to keep from laughing himself.

"Well, you know what I mean, Lavina," Winnie said, shifting her handbag that sat between them on the unwrinkled leather sofa. The humor had obviously escaped her. Lavina just shook her head and pressed her lips together.

"Now, then . . .," Sheriff Arthur resumed in a deeper voice that Lavina knew was part of his official put-on. He strode over to the desk and grabbed the back of one of the upholstered, wooden chairs, then dragged it back across the rug to set it up facing them. He sat down and shifted his weight, his long legs spread apart. "Suppose you let me have your side of the story, Lavina," he said, lifting a small notepad and pen out of the pocket of his long-sleeved shirt. "Just tell me what happened here after you arrived. Winnie can fill in later if she feels you've omitted anything."

She had performed in too many mystery stories in the course of her long radio career not to have anticipated the man's request. As a matter of fact, she had gone over the incident in her mind while she and Winnie had been waiting. She told him everything she could remember as best as she could, from the moment she had first spied the hanging plants in the bay window to Jeffrey Marcus's practically barricading them in the office, omitting only one thing that she was deliberately saving for later. When she was finished, she heaved a deep sigh and sat back on the sofa.

"You should have been an investigative reporter, Lavina," Sheriff Arthur said without looking up as he continued making notations in his notepad. "You've got a fine eye for detail."

"That's true," Lavina agreed in all humility. "It comes from my background, I suppose. I used to be in radio, you know."

"Yes, so you've told me several times in the past." The sheriff smiled and looked up from his pad.

"I guess I do have a tendency to go on sometimes," Lavina admitted, a smile crossing her own unglossed, pink lips, as well. "Kenneth used to take me to task about that now and again."

"How about you, Winnie?" Sheriff Arthur asked, turning to Winifred O'Kirk. "Anything to add?" His pen was poised in midair, the pad cupped in his palm.

"Just that I nearly had a heart attack when Mr. Marcus opened that lid on the coffin."

"Casket, Winnie," Lavina corrected.

"Coffin, casket. What's the difference? A box is a box is a box—especially for someone who's dead and couldn't care less." And a box by any other name, Lavina thought. It reminded her of how her brothers used to put dead insects—at least she hoped they were dead—in little sliding matchboxes when they were children and then bury them with pomp and dignity in their homemade cemetery in the backyard behind the canvas hammock. She wondered if Leo Frame had ever played at being undertaker. Somehow, she doubted it.

"You noticed the blood, of course," she said nonchalantly as she saw Tod Arthur was on the verge of pocketing his notepad and pen.

"How could I miss it, Lavina?"

"I wasn't referring to the blood on the man's body, Tod."

"Oh?" Sheriff Arthur drew his knees together and sat up straight.

"On the floor tiles."

The pad and pen were out again. "You *are* astute, Lavina. I didn't notice it myself, but of course the boys are still busy down there. They're trained to look for such things."

"I suppose so," Lavina said, not fully convinced. "I just thought I'd mention it for what it's worth. It looks as if someone tried to wipe it up and did a lousy job. I noticed it in a few spots."

"Maybe I'll go down and have a look for myself," Arthur said, sliding the pad and pen back again in their pocket. "Just to be on the safe side." He rose and swung the chair around, carrying it back with one arm to its place near the desk. "I guess that will be all for the time being," he said, heading back toward the door. "I'll get back to you when I need you. No need for you to hang around."

"What about the casket for my father?" Winnie asked as they rose to join him. In the midst of all the excitement, they had almost forgotten what they had come for.

The sheriff stopped and rubbed his nose between two fingers. "Right," he said, and then after a hesitation added, "I'll send Mr. Marcus back in. Maybe you can make your choice from photos. I'm sure they must have a catalog of such things. No one will be allowed downstairs for a while, I'm afraid. Will that be all right?"

"I suppose it will have to be," Winnie said, and then added, "Come to think of it, I have no desire to go back downstairs anyway, as far as that goes."

"Good. That will satisfy all of us." When he finally reached the door, Tod Arthur stopped again and turned around to face them. "You didn't happen to see Mrs. Frame when you arrived, by any chance?" he asked, looking from one to the other. The two women shook their heads in unison.

"Why, is she missing?" Lavina asked, more intrigued than ever.

"No. Just wondering. I'm going up to try and question her now. They have an apartment upstairs over the funeral home." It wasn't news; Lavina had noticed it even before the establishment on Route 17 had officially opened three years earlier. She had often wondered what it must be like living above a funeral parlor—especially at night.

"I'm surprised you didn't talk to her first," Lavina said, hoping to elicit a bit of information from the far too closemouthed official. She wasn't entirely disappointed in her expectations.

"She was still a bit too upset—or so Marcus claimed. Said she hadn't known anything about the death until he broke the news after phoning us—which is probably true."

"Unless, of course, she's the one who killed him." Lavina smiled.

"Also true."

"When did he die, by the way? You have any idea?" Lavina asked. Winnie had deserted them and was now at the bay window poking at the soil with her fingers in one plastic pot after another.

"We won't know that for a while, Lavina, but it couldn't have been too late this morning judging by the early signs of rigor mortis Dr. Errol says are already present." He paused, then raising his voice added, "Lucky for the three of you he didn't sit up in the casket to greet you when Marcus opened it up." Tod Arthur chuckled between closed lips, then rubbed the back of his hand across his mouth.

Lavina laughed. "That would have made our morning for sure."

"Don't be such a ghoul, Tod Arthur," Winnie scolded, pinching out a dead begonia head.

"It *was* murder, though," Lavina prompted with a hint of a question in her voice. She certainly didn't want to be spreading information that wasn't true.

"Unless he banged up his face like that on his own and then hopped into the casket for a nap," Arthur said, turning and walking out of the door.

Chapter Five

Elenice Frame stood back from the double bedroom window and looked down into the front parking lot through the sheer, voile panels. She ran her tongue across her lips as she watched the sheriff giving what seemed to be final instructions to two troopers already on their motorcycles. When he ducked into his car and followed them out onto the now almost empty highway, she noticed that there were still two official vehicles nosed up to the yews in front of the building. She turned and walked over to her bed where she sat down on the satinlike comforter, and lifted the receiver of her private Princess phone. She hesitated, then dialed.

There were four rings before someone answered. "Evergreen. Can I help you?"

"Mr. Creighton, please."

"Sure, Mrs. Frame. Hold on." Shit. And she thought she had been so clever disguising her voice.

She waited about five seconds, then slammed down the receiver, almost knocking the phone off the night table.

She got up off the bed and moved across to the closet, opening the wide pair of louvered, folding doors. She ran both hands through her frosted hair, kicked off her white scuffs, and stared at the rack of dresses in front of her. She never wore black, and certainly didn't intend to wear it now—not that anyone really expected it anymore. Except maybe the real old-country types. Elenice was far from that; if anything, she was completely up-to-date, or so she liked to think. This morning she felt more "with it" than ever. And this was only the beginning, a new chapter, as they always liked to call fresh starts in life. Well, this was hers, and she deserved it.

She slipped out of her red-and-white-striped breakfast coat and turned to look at her full profile in the full-length mirror on the wall to her left. She sucked in her tummy under her white, lace teddy and pursed her lips. Then she ran her hands slowly down the curves of her firm body, letting them come to rest on her buttocks. She smiled at her reflection as she thought about Leo. Well, she'd never have to put up with his pink flab weighing her down anymore, pumping away like a relentless plunger until he got his rocks off. On and off in thirty seconds, that had been Leo Frame. Like an Olympics hopeful, he always seemed to be trying to break his own record. In a way, it had been just as well, even if it always meant ending up unsatisfied and frustrated. Not that she really ever needed him, of course. Poor, stupid Leo—him and his funereal friends. Deadheads all. She chuckled, enjoying the silly pun. Well, he had probably been no angel either. She had always suspected that he took his quickie sex wherever and whenever he could, probably even with a few of his dead, defenseless clients. Embalming fluid probably wasn't the only thing he'd pumped into some of them. She shivered, as she always did, at the thought, feeling dirty at the idea that he might have entered her afterward. That it might have been without a shower on his part made it even worse.

With a clatter she slid the clear-plastic hangers from left to right on the long bar, quickly inspecting and dropping one item after another until, by the time she reached the last hanger, she was standing in the midst of a veritable pyre of fabric, which if ignited would have sent her up in smoke like the Queen of Carthage. She picked up a simple beige skirt, kicked her way out of the pile, and walked over to her dresser. She pulled open the middle drawer and dug out a coordinated polo top. She slipped them on, combed her bangs forward over her high forehead, and ran a few brush strokes through her short, dark, platinum-frosted hair. Then she climbed back over the pile of clothes and took a pair of brown flats from the shoe rack on the closet floor. Sitting back on the bed, she squeezed into them with the aid of a finger, being careful not to break any of her long, polished nails.

She pushed her way across the bed and swung her legs around until she was able to reach the intercom on the night table on the far side. She pushed the button that buzzed the office downstairs. When Jeffrey Marcus finally came on, he quickly informed her that most, but not all, of the police officials had gone. And yes, Leo with them. After a brief conversation, which included specific requests on the part of the grieving widow, he promised to take care of the funeral arrangements and call the Frame's lawyer. When she released the talk button, she tilted her head back against the headboard and let out a deep sigh. She could always count on Jeffrey—most definitely she could always count on Jeffrey.

In the attic she found three, large cardboard cartons that she tossed down the flight of stairs to the landing below. She then dragged them into the bedroom where she quickly filled them with carelessly folded garments that she gathered from the heap on the floor. A quick glance back into the closet convinced her that she didn't have a thing to wear, which meant a trip up to Monticello, like it or not. Personally, she loved the idea. Leo, of course, would have had a royal fit; instead she would have what would amount to a royal fitting. After all, a widow of her standing had to have a proper wardrobe, didn't she? Clothes, a visit to the hairdresser, and of course a stop at the Barth Nurseries on the way. Annis Barth would be more than happy to whip up something special in the way of a floral tribute for a dear, departed spouse. A big, bleeding heart, maybe. Yes, Annis would be more than happy. Of that she was quite sure.

She hummed as she tucked in the flap on the last of the cartons and lifted it on top of the other two, leaving them stacked in the corner until she had a chance to contact the Mount Carmel Guild. They would take them off her hands and pass the clothes on to some deserving souls. Elenice was definitely in a mood to share her good fortune now that fate had cast her in the enviable role of young, merry widow. Life begins at forty, she reminded herself—give or take a couple of years.

She stood and looked at herself approvingly in the wall mirror again, then turned and grabbed her handbag from the vanity, careful to check her wallet for her credit cards. She'd wait and call the cemetery again later when she got back; it might be foolhardy to take the chance of appearing overeager. In the meantime, Jeffrey would make an official call with the bad news and arrange for the cremation. She smiled at the thought as she snapped her bag shut. If not for the fact that he was already dead, Leo Frame would have had heart failure at that ironic prospect for sure.

Gregory Creighton let the phone ring seven times and then hung up. He flipped closed the latest issue of *The American Cemetery* and pushed it aside on the desk in front of him. While ostensibly the mere operator of Evergreen Memorial Park, Gregory Creighton was, in fact, one of three promoters who owned the land on which the cemetery and crematory now stood, and who controlled the "nonprofit" cemetery corporation that went by the same name. This in spite of New York State legislation enacted to put a halt to such shenanigans, as the outraged general public was quick to call them; there were always ways of circumventing the law. Not one to sit back on his duff, Creighton had also insisted on being installed at the Park in the capacity of on-the-spot operator and overseer, a position that gave him the opportunity to keep an eye on anyone who might just prove to be as unscrupulous as himself.

He tilted back now in his swivel chair and looked

vacantly across the large office at the back of Karl Janowitz, his right-hand man and top pre-need promoter and salesman. "Buy now and let your *mind* rest in peace" had been just one of the man's successful advertising gimmicks. The slogan could be found on the back of the Sunday bulletin of just about every church in the county, not to mention the billboard on Route 17 just this side of Monticello. The man would have made a killing on Madison Avenue, Creighton thought—not that he had any intention of saying so to his face and thereby risking losing him to the advertising world. No way! If the man was satisfied here in his salary-plus-commission job, so be it. Some guys just didn't have the self-confidence and drive it took to get ahead in this dog-eat-dog world. Which was all right with him.

"Are you sure that was Mrs. Frame calling before, Karl?" he asked, straightening up in his chair.

"That's what Theresa said," the salesman answered, turning away momentarily from the green phosphorescent characters on his monitor. "She should know her voice by this time, don't you think?"

"There's no answer there now."

"Maybe she wasn't calling from the Home." He experimented with a few more keys on the new office addition, squinting to see the screen in the glare of the morning sun through the multi-paned, front window behind him. He went over and lowered the Levolor blinds, and then returned to take up his position at the computer-center desk that confronted him on three sides like a flat wooden triptych.

"Where else would she be calling from at this time in the morning?" Creighton asked with a glance at his watch.

"You mean there's no answer at the Home at all?" Janowitz turned again, this time with a quizzical look on his face. "That's odd."

Creighton could have kicked himself for his stupidity. He certainly couldn't tell the man that he had dialed Elenice Frame's private number, which itself had been a stupid thing to do in the first place. "It doesn't sound very likely, does it?" he said, after some very quick thinking. "Maybe I dialed the wrong number." He flipped open his personal phone directory on the desk and ran a finger down the entries under *F* until he reached Frame. Holding one finger of his left hand under the number, he reached over and picked up the receiver with his right, and dialed with the same hand. "I'll try again. I think I dialed eight nine instead of eight eight."

"You must have done something," Janowitz said. "Someone must be there, even if they're downstairs showing caskets." He quickly glanced at the clock over the front door behind him. "It's ten after eleven."

"Hello?" Creighton said into the phone, nodding his head toward Karl Janowitz and gesturing at the same time with his thumb and forefinger in the unmistakable O.K. sign. "Who's this—Mr. Marcus? This is Gregory Creighton at Evergreen Memorial Park. . . . Fine. You, too. Is Mrs. Frame there?"

He stopped talking and listened, occasionally nodding his head of wavy, sandy-colored hair, all the while maintaining eye contact with Karl Janowitz. "No kidding! . . . Incredible! . . . I see. . . . Yeah, sure. So I saved you a phone call. I'll put it on the tab." He laughed, and winked at the younger man across from him. "They have any idea who did it? . . . Yeah, I guess so. . . . Who else? Hold on till I get a pen here. . . ." He slid a thin, gold, mechanical pencil out of the desk holder and started jotting on a large, lined, yellow pad on the desk. "O.K., go on. . . . They already have a plot? . . . Her mother? What's—no, of course, that would be the same name then. . . . O.K. . . . No, I don't think so." He rolled his brown eyes up toward the top of his head in jest and then stared across again at Karl Janowitz. A couple of nods more into the phone and finally, "What did I call about? Oh, nothing important. Nothing that can't wait until after the funeral, certainly." He shook his head this time. "No, just tell her I called and that I'll see her at the service. And, Marcus, extend my sympathies, will you? . . . No problem. . . . O.K. Take care." With that, he replaced the receiver, pushed the chair back from his desk, got up, and headed toward the front door that stood open now in the warming May sun. He took a deep breath, catching the heavy fragrance of hyacinths planted in front of the pink-flowering azalea shrubs in front of the modern, white building. He looked out toward the wide drive that led up to the cemetery through the tall iron gates off to his right.

Karl Janowitz sat watching him, his hands motionless on the computer keyboard in front of him. "Anything wrong?" he finally asked when Gregory Creighton remained silent.

"Leo Frame is dead," Creighton said without turning around. He spoke as if he was giving a morning report over the local radio station. "Murdered, it would seem," he added by way of punctuation after a few seconds. His eyes followed the winding, blacktop road off to the left until they came to rest at the top of the knoll on a white-marble reproduction of Michelangelo's *Moses*.

Karl Janowitz shut off his machine and narrowed his eyes. "Who's shelling out for the champagne—you or me?"

Chapter Six

After she digested the essentials of the overblown obituary, Lavina London shifted back to the front page and started to reread the reporter's account of the murder of Leo Frame. Not once, however, did the writer actually use the melodramatic term; "homicide" or "slaying" seemed more in vogue, unless of course the reporter was just unaccustomed to writing such features. She separated the two sections of the newspaper and laid the one no longer under scrutiny on the end table to the right of her recliner.

"How often are you going to read that account, Gran?" The blond girl was curled up on the floral-print, beige sofa with a Diet 7-Up in one hand and a folded-back copy of *Swimming World* in the other, her red-trimmed, white tube socks barely visible underneath her trim figure. She wore a pair of red, satin running shorts and a flimsy white T-shirt that simply said SWIMMING, the faded iridescent figures on the front vaguely resembling swimmers performing various forms of aquatic activity.

Lavina looked across from her chair over the clear rims of her reading glasses and lowered the paper. "If you intend to sit around all morning in that skimpy outfit, Susanne, you'd better go and turn up the thermostat. I don't want you going home to your mother with a spring cold. They're the worst kind to get rid of."

"Oh, Gran, come on! I'm fine. Besides, you can't catch colds from the way you dress."

"Oh no? Then why did you bother with that warm-up outfit when you went out jogging earlier—or whatever that was you were doing this morning?"

"Because it was a little chilly out, that's all. I could have gone like this, though, without catching a cold —even if I worked up a sweat. That's a fact; I heard it on the health cable or somewhere."

Or somewhere. Lavina just shook her head, her lips pressed together. "You young people have all the answers nowadays, it would seem. We can't tell you anything. I honestly don't know what grandparents are for anymore, except maybe to side with you against your parents." She smiled and lifted up the paper again. She could never keep a straight face for long where her granddaughter was concerned—not when, as now, they were having one of their little exchanges of opinion, anyway.

She had found Susanne in the lake when she and Winnie arrived back at the house late yesterday morning following the unexpected turn of events at the funeral home and their subsequent visit to the Barth Nurseries. On her way home to New York on summer break from college up in Boston, the girl had stopped off for a surprise visit with her grandmother. Lavina had recognized her granddaughter swimming out beyond the dock as soon as she got out of the car and saw the splashing feet and bobbing blue-on-yellow Speedo bathing cap. "My granddaughter, the swimmer," was the way she usually introduced the girl to those of her friends unfortunate enough not to have met her pride and joy—and, if Susanne had any say in the matter, a future Olympics hopeful as well. She was just determined enough, too—just like her grandmother, Lavina often thought—to go out and do it. As it was, she seemed to spend half her waking day in one pool or another. Lavina found it impossible to keep track of all her meets and medals; even worse, she could never remember whether the Boston school was College or University, and since there actually were two such different institutions, she was always extremely careful whenever the subject came up.

"In answer to your original question, young lady," she said now behind her newspaper, "I'm going to read these accounts until I have absorbed all the facts there are to be absorbed." She gave the paper a crisp snap by way of emphasis. *So there*, it said.

"And then what?" Susanne straightened out her long muscular legs on the sofa and took a swig from the can of soda. Lavina could see her out of the corner of her eye.

"And then . . . then, we'll see."

"It sounds to me like you're up to something." She narrowed her eyes. "What is it?" She tossed the magazine onto the cocktail table in front of the sofa and, swinging her legs around until they reached the rug, sat up. "You can tell little Susu, Gran. . . ." Her blue eyes, pale like her grandmother's, seemed to twinkle in anticipation of some juicy tidbit known only to her grandmother.

The girl's resorting unexpectedly to using their private, childish nickname brought a smile to Lavina's lips. "Like you tell me everything now that you're all grown up?" she teased, peeking with a grin around the edge of the newspaper.

"I tell you more than I tell mother." The nineteen-year-old college sophomore sounded to Lavina more like that pouting little girl she used to know. "I told you all about Marty, didn't I?"

Lavina mulled a few seconds behind her newspaper, then, without putting it down, said, "You told me some things. I'm not sure I got the complete story, though."

"Gran, stop that! I told you everything there is to know—that I have this thing for him like I've never had before for *any* male." In Lavina's day, of course, it would have been "boy."

" '*Have*', did you say? Well, there you are! You told me that story nearly a year ago. I thought it was all over last fall when you went back to college. You never mentioned him after that. How was I supposed to know you're still in love with him?"

"I'm not *in love* with him, Gran. But yes, I still like him. I really thought you knew, that I told you. We kept in touch after I went back to school. Letters, phone calls. You know." It was something Lavina had guessed, of course, but not really known for sure. Susanne had spent the previous summer at the lake in Boulder with her. In a way, it had been like old times for both of them. It hadn't actually been on the girl's agenda, of course—not until she'd met the young man in question while she was making a routine stop at the nursery for additional bedding plants for her grandmother. That very evening she phoned her mother to let her know she was "staying on to keep Gran company." And from that point on, with the exception of her rigorous daily swimming schedule and the boy's job, they were together almost constantly.

"Hmmm. And, of course, you stopped by here now on your way home just to see your poor, old grandmother," Lavina said. The paper vibrated with her silent chuckle.

Susanne laughed. "Put down that silly paper you're hiding behind there, Gran. I know you're laughing."

Lavina lowered the paper to her lap, a broad grin on her face. "Too bad you weren't here Sunday to tell me all this."

"Why?"

"I was at the nursery only yesterday."

"Oh, Gran . . . not Barth's!" The athletic shoulders collapsed under the disappointment.

"Well, Winnie and I had to get the floral pieces for her father, didn't we? How was I supposed to know you had a crush on that . . . young man"—she almost said *boy*—"or that you were even going to be here, for that matter?"

"Don't call it a crush, Gran. You make it sound so adolescent."

"I'm sorry, dear, I didn't mean it that way. You'll have to forgive your old grandmother's old-fashioned vocabulary."

"Stop calling yourself old all the time, Gran." The girl leapt up from the sofa and made her way around the cocktail table over to her grandmother, crouching down and throwing her arms around her. "You're not old. You're the same as you've always been. And you're not going to change either. I forbid it. Do you hear?"

Lavina pulled the girl to her shoulder, smoothing and patting the tossled, blond head. "Whatever you say, dear." Then, to keep the tears from overflowing, she suddenly said, "Did you ever know Peter Frame?"

A startled Susanne jerked her head back and looked up into her grandmother's face. She was still on her haunches on the floor. "Who?"

"Peter Frame." Lavina picked up the newspaper again and ran a finger down the account on the front page. "It says here that Leo Frame has a son named Peter who is supposed to be away at college. It doesn't say where or what year he's in."

Susanne shook her head and rose to her feet, tucking the T-shirt into her shorts. "Never heard of him. But, then, I really never knew any of the Frames."

"Nor I," Lavina admitted. "It says here 'Leo Frame's son.' It doesn't mention the mother. I wonder . . ."

"If he went to high school up here, Marty might know him."

"Perhaps."

"Gran, what's this all about? Why are you so interested in this morbid business anyway?" She stood over her grandmother, her hands on her hips.

"I don't remember there ever being a murder here in Boulder—not in my time, anyway, which is pretty long when you stop to think about it. I don't like the idea, that's all."

"What about Mr. Davies down at the old general

store?'' The "old general store" just about *was* Boulder back in those days before the town expanded. Even housed the post office. Lavina and Ken were still summer residents at the time, building the original house. Not that Boulder was all that big now, of course, but at least it was pretty much self-sustaining, stretching out on both sides of Route 17 and embracing two lake communities as well.

"That's not quite the same thing, Susanne—not what *I* mean, anyway. That was an accidental shooting during the course of an attempted robbery —by some young punk if memory serves me correctly.''

"And this?''

"This is more personal. Closer to home, if you know what I mean. Not only do we know the people involved—however slightly—but we might even know the murderer as well." Lavina shook her head, staring blankly at her granddaughter. "I don't like the thought of it. . . . No, I don't like it at all.''

"What makes you think it wasn't a stranger this time? Someone passing through town? Doesn't the article say one of the side doors was found unlocked?''

"Yes, but according to the account there was no actual robbery of any kind, nor any indication of attempted robbery.''

"Maybe whoever it was got scared of something and ran?''

"After taking time to put Mr. Frame in one of his own caskets? No, dear, I hardly think so. That touch was just a little too clever, I think. The murderer's idea of irony, perhaps. It might also be his own undoing." Lavina turned again to look at the newspaper, though she didn't actually read it. "Frame was struck about the face—his mouth was a mess—and then put into the casket. It had to be that way, of course, and not vice versa—"

"How do you know?"

"From the blood stains on the floor, dear. I guess I forgot to tell you about that." She then proceeded to fill her granddaughter in on the particulars she had been mulling over in her mind since the night before, but that, for some strange reason, she had failed to mention to the girl.

"You sound like Nancy Drew, Gran."

Lavina ignored the remark and tapped on the paper with her fingernail by way of emphasis. "Somewhere along the line, though, something happened so that the actual death is listed as the result of asphyxia."

Susanne smiled. "That means the man died of shortness of breath, right, Gran?" Even before her grandmother had a chance to respond, she held up both hands in front of her reddening face by way of apology. "I'm sorry, Gran. Forgive me. I just couldn't pass that one up. I know it isn't funny."

"Indeed, it's not." Lavina shook her head, the makings of a smile at the corners of her lips.

"So he died of suffocation," the girl reiterated. "What does that prove? What difference does it make?"

"I suppose it all depends on what actually caused the asphyxia," Lavina said, folding the paper in half and laying it on her lap again. "The man could have choked accidentally, or been choked—strangled— which would mean the difference between man- slaughter and murder, I suppose. Perhaps he was smothered. Judging by this article, the police obviously haven't told the press everything. There's no mention of those stains on the floor I pointed out to Tod, either.''

"Sheriff Arthur would know, though, wouldn't he, Gran? About the form the asphyxia took, I mean."

"I should certainly hope so," Lavina said, as if she intended to straighten him out in case he didn't. Then, tapping her fingers on the vinyl arm of the recliner, she looked up at her granddaughter who was standing now with her legs apart, her arms folded across her small T-shirted breasts. She narrowed her pale blue eyes and halted the tapping. "When was the last time you saw Tod, Susanne?"

"Sheriff Arthur?" Susanne shrugged her shoulders and stared off into a corner of the living room beyond her grandmother. "I saw him a couple of times last summer. Once out at the post office—I remember that because he stopped me and asked about Mom and Dad. And then again later outside one of the movie theaters up in Monticello I think it was. Marty and I were just going in or coming out, I forget which. Why?" She slid one leg over to meet the other, keeping her arms across her chest.

"Tod Arthur used to be quite a swimmer in his day, you know," Lavina said, lifting off her reading glasses.

"Yes, I know."

"He could probably answer any questions you have about your backstroke or butterfly, or whatever."

Susanne gave a little laugh, then turned and went back and sat on the sofa. "I don't have any questions about swimming, Gran. If I did, I'd ask my coach. And besides, swimming has undergone quite a few changes since Sheriff Arthur's day, you know."

"Yes, dear, I'm sure it has, but that shouldn't stop

you from asking. You could pretend, you know? Come up with a couple of technical questions he'd probably know the answers to. That sort of thing. I'm quite sure something like that—especially coming from a rising, young swimming champion—would make him feel good. Boost his male ego. You know . . ." Lavina gave the girl her most concerned smile.

"I know all right. You're not fooling me with any of that malarkey, Lavina London. This is your granddaughter you're talking to, in case you forgot —the one you taught to be on the ball at all times. You think two years away at college has suddenly turned me into some sort of naive preppie?"

"Susanne! Shame on you! You're not hinting that your grandmother would ever—"

"That's exactly what I'm doing, you old faker, although I would hardly call it hinting. I'm supposed to be your *billet d'entrée*, your excuse to see Sheriff Arthur so you can find out about the cause of that man's death." She laughed. "I really hope you're not planning on playing amateur detective, Gran. The police have enough problems, I'm sure, without having you snooping about."

Actually, the idea had never really taken shape in Lavina's mind, but now that Susanne mentioned it in so many words, it got her thinking. It reminded her of a role she'd played once in a *Crime Club* show—or was it *Mystery Is My Hobby*? Well, no matter. It was a role she had thoroughly enjoyed. Would it be the same, though, in real life? She wasn't quite sure she wanted to find out.

"Don't be silly, Susanne," she said. "I just want to make sure that Tod knows how strongly I feel about this whole business, and that I want to see it cleared up as soon as possible. Murder in our own little community . . . it's like . . . like someone invading the privacy of your own home. I have that same feeling of violation you always hear about from people whose houses or apartments have been broken into."

"Gran, you're absolutely incorrigible!" The girl shook her blond head. "But, you know, it does sound a little like fun." She paused and then added, "I wonder if the sheriff would catch on, though."

The relaxed body in the recliner suddenly seemed to take on new life, with the pale blue eyes becoming bigger and brighter. "That depends on how clever your questions are, dear, don't you think?"

Chapter Seven

When he left the bus depot in Monticello that Sunday afternoon, Peter Frame had every intention of going directly to the house and having it out with his step-father once and for all. What precisely had made him change his mind he wasn't quite sure. The possible funerals maybe, or just the thought of Elenice—he didn't know. He had just decided that he wanted to spend some time alone first, before facing the man. The motel had been a spur-of-the-moment decision and he'd taken a cab to the modern, two-story establishment out on the highway. After dropping off his bags, he settled down to some serious drinking in the motel lounge.

He looked through the upturned pyramid of cocktail glasses stacked on the shelf facing him into the fluorescent-lighted mirror beyond. Although it was only a little past noon, the darkened bar had all the appearances of five-o'clock happy hour. His reflected face looked like something in an incomplete jigsaw puzzle, chopped up as it was by the glasses. It had seemed a bit clearer a while back, he thought—one or two martinis ago.

"I'll have another, Ralph," he said, tipping back the glass to let the remains of an ice cube slip into his mouth as the bartender advanced and deposited two sours in front of the couple seated to his right at the curve in the red leather-padded bar.

"The same, sir?"

"Right. A little lighter on the vermouth this time, though, O.K.?"

"Whatever you say." The short, blue-jacketed, bow-tied bartender grabbed the neck of the squat green Tanqueray bottle from the bottom shelf behind him and clinked a shovelful of ice cubes into the tall glass mixer. The dry vermouth was there and gone even before Peter Frame had a chance to check the label. The swift motion of the long, silver cocktail spool created an eddy in the clear liquid. It and the clinking of the cubes produced a temporary hypnotic effect as Peter stared vacantly into the glass. Ralph replenished the cubes in the rocks glass and with the aid of a bar strainer poured the cocktail, at the same time yanking the tab from its face-down position on his side of the bar. Then, off to the register for the inevitable tally, the clicking of the machine breaking Peter's trance.

Peter lowered his head to the brim-filled glass and took a sip, then lifted it to his lips for another. Running his tongue over his lips, he set the glass down again on the soggy, paper cocktail napkin that clung limply to the smooth bar, and slid the newspaper out from the recess under the bar ledge. He opened it, leaving it folded in half, and set it down against the leather padding. He stared down intently at the headline blazoned across the upper portion of the front page, blinking his eyes a couple of times in the dim light, and proceeded to reread the article.

"Lousy thing, ain't it?" he heard to his left when he was about half-way into the third paragraph. Looking up, he saw a young man with a flattened nose thumbing in the direction of the paper. His rugged, beardless face under the yellow construction hat was almost as dirty as his soil-encrusted white T-shirt and tight, faded jeans. When Peter looked back down without replying, the man added, "He lived here, you know, in an apartment over the funeral home."

"Yeah, so I see," Peter said finally, hoping that would be the end of it. He wasn't in the mood for small talk.

"Guys like that make a lot of enemies, I guess," hard hat insisted. The hair that protruded from underneath the hat, Peter noticed, seemed almost as yellow.

"Yeah? Like who?" He hadn't intended it to sound sarcastic, but that was the way it came out. His companion, however, didn't seem to notice, or, if he did, didn't care.

"Oh, I don't know. Business associates, I guess."

"Couldn't be a dissatisfied customer, that's for sure," Peter said, surprising himself with the bit of black humor. He lifted his glass for another sip.

Hard hat shook his head, the beginnings of a smile on his parched lips. "You got me there, pal," he said, lifting the sweating, long-nosed Schaefer bottle the bartender had set before him, and downing half its contents.

"Unless, of course, you believe in ghosts," Peter

said, letting his eyes drop surreptitiously down the length of the man's body. Unfortunately, the soiled jeans and dim lighting made it impossible for him to see anything beyond his own vivid imagination.

"Naw, only in the movies," the man said. "It will probably turn out that the wife did him in after all."

Peter gave a little start, then resumed his affected poise. "Why do you say that?"

"Well, it's usually the husband or wife, isn't it?"

"I don't know, is it?"

Hard hat shrugged. "Who do you think it was, then? Besides those ghosts, I mean." The lips parted this time in a full smile, a handsome sort of smile, Peter thought.

Peter shoved his tongue in one of his cheeks and squinted up at the man who had remained standing alongside his stool. "My money's on that son who's supposed to be away at college." How he had ever managed to be mistaken for the man's flesh and blood, he couldn't imagine. Being his stepson was curse enough.

"How could he if he was away at college?" Another slug from the bottle that he then raised aloft against the dim light for closer scrutiny.

Peter cringed. The guy was obviously more of a jerk than he'd thought, in spite of the outdoors physique. "He probably snuck into town without anyone knowing it, that's how." The lack of condescension in the delivery surprised even him.

"Could be, I guess," the man said, tossing off the remains of the beer and signaling with the empty bottle for another. He reached into his left-hand pants pocket and eased out a folded wad of bills between two fingers. He sorted out three singles and tossed them on the bar. "What motive, though?" he asked, looking across again to meet Peter's eyes, an I've-got-you-there grin on his strong face. "There has to be a motive." It sounded to Peter as if the man thought he was telling him something he didn't already know. Stupid, macho bastard.

"Maybe he had the hots for his stepmother," Peter suggested, barely managing to keep a straight face.

"Jeez, that would be real kinky, wouldn't it?" hard hat said, slipping the fingers of his left hand into his waistband and grabbing for the fresh, amber bottle with the other.

"It would be even kinkier if he was in love with his father." This in Peter's best mock-enigmatic voice.

Something in the suggestion obviously struck the man's funny bone because he burst out laughing, sending a spray of beer across the bar and causing heads to turn in the semidarkness. He set down the bottle and drew the back of his free hand across his mouth. "'Scuse me, but that one was a real corker." He swung up a tattooed arm, smacking Peter on the back, then lifted it to the younger man's shoulder in an obvious gesture of camaraderie.

Peter flinched and jerked away his body as if a reptile had alighted on his back, almost tipping over his barstool in the act. "Don't do that, buddy, okay?"

"Do what?" The man was still laughing, his arm resting lightly now on Peter's left arm.

"Touch me."

"Oh. . . ." The man slowly let his muscular arm drop to his side, an injured look furrowing his brow. "Sorry. I didn't mean—"

"Look, forget it," Peter said with a wave of the hand. "I shouldn't have flown off the handle like

that. It's just that, well, I recently had a back operation and it's still a bit tender, you know what I
mean?"

"Sure. Stupid of me in the first place. I have a
tendency to be too free with my hands sometimes."
Peter's imagination went sort of wild for a few
seconds pondering the possibilities of that one.

"Forget it," he said. He finished his martini and
nudged it along with the soggy napkin toward the
inside ledge of the bar. When he caught Ralph's eye,
he raised a finger, then turned back to his new companion. "It doesn't say anything about the funeral in
here, you know?" he said, tapping the paper with a
stubby finger. "Are the cops holding the body, I
wonder? I mean, the guy was killed Sunday night,
Monday morning, right?"

Hard hat nodded, comprehension in his deep-set
eyes.

"And there's no more in today's paper than in yesterday's." Peter folded the paper again and shoved it
back into the recess under the bar ledge.

"Some of the guys down on the job were talking
about that this morning. We're doing construction
work down on 17 at Neversink, just south of the
funeral home. One of the guys knows a couple of the
troopers real good. According to them, they're supposed to release the body sometime today."

"Did he mention if they found anything important
—anything that wasn't mentioned in the papers, I
mean?"

Hard hat paused to mull over the question, the
mouth of the beer bottle in midair just short of his
lips. "No, I don't think so." He raised the bottle and
completed the slug. "Hey, wait!"—the bottle was

barely out of his mouth again—"There *was* something. Nothing about the death or anything like that, nothing from the police or their lab guys, I mean, but —now get this—this guy's widow, this Frame dame— hey, that rhymes—"

"Sure," Peter said, "you're a poet and don't know it. Your ... legs are so big, they call you Longfellow." It wasn't even out of his mouth when he regretted saying it, and he closed his little eyes waiting for another shower bath. His companion, however, didn't even chuckle. Instead, he just went on as if he hadn't even been interrupted.

"Anyway, this guy's widow wants him cremated." He gave Peter a knowing wink. "Get it? Burned to a crisp. Sounds fishy to me. What do you think?"

Peter Frame smiled, more to himself than to his new drinking companion. "Cremation, huh? I bet that would have given the guy a slow burn if he'd still been alive to witness it." He gave a little laugh, staring down into the refilled rocks glass sitting in front of him. "That's funny, really very funny."

Hard hat looked puzzled. "Why? Probably get it done for nothing, don't you think? I mean, one of his cronies is probably in the business. Wouldn't cost him no more than a regular burial—not that he has to worry about that now." An elbow to Peter's upper arm. "Oops, sorry."

Peter ignored the poke and merely shook his nearly neckless head. "I'm afraid you don't know much about the funeral business, friend. Funeral directors, like this guy, are definitely—I mean, de-fi-nite-ly— anticremation."

"How come? Seems the way to go nowadays."

"That's the problem. The bottom line, you can be

sure, is cold, hard cash. This guy probably spent half his miserable life fighting a trend that's obviously becoming more and more acceptable and popular —Look at your own reaction just now, 'the way to go.' For funeral directors, cremation cuts into profits.''

''How come you know so much about the undertaking business?''

''All you've got to do is read the papers, friend, just read the papers.'' His tapped the one in the recess under the bar.

''The wife should have known that, though, don't you think?'' Hard hat said. Another of his brilliant deductions.

''Unless she's deaf, dumb, and blind.''

''Jeez, then she's really sticking it to this poor stiff, ain't she?''

Peter Frame smiled across at his distorted reflection that now seemed like something in a rippling pond. He wrapped a meaty mitt around his fresh drink and shifted his short, two-hundred-sixty-pound carcass on the inadequate bar stool. ''So it would seem, friend, so it would seem.''

The restaurant annexed to the Seventeener Motel was the latest addition to the sprawling unit, and for Lavina's money, equal to any in the county. What the motel itself had to offer, Lavina couldn't say, at least not from firsthand knowledge. She sat in one of the latticed, corner windows fronting the highway, with one whole side of a sumptuous, blue-velveteen booth for four to herself. Opposite her sat Winifred and Sean O'Kirk, their heads buried in their menus. She was glad to see that Winnie had been sensible and avoided black after all. When she had gone to meet her and Sean yesterday evening for the initial visit to the funeral home to view the body of old Mr. Shaw, she wasn't at all sure what to expect, since her friend had been torn between an age-old family tradition and the more practical practice of the eighties. Modernism, it would seem, had won out—at least this time around.

"What are you going to have, Lavina?" Winnie asked in a faint voice.

"I'm not sure, Winnie. The scallops look tempting." She repositioned her reading glasses and looked down into her own huge, glossy luncheon menu, opened now on the table in front of her.

"Well, take your time, dear. We can't get to the home before two, you know, so there's no sense rushing."

"Thank God for little things," Sean piped up from behind the colorful wall of his raised menu, which he subsequently lowered.

Lavina smiled and lifted off her glasses, letting them hang on their thin, silver chain over her bosom. "Yes, indeed. You remember the days when wakes went on continuously from early morning till night without a break even provided for meals?"

"How could I forget?" Sean said. "And they lasted three days at least, into the bargain."

Winifred O'Kirk sighed and closed her menu, setting it down on the table after shifting the white, linen napkin to her lap. "The only thing worse, as I recall, were those wakes held at home," she said. "I remember one I had to go to—I'll never forget it—for a little four-year-old lad who'd fallen out of a fifth-floor—

or was it sixth-floor?—apartment window. He was absolutely—"

"Winifred, *please*!" Sean scolded, his eyes heavenward. "Not before lunch."

Lavina laughed, causing her friends to join in, thus easing the mounting tension she knew they were all feeling. Death, she well knew, was never easy to face, even when expected, and the trappings surrounding it, artificial as they often were, were no less so, even when the bereaved were among friends, as now. Lavina caught Winnie's eye and just smiled. It had all the magic of a little hand-squeeze, and her friend responded in kind.

"I haven't eaten here in ages," Lavina said, looking out the wide window on her right. The sea of yellow daffodils she vaguely remembered from an earlier spring was replaced now with mammoth, red Emperor tulips that stubbornly held their royal heads erect against the periodic gusts of wind from the west. On the far side of the highway, up on a slight knoll, she could see the chalk-white Methodist church, set against a cloudless, blue sky. Even in its utter simplicity of line and its rural setting, it was somehow stately.

"Would you folks care for a drink?" Lavina turned her head, looking up to find a black-and-white clad waitress at their side, her pad palmed and pencil poised. The smile on the too-thin lips had to be sincere. She could have used a few more pounds, Lavina thought.

"A manhattan straight up for me," Winnie said without hesitation.

"Dry?"

"No. Regular. Just sweet vermouth."

"Right." As the pencil started writing, the tip of the woman's tongue appeared at the corner of her mouth.

Sean looked across at Lavina and waited.

"Oh, just a Diet 7-Up for me, if you have it," she said. The quick scribble in the woman's pad was answer enough.

"Johnnie Walker Black on the rocks," Sean added when the waitress looked up from her pad. After the final notation, she smiled again and turned on her flats and headed toward the lounge on the opposite side of the dining room.

"I thought Susanne was coming along, Lavina," Winnie said as she turned her eyes back to the again open menu.

"She is. She'll meet us at the funeral home. She wanted to stop off and see Tod Arthur first."

"Tod Arthur? Whatever for?" Winnie was looking across at her again.

"Something about swimming. Don't ask me. You know how athletes can be sometimes." Lavina returned to her own menu but kept talking. "She said she had a question she wanted to ask him about some kind of stroke or something. She mentioned the name but it didn't mean anything to me, so of course I don't remember what it was."

"Arthur was quite the swimmer in his day, I hear," Sean said, patting his jacket's breast pocket.

"This is the nonsmoking section, dear, so you'll just have to suffer through it until we leave." It would have been hard for Lavina to miss the twinkle in Winnie's eye that accompanied the devilish grin. She had to smile herself.

"You're right about Tod," Lavina said. "I'm sure

there are lots of things swimmers could learn from him even now.''

"Susanne is smart to be taking advantage of his knowledge,'' he said.

"Yes, that's true.'' How true, Sean would never know. Lavina wondered how the girl was making out with their little ploy, or if she had even gotten in to see the sheriff.

"I wonder if the Frame woman will be at the funeral home this afternoon,'' Sean said as he cut a heel from the small, round loaf of homemade bread that had been set on the table.

"Elenice?'' Winnie said.

"Is that her name?'' He sank his dentures into the slice of soft, warm bread.

"Yes. Well, I told you what Reverend Quirk told me this morning. . . .''

Sean O'Kirk nodded his white-fringed head. ''That doesn't tell me whether she'll be at the home or not. It would be interesting to see her, considering . . .''

"You sound like a callous old man, Sean O'Kirk. I'm surprised at you!''

Lavina kept looking from one to the other. She knew she had missed something someplace along the line. "What's all this about Reverend Quirk?'' she asked, leaning forward across the table.

"I thought I told you, Lavina,'' Winnie said.

"No.'' Lavina waited without changing her position.

"Well, just that when I spoke to him this morning about the death—Leo Frame's, I mean, not Father's, although, of course, we did—''

"Winnie, *please*! Get to the point.''

"I am, Lavina, I am. Give me a chance.''

Just then, the waitress returned and set their drinks

on the table, and said she would return to take their lunch order when they were ready.

"Well, anyway," Winnie continued, looking across at her friend, "when I brought it up, Reverend Quirk told me that Elenice Frame had called him— no, that's wrong; someone from Evergreen called him. Anyway, she wants him to perform the service at the cemetery after the cremation."

"Cremation!" Lavina was sure she had misunderstood. "Are you sure he said cremation, Winnie?" She sat straight up in the booth.

"Yes. Why are you acting so shocked? Cremation is perfectly acceptable nowadays among most Christian denominations."

"I wasn't thinking along religious lines, Winnie, to be perfectly honest. Doesn't it seem strange to you that a man who spent most of his adult life making a living providing Christian burial—or what used to be regarded as Christian—for everyone else should end up in a crematorium?"

Winnie pursed her lips. "Yes, I suppose so, when you put it like that. You don't think it could have been a request in his will?"

"Hardly, Winnie. Unless I'm greatly mistaken, crematorium operators are among the opposition in his business." She ran her tongue over her lips and lifted her glass tumbler, its plastic straw rising to the top. "It had to have been his wife's decision," she added, holding the straw in check.

"You hear that, Sean?" Winnie said. "You'd better watch your step if you know what's good for you, or when you go—"

"And what makes you think *I* will be the one to go first?" Sean countered with a smile.

"Those cigarettes, for one thing," Winnie said.

"I suppose it's all right with the police," Lavina said, a hint of a question in her voice.

"What's that, Lavina?" Sean asked.

"The cremation."

Sean shrugged and looked at his wife alongside him. "I suppose so," he said.

"When is this cremation and service, do you know, Winnie?"

"Sometime tomorrow morning after Father's. Reverend Quirk mentioned he'd stay on at the cemetery and come back to the lake later for a bite of lunch."

"It seems so final though, doesn't it?" Lavina said, her mind suddenly elsewhere as she took her first sip of 7-Up through the straw.

"I should have thought that death itself was rather final," Sean said with a chuckle as he bent his head to meet his raised glass.

Lavina smiled and set down her glass. "What I meant, Sean, is that once the man is cremated, they can't perform any more tests or anything."

"The police, you mean?"

"Yes. The pathologist."

"I imagine all their tests will be completed before permission is granted for cremation, Lavina, don't you think? I mean, we may live in the sticks up here, but our law enforcement isn't exactly stupid, you know," said Sean. To Lavina, it almost sounded as if he had taken the unintended innuendo personally.

"No, of course not, Sean, nor did I mean to imply such a thing. I'm quite sure Tod runs a tight ship and knows exactly what he's doing."

"That medical examiner and pathologist—Dr. Errol—is no hayseed either. I've had many a conversation with him at the Elks over one thing or another. Quick mind, believe you me."

"You seem to know an awful lot of people from the Elks I've never heard you mention before," Winnie said with a sideward glance at her husband.

"Man-talk, Winnie. Nothing that would interest you."

"I mean the people. You never mentioned Dr. Errol before to *me*. Nor even having met Mr. Frame."

Sean merely shrugged. "You probably weren't listening when I told you, that's all. On the phone more than likely." Winnie gave him a slap on the arm with the back of her hand.

"I wonder when they'll release his findings on the murder," Lavina said, her fingertips toying with the straw. "You haven't heard anything since this morning, I suppose? The paper had nothing new."

"Oh!" Winnie's face turned a telltale shade of strawberry as she set down her glass. "I guess I didn't tell you, did I, Lavina?"

Lavina looked across at her friend through squinted eyes. "What now, Winnie?"

"Brad Reeves told me this morning that the man had been smothered." Winnie tugged at the dark-blue ribbon at the nape of her neck that held back her bottle-titian hair.

Lavina sighed audibly. That made two things the woman had neglected to confide to her earlier. While it was difficult to be actually angry with her friend, especially under the present, trying circumstances, Lavina was nonetheless having a hard time biting back her annoyance. There was poor Susanne off on a wild-goose chase while the friendly mailman calmly delivers their sought-after piece of information to Winnie's doorstep. Talk about irony!

"I'm sorry, dear, really I am," Winnie said. "I know how interested you are in the murder and all. It just slipped my mind, what with the wake and everything."

"Brad didn't happen to leave off a copy of the medical report, I suppose," Lavina said, and could have bit her tongue as soon as it was out.

"The medical report?" Winnie cocked her head.

"A joke, Winnie, a joke." Lavina lifted her glasses back onto her nose and took a last quick look at the menu before closing it.

Obviously relieved, Winnie took a sip of her manhattan after sinking her teeth into the cherry at the end of her plastic cocktail pick. "According to Brad," she said, "he was smothered by the pillow in the cof—casket—we found him in. Can you imagine, Lavina? It gives me goose bumps just thinking about it."

"How did they come to that conclusion?" Lavina asked.

"It seems that when the police turned the pillow over, they found it covered with blood. Since Mr. Frame had only bled from the nose and mouth, they put two and two together and did further tests that seemed to bear out their theory."

"Meaning, of course," Lavina concluded, "that he was smothered after he'd been beaten—or whatever it was that caused that mess to his face."

"Why 'of course'?" Winnie asked.

"He wouldn't have bled very much if he'd already been dead, Winnie," Sean clarified for his wife, both hands hugging his glass.

"Oh."

"He may even have been on the floor when he was smothered," Lavina added. "Not that it makes much difference, I suppose."

Winnie cocked her head again and narrowed her eyes. "On the floor? What makes you say that?"

"The bloodstains, Winnie—or what I assume were bloodstains—that someone seems to have tried to wipe off the white tiles. Either the murderer didn't have time to do a good job, or the lighting misled him into thinking the floor was clean, I don't know which. You remember my mentioning the stains to Tod, Winnie."

Winnie pursed her lips. "I vaguely remember your saying something about blood, Lavina, but outside of that . . ."

"What puzzles me," Sean said, tapping the rim of his glass with a free index finger, "is how the body got into the casket in the first place. Could one person do that, do you think? I mean, Frame wasn't exactly a lightweight, as I recall."

"Oh, I think so," Lavina said, convinced. "If anyone was determined enough, I mean. I think people—even the police—sometimes tend to under-estimate the strength of murderers. Surely they must have more adrenaline or something coursing through their bodies once they've reached the point of being able to actually kill another human being. In a way, they're no longer themselves. Not that I mean they aren't sane—or guilty, for that matter—I'm sure they are. It's just that something seems to temporarily alter their normal personalities and capabilities." She gave a dismissive wave of a long, slender hand. "I'm not sure, of course, I never really sat down and tried to figure it out. I may even have read it somewhere."

"Maybe there were two people involved," Winnie suggested.

Lavina nodded. "That's possible, too, of course, but there's also something else that came to mind last night as I was lying in bed trying to sleep. Those casket stands with castors—aren't they collapsible? I seem to recall seeing them used at a funeral mass and then folded up and slipped into the hearse with the casket."

"I know the things you mean, Lavina," Sean said, "but you're not suggesting they can be lowered and raised with a casket on them, are you?"

"I'm not?" Lavina could feel the warmth of the flush rise to her face.

"I hardly think that's possible, Lavina, but, of course, you can check it out for yourself when we get to the funeral home."

"If it is," Winnie said, "whoever killed Leo Frame would have had to know how to operate the contraption, wouldn't he?"

"Yes," Lavina agreed, "but then no one has suggested the murderer was a stranger to the funeral business either, did they, Winnie?" She looked from Winnie to Sean, then back again, with no one venturing further comment. Instead, they lifted their glasses in unison to their lips as if in tacit agreement.

"How did Brad get all his information, by the way?" Sean asked, setting down his glass and turning to his wife.

"He works at the post office, doesn't he?" Winnie said. "That's practically the central clearinghouse for information in this town. You should know that by now, Sean."

"Not being one to listen to gossip, my dear, I'd hardly be expected to know anything of the sort." He cut another slice of the cakelike bread and smiled across at Lavina.

"I suppose that's not gossip you dish out over at the Elks on Thursday nights." Winnie chuckled and Lavina smiled and shook her head at the husband-and-wife banter she was, by now, so used to. For a few seconds she thought of Ken, smiled to herself, then tucked the pleasant memory away.

Sean, meanwhile, shook his own head, then, as he chewed on his bread, suddenly stared beyond Lavina toward the reception area of the dining room.

"Don't turn around now, Lavina, but guess who just walked in the front door."

"Sean, don't stare like that!" Winnie reprimanded, lowering her own eyes and toying with the silverware in front of her.

Sean paid no attention but, instead, was intent on the party whose movement he followed from the doorway to a table in the center of the dining room, though they were still out of Lavina's peripheral view.

"Don't just sit there, you two. Who is it?" Lavina lowered her reading glasses again on their chain as if to emphasize her plea.

"It's Elenice Frame," Winnie said in a near whisper, the eyes in her lowered head looking up to meet her friend's. "With some man."

"This is silly," Lavina said, turning around to glance over her left shoulder, and catching a clear glimpse of the couple sitting in adjoining seats at a table for four. She surprised herself to find that she was momentarily taken aback by the appearance of the woman, dressed as she was in a tight, off-white crepe de chine dress that was a near match for the frosting in her dark hair with its long, attractive bangs. The one shoe Lavina could see wrapped around the chair leg was a white, strippy sandal with a sling strap and spiked heel.

"Lavina, please! You're as bad as Sean," Winnie said.

"Who is he, do you know, Winnie?" Lavina asked without taking her eyes off the couple. The man's elbows were planted on the table, his chin resting on top of his folded hands. Lavina stared, intrigued by the dense, sandy hair that covered his wrists and the back of his hands. A lock of his wavy, sandy hair fell across his forehead as he spoke, in what seemed like hushed tones, to his female companion.

"I've never seen him before. Have you, Sean?" Winnie turned her head to her husband. "Another Elks buddy, maybe?"

"Don't be funny, Winnie. No, I don't know the man either."

"*She* seems to know him very well, though, doesn't she," Lavina said, turning back around to face her friends.

"Lavina, sometimes you can be absolutely exasperating with your innuendos. He's probably the poor woman's brother, for heaven's sake."

"Does she have a brother?"

"How should I know? It's just a for instance."

"Well, if that's her brother she's looking at like that, the situation's worse than I suspect."

Sean chuckled behind a raised palm while his wife grabbed her glass, almost spilling the drink. She took a deeper-than-usual swig, all the while glaring across at her friend.

"Don't get your bowels in an uproar, Winnie," Lavina chided. "I'm not broadcasting scandal. This is just between the three of us. And besides, I'm sure there's nothing I could do to harm the woman's reputation in the least."

Just then, the waitress returned as promised to take their order. Lavina had just asked for an extra portion of tartar sauce for her scallops when they were interrupted by the commotion in the middle of the dining room.

Lavina turned her steel-gray head in time to see Elenice Frame propel herself up from her arm chair, beckoning to someone across the dining room in the direction of the lounge. Lavina followed her eyes to see a young man plodding across the room toward the woman's table. Staggering might have been a better word for it, Lavina thought. She looked back at Elenice Frame, who had regained her seat, if not quite her poise. Then she looked again at the young man. He looked all of five feet tall, and the excess weight certainly didn't detract from the impression. Not quite "Mr. Five by Five," but not far from it either. His jowls all but sat on his collarbone, and his neck, what there was of it, was swallowed up in his stained sport shirt, which, even though unbuttoned, seemed about ready to burst. He was carrying a wrinkled, lightweight jacket across his fleshy, pink arm, and looked as though he'd slept in the nondescript, non-matching trousers.

Lavina followed his progress as he made his way over to the table, where he finally stopped without sitting down, his full face in clear view. While she could hear Elenice Frame's somewhat authoritative voice, she was unable to make out much of what the woman was saying. It was different with the young man, whose advanced state of inebriation caused him to dispense with all inhibitions.

"What's it to you anyway?" he said, pushing a fall of baby-fine hair off his high forehead with the heel of his small, thick hand. "It's none of your damn business."

"Really, Peter . . ." was all she could make out of Elenice Frame's retort, which in any event was promptly cut short by the young man, who was rapidly growing red in the face.

"What fuck do you give 'bout me—or him, for that matter? You got what you want"—Lavina couldn't be sure whether the vague sweep of his arm indicated the woman's companion or not—"You should be grateful to whoever did it."

Lavina's eyes shifted to the older man now to see if he would come to the woman's defense. He didn't. He just kept staring up at the younger man, seemingly trying to figure him out, or maybe just biding his time.

"That's the stepson," Winnie said, slapping Lavina's wrist from the other side of the table. "That's Peter Frame, I'm sure of it."

"Stepson?" Lavina said, turning again to face her friend. "The paper said son, Winnie. Are you sure?"

"Certainly I'm sure. He used to go to our church when he was still living at home. Before he went away to college, I mean. I remember Reverend Quirk pointing him out to us one Sunday after services." She turned to her husband. "You remember, Sean?"

"Vaguely," the man said.

"Hmmm. That's interesting," Lavina said, turning back again to face the other table. "I don't recall the paper mentioning that he'd shown up though."

"The poor boy," Winnie said, shaking her head. "He's obviously distraught over the whole wretched business. The drink must have gone straight to his head. I bet he hasn't had a bit of solid food since he heard about his father."

"Stepfather," Lavina corrected, cocking her ear toward the farther table.

"I wonder if maybe I should ask him—"

"Winifred O'Kirk! Don't you even consider it!" Sean said with finality. "It's a family matter, and you make sure it stays that way."

"Shh. . . ." Lavina interposed with a brusque wave of her hand.

Winnie shook her head without looking at her husband.

Peter Frame suddenly backed away from the table, yanking his arm away from Elenice Frame's grasp. In so doing, he bumped into the empty table behind him, causing a clatter of silverware, and upsetting a small, glass vase of lily of the valley. Oblivious to the accident, he turned and angled through the tables toward the lobby. He reached his destination without further incident, pulled open the heavy, glass door, and was gone. Lavina turned to watch him through the window as he headed across the walk in the direction of the motel unit off to the left. When he reached the end of the building, he rounded the corner and was soon out of sight.

When Lavina turned her attention back to the dining room, Elenice Frame and her companion were already on their feet, ready to make their own hasty exit. They were speaking with the hostess.

"You know, Sean," she said, turning back to her friends opposite her, "I think maybe Winnie was right. Maybe we should go over and see if the boy's all right. After all, he's only a lad." Twenty, twenty-one, Lavina figured, not much older than Susanne.

Sean eyed her suspiciously over the rim of his glass. "You think you two are going to get a better reception than his own mother—or stepmother—whatever she is?"

"You know, Sean, that's an interesting point. I wonder what their relationship is. I hadn't even thought about that. I don't suppose your Reverend Quirk mentioned it, did he, Winnie?"

Winnie thought for a few seconds before replying. "No, I'm sure he didn't, Lavina, now that you mention it." She turned to her husband. "And in answer to your question, dear, I'm sure that once we mention the Reverend's name, Peter will be as gentle as a lamb, and quite willing to listen to us." Talk, of course, more than listen, was what Lavina had in mind.

"Okay," Sean said. "If you two want to make fools of yourselves, be my guests. But don't think you're going to get me to traipse along with you. I'll wait for you in the bar."

"You'll wait for us in the car," Winnie corrected with a little tug at her hair ribbon.

Sean shook his head, a smile on his lips. "Why don't you at least wait until the boy sobers up a bit," he said. "Lord knows how he'll rave on in his present condition."

"Exactly," Lavina said with a twinkle in her pale blues as she dug into the fried sea-scallops and French fries the waitress had set before her.

Chapter Eight

"She didn't tell you what was so important, Sheriff?" Rob Uberon asked as he nosed the Sullivan County police car onto the highway and headed north.

"Nope. Just told me she had to see me about her husband's death."

"Think she's going to 'fess up?" The officer kept his eyes on the road, and as a result, was unable to appreciate the smirk on Tod Arthur's face.

"Elenice Frame is hardly the confessing type, Rob."

"You know her well?"

"Well enough. Well as I know any other businessman or woman in the area, anyway."

"Did she have much to do with the business? I would have thought the husband had been in complete charge."

"You're right, he was. But where money's concerned, you can be sure Elenice Frame has her two cents worth in at all times."

The morning wind had died down, leaving the highway and roadside strewn with paper refuse carried down from the surrounding hillside. Tod Arthur gave a little start as Rob Uberon narrowly missed a small cardboard carton while turning into a sharp curve in the road.

Five minutes later they reached the Frame Funeral Home and Uberon turned into the driveway. He headed up the blacktop to the front of the building, where he pulled in head-on to the low-spreading yews that hugged the base of the red-brick establishment with its double, white-enameled front doors. Tod Arthur noticed a quick movement behind the plant-filled bay window off to the right. Elenice Frame, he thought. Or one of her hirelings. Marcus, maybe.

"You want me to come in?" Uberon asked, shutting off the ignition and grabbing for the pack of cigarettes in his gray shirt pocket. The plea in his young voice was unmistakable.

"No, I guess not," Sheriff Arthur said. "Stay and enjoy your cigarette. But make sure that noise you're going to put on the radio is off before I get back." He smiled, pushed open the door on the passenger side, and got out. He wasn't even halfway up the six steps leading to the front doors before he could hear the pounding and throbbing of the rock music behind the closed car windows. He shook his head and continued up the steps.

The door to the right opened before he had a chance to reach for the antique-brass, thumb-latch handle. Jeffrey Marcus in one of his best, dark-blue suits flashed a dimpled smile from the shadows, then stepped aside to let him enter. "Sheriff," he acknowledged, closing the door behind the visitor. "It certainly didn't take you long to get here."

"I think the department can pride itself on its efficiency, Mr. Marcus," Sheriff Arthur said, a smile on his face as he followed the younger man toward the office.

Elenice Frame was sitting behind the huge desk in front of the bay window, the healthy greenery a perfect backdrop to her white dress and platinum-frosted hair. Arthur was surprised when she rose to greet him, extending a braceleted arm across the deep-mahogany desk, her breasts firm behind a tight crepe bodice. She was a handsome woman, he thought, a mighty handsome woman.

"Thank you for coming, Sheriff," she said, sitting again once the amenities were dispensed with. "I'm sorry I was so mysterious on the phone. It's just that I thought it better to see you in person." She waved a hand in the direction of the younger man, setting off a percussion of bracelets. "I think you already know Mr. Marcus."

"Oh, yes," Arthur said with a quick turn of his now hatless head. Marcus nodded with only a trace of a smile.

"You can go now, Jeffrey, and thank you," she said, quickly adding, "Any parties here for an afternoon viewing, by the way?"

"Not yet, Mrs. Frame," Marcus said with a quick glance at his watch. "And there's still just the one this afternoon—Mr. Shaw."

"Oh, yes, that's right, Mrs. O'Kirk's father. When she comes in tell her that I'll try to drop in a little later, will you?" She turned back to the sheriff, motioning for him to sit in one of the leather-upholstered chairs on either side of the desk. "A lovely woman, Mrs. O'Kirk."

Tod Arthur watched Marcus as the young man went out the door, pulling it closed after him. "You know Winifred?" he asked as he sat down, conscious too late of the marked surprise in his own voice.

"Oh, yes, pretty well. From the county arts and crafts show, for one. We worked on the same committee last fall, and then again during the last political campaign. I gather from your use of her first name that you know her better than I do," she said.

The sheriff nodded, inching forward in the leather chair. "For a number of years, Mrs. Frame." He looked down to find himself toying with the wide-brimmed, gray trooper's hat that sat on his lap. He lifted it up, then slapped it back down against his thighs. "Now, what's this all about, anyway?"

Elenice Frame reached for a cigarette in the Florentine-leather case on the desk, then gathered up the heavy, silver lighter with a swoop of the same hand. She ran the tip of her tongue over her deep-rose lips, then inserted the filter-tip cigarette between them. After lighting it, she exhaled a rushing geyser of white smoke with an upward toss of her head. Then she looked across the desk at Tod Arthur through intent green eyes. "I have just left my husband's stepson." She took another quick puff on the cigarette. "I have the strangest feeling that he's responsible for his father's death."

Outside in the corridor, Jeffrey Marcus pulled his

head away from the office door and smoothed back the side of his brown hair with a manicured hand. He then headed toward the front of the funeral home, his steps cushioned by the deep pile of the dark-olive carpet. When he reached the front door, he inched aside one of the sheer, white, voile panels covering the sidelight windows and peered out into the driveway and parking lot. Satisfied, he turned and went along the opposite corridor to a small office in the rear of the building. Once inside, he lifted the receiver off the phone on the desk and dialed.

An annoyed female voice answered on the third ring. "Barth Nurseries," it said.

"Annis, Jeff."

A hesitation at the other end. "Where are you?"

"At the funeral home."

"Anything wrong? Can you talk?"

"No. I mean, nothing's wrong. I just thought you'd like to know that the sheriff's here. Elenice called him. It seems she ran into Peter at lunch today, and is suddenly convinced that he's responsible for Leo's death. Being the good citizen that she is, she naturally contacted the police."

"Naturally."

"She's inside now trying to convince the sheriff. She claims he was bombed out of his mind when she saw him."

"Alcohol, again?"

"So it would seem."

"Stupid bastard. You'd think he'd lay off the stuff if he can't control it."

Marcus was going to say something, but changed his mind. "Yeah," he said.

"Where is he now?"

"At the Seventeener Motel."

"Have you seen him yourself?"

"No. I've been holding down the fort here all day. We had the judge's funeral this morning, and there's another viewing here now. That, and the preparations for Leo's service."

"Who's taking care of your embalming and what-not down there now that Frame's gone?"

"Dan De Georgio came down and took care of this one for us, but I suppose we'll need someone permanent. Elenice was in no frame of mind to make any decisions when I asked her this morning."

"There's nothing being held there, is there? For Frame, I mean?"

"No. Nothing till tomorrow at the cemetery after the cremation. So, actually, his preparations were the least of my worries. The police still have the body, as far as I know, and will be shipping it directly to the crematorium at Evergreen."

"I suppose they have no leads? To the murder, I mean?"

"Nothing they thought important enough to call me up about," Marcus said with a snicker.

"Don't be such a smart ass."

"Then don't ask such stupid questions. How the hell would I know if they learned anything? I'm hardly in their confidence, you know—though I may well be on their list of suspects."

"As well you should be," Annis Barth said.

"What's that supposed to mean?" Immediately conscious of his raised voice, he added in a near whisper, as if to cover up the boner, "And what about you?"

"Don't worry about me, lover. Little Annis can take care of herself." And a good thing, too, he thought.

"Well, I've told you everything I've learned at this end," Marcus said, shifting his weight from one leg to the other and staring unseeing at the black-and-white hunting print on the wall behind his desk.

"You didn't overhear the police say anything to his wife?"

"To Elenice? No. I left them alone in the office with the door closed."

Annis Barth laughed again, heartier this time. "Oh, Jeffrey, that's precious. I can just picture you—a vision of innocence."

"Well, I didn't overhear anything important, anyway—nothing I didn't already know," Marcus said, feeling the flush in his face even as he stood alone in the office.

"What's making you so nervous all of a sudden, anyway?" she asked. "I would have thought your veins were icier than that poor dead ass's."

"Well, you thought wrong."

"What happened to you last night, by the way?"

"Under the circumstances, I thought it better that we not chance being seen together."

"Don't tell me you think you're being shadowed or something."

"Don't make it sound so melodramatic. No, I'd just rather not have to explain anything right now, that's all."

"What's to explain?" She gave another little laugh. "You're becoming paranoid all of a sudden. Maybe Frame's come back to haunt you."

"Cut it out."

"What you need's a little relaxation. Stop by the house tonight."

"No, I told you! Not until after the funeral."

"Suit yourself," she conceded. Another little hesitation, then: "Unless, of course, the merry widow is taking care of you, now that the two of you have the place practically all to yourselves."

"Cut the crap, Annis, will you."

"What's she planning on doing with lover boy's ashes, by the way?"

"As far as I know, she's getting a niche at the cemetery. She mentioned earlier that she wanted to discuss it with Creighton. I haven't heard anything more about it since."

"I would have thought she would have had them scattered."

"She probably never thought of it, though I'm sure Creighton would talk her out of it if she did."

"The city dump would have been the perfect place, don't you think?" When Marcus didn't answer, she added, "Have you heard anything yet about his will?"

"Hardly. The man's barely cold."

"You mean she hasn't gotten in touch with their lawyer yet?" Annis asked. "That doesn't sound like the Elenice Frame *I* know."

"I really have no idea. Look, Annis," he said, planting his weight equally again on both feet, "I've got to go. I'll give you a ring tomorrow."

"You'll see me tomorrow," she corrected, with no trace of humor in her voice.

"I'll try. Right now I've got a lot to do here."

"I have a few more floral pieces to finish this afternoon myself," she said.

"Are they for Shaw?"

"Yes." A slight hesitation again, then: "Too bad I had to miss out on Leo. It would have been sheer joy making up a big bleeding heart for the dear."

When Marcus replaced the receiver in its cradle, he remained standing at the desk, his eyes glued on the hunting print on the wall.

"Excuse me, Mr. Marcus," a female voice said from the doorway, causing him to start and spin around to face the door he now saw he'd left open. "I didn't want to disturb you while you were talking on the phone. We didn't see anyone out front, and we'd like to discuss arrangements for tomorrow morning." Lavina London beamed, carefully taking in the man staring at her blankly from across the small room. Was she right in thinking the lips she'd found so sensuous earlier were quivering now just a bit?

Chapter Nine

It was the laughter that woke him up, or so it seemed.

The television set across the room behind him as he lay sprawled on his stomach on the bed flickered its ever-changing images in the otherwise darkened room. He half opened his eyes.

The pillowcase beneath his head was damp against his fleshy cheek. Although he couldn't actually see it in the gloom, he knew he was on top of the bedspread. He let his left hand run slowly across the fabric to make sure. It was rough. The light from the television just barely indicated the outlines of the sparse furniture in the small room. He closed his heavy eyelids again for a few seconds to get his bearings. Gradually, it came back to him. He was in the motel room. He opened his eyes again, more completely this time, and lifted his head to get a better view of the double window. As far as he could judge, it was darker outside than in. He had no idea of the time, or even what day it was. He felt for his watch on his wrist; it wasn't there.

It had happened again—the frightening blackout. He tried to think back, tried to recall everything. It was senseless, of course, but he tried anyway. He remembered the yellow hard hat and the handsome stranger. He couldn't be sure, of course, but he was almost positive he hadn't said anything to give himself away . . . certainly hadn't invited the man to his room. That was something he'd never done, would never do.

He forced himself to turn in the bed so that he was lying on his back, his eyes on the low ceiling that somehow seemed to get brighter the longer he stared at it. He'd bought the guy a drink, that he remembered, a beer . . . yes, a Schaefer. Ordered himself another martini. His fifth, was it? That, he couldn't recall, or even if it had been his last. Funny . . . he could picture the man's face as if he was still there at his side. It was a strong face, a face that had become more and more handsome as Peter downed his drinks. Still, he was sure in his heart and soul that he had done nothing stupid. But, then he could never be completely sure, could he? *Shit!* He dragged a heavy arm up from his side and rubbed a sweaty palm over his face. He couldn't feel any pain anywhere in his body except for the inevitable pounding in his head. Running his tongue continually across his lips did nothing to alleviate the dryness.

He let his meaty mitt travel down his chest as far as his stomach.

He was still in his slacks and shirt, the latter completely unbuttoned now down to his waist. The belt buckle and pants button were open, the fly unzippered. He screwed up his face in the darkness.

He stretched his left arm out across the full-sized bed and instantly recognized the object that met his fingers. A towel. He grasped it and yanked it back across his chest. He held it up to the faint, fractured light from the television, now in front of him across the room. Then he lowered it to his face. The pungent odor confirmed what he really didn't need to be told. He gathered it up and flung it across the room where it landed on the floor by the front door and once more closed his eyes, trying again to call forth the memory of the night before. The mind was relentless, like one of his stubborn bowel movements. Try as he might, he couldn't remember anything beyond that period in the lounge. Not leaving, not getting back to his motel room, nothing.

He opened his eyes again and rolled over on his left side until he faced the bathroom door in the shadows in the corner beyond the head of the bed. He swung his squat, leaden legs across the bed and planted his stockinged feet heavily on the soft rug. Behind his tiny eyes his head spun like a whirlwind. Once he was sitting up on the edge of the bed, he lowered his head between his knees until the dizziness abated. Then, he raised it, and this time his whole body with it, and dragged himself across to the bathroom.

Inside, after a bout of the dry heaves, he relieved himself without turning on the light, then went over and turned on the right-hand faucet to the sink. He cupped the cool water in the palms of his hands and splashed it over his face, three, four, five times, until he lost count, it felt so good.

It was when he was turning off the squeaking faucet that he became conscious of it. First, the click, like the sound of a door opening or closing, then the rise in volume of the television. The idiots were still laughing. Why he hadn't turned it off in the first place, he didn't know. It was certainly something he could have done without.

Driblets of water fell from his nose, chin, and earlobes. He reached out and grabbed for the towel he saw on the wall rack. He tossed it over his head, drying first his fine, thinning head of hair, then his eyes, and finally his whole face and the back of his thick neck.

He had just flipped the towel up over the shower rod and turned around when he spotted the shadowy figure approaching the bathroom door from outside. God, he *had* invited somebody back after all. He couldn't believe it. He was suddenly sick to the pit of his stomach. But where had the guy been all this time? He only had time to blink his eyes two or three times in rapid succession before he saw the swift downward motion, felt the slight, cool breeze against his recently dampened brow, felt the blow that caused a blackout of its own.

Chapter Ten

"Jupiter *Pluvius*, Rainmaker!" Lavina exclaimed as their gray limousine crackled across a pebbled patch of road leading past the cemetery office in the direction of the massive iron front gates. She turned around in the spacious seat next to Winnie O'Kirk to squint out the rear window toward the modern, white building off to their right before it passed out of sight behind a dense stand of rhododendron just inside the high, spiked-iron fence that completely enclosed the grounds of Evergreen Memorial Park. Satisfied, she turned around again to face Winnie and Sean at her side. "Did you see him?"

"See who?" Winnie said.

Lavina darted a hesitant glance at the white-haired chauffeur, who was preoccupied with the oncoming traffic. She lowered her voice just the same. "The man back there outside the cemetery office. In the doorway."

"I didn't notice, Lavina," Winnie said as she dabbed at the corner of each eye with a small, neatly folded hanky.

Sean merely shrugged his shoulders and shook his head.

"It was him," Lavina said, folding her hands complacently in her lap.

"Him who?" Winnie asked, tucking the hanky into the top of her simple, dark-blue dress.

"The man we saw at the Seventeener with Mrs. Frame. The one she was having lunch with—or going to have lunch with, I should say, before that unfortunate encounter with young Peter."

"Who *is* he?" Sean asked, bending forward to see Lavina on the other side of his wife.

"I don't know," Lavina said, "but from the way he was lounging in that office doorway, I'd say he was connected in some way with the cemetery."

"Maybe he's the caretaker," Winnie said.

"Depends on what you mean by caretaker, I guess, Winnie. He was certainly all dolled up."

"With no place to go," Sean added with a little laugh.

"I don't remember seeing him when we buried Kenneth . . . not that that means anything, of course." Lavina sat back in her seat and grabbed hold of the sturdy strap hanging near the window. "Hmmm."

"I don't like the sound of that, Lavina," Winnie said.

"The sound of what?"

"That *hmmm*."

"Hmmm," Lavina added unconsciously.

"There you go again."

"You know, Winnie," Lavina said, ignoring the comment, "I think everything went very well, all things considered. Yesterday and today both."

"Well, I have you to thank for that, Lavina, for all your help. As usual. You were Johnny-on-the-spot."

"You know what I was just thinking? When I go, I really don't want Tracey and Damian to have all those things to worry about."

" 'Fraid there's no way of avoiding it, Lavina," Sean said, looking out his window. "We all have to go sooner or later."

"That's not what I mean, Sean. Of course we do, but we can be prepared so that things are a bit easier for those we leave behind."

"What are you getting at, Lavina?" Winnie asked, suspicion clearly present in her voice.

"What I mean is that I want to have as many of these difficult things taken care of ahead of time while I can attend to them myself."

"That makes sense," Sean said. "And I think it's something that's becoming more common nowadays, too."

"You mean like selecting your own coffin and all?" Winnie said with an audible shudder.

"Well, yes, that, too, of course," Lavina said. "But what I was thinking of first was the burial site."

"But you already have a plot, don't you, Lavina?" Winnie turned again to stare at her friend. "Wasn't that a double or triple grave you purchased when you buried Ken?"

"Well, yes, of course, but . . ." She hesitated, her eyes fixed on the windshield ahead of her. ". . . well, I was thinking more in terms of a mausoleum, and—"

"A mausoleum!" Sean and Winnie in unison this time.

"Well, not a mausoleum exactly," Lavina corrected, "but one of those new kind of aboveground graves. What do they call them?"

"Condominiums?" Winnie suggested, setting them all laughing.

"Aboveground vaults, I think," Sean said. "The whole building is probably called a mausoleum."

"Well, whatever," Lavina said. "I could have Ken moved once I get it, couldn't I?"

"I don't see why not." Sean reached inside his jacket to the breast pocket of his shirt.

"No smoking in the car," Winnie scolded without even looking in her husband's direction. "What put all this in your mind, Lavina?" she asked, suspicion still in her voice.

"Oh, I don't know. I've read about them, of course. Being here and all just brought it to mind, I suppose. That, and helping you run around getting everything done. When I get home I think I'll give Evergreen a ring and have someone come out to the house."

"That man you just saw back there at the cemetery office is who you mean," Winnie said, her eyes darting accusingly at her friend.

"You think they'll come to the lake?" Sean asked. "Do they conduct business that way, I mean?"

"I imagine so," Lavina said. "And if not, I'll just make an appointment to see them out here, that's all."

Sean shifted in his seat, yanking his jacket out from underneath him. "Are you sure they have those type of vaults up here? I don't remember seeing any."

"Oh, yes." Lavina turned now to face her two friends. "They put one up two years ago or so; that's how I first read about them."

Winnie shook her dyed head, tightening the dark-blue ribbon at the nape of her neck with both hands. "You're not fooling me, Lavina London, in case you think you are. You've got more than personal business on your mind. I know you too long and too well. It's this silly murder you're interested in."

"Nonsense, Winnie!" Lavina turned to look out the closed window. "I'm just being realistic in my old age, that's all. I suppose you can thank your father for that. Him or Leo Frame."

"I wish you wouldn't go to all this trouble, Mrs. London."

"It's no trouble at all," Lavina insisted as she set the blue, plastic tray on the cocktail table in front of the floral-print, beige sofa. "I wish you'd take something with your coffee, though. I have some nice homemade coffee cake."

"That's all I'd need," Karl Janowitz said, jokingly patting his trim waist. His shoulders and back threatened to split the lightweight, mushroom-colored jacket, as did his thighs the matching slacks.

"You do much swimming?" Lavina asked, still standing in front of him, looking down. It gave her a good personal opening, if nothing else.

"Not really," Janowitz said, replacing Susanne's magazine on the table. "I was just thumbing through it while you were in the kitchen."

Lavina laughed and tossed her short-cropped, steel-gray head. "I wasn't referring to the magazine

—It's my granddaughter's, by the way, in case you were wondering—but rather to those shoulders and chest of yours. You look like a swimmer."

Janowitz looked down at his upper torso as if he hadn't checked it out in a while. "Oh, no. I just work out quite a bit, that's all. Have since I was in high school." It reminded Lavina of the old Charles Atlas cartoon ads of the scrawny wimp on the beach always getting sand kicked in his face and losing his girl until he wised up and literally shaped up.

"It has certainly paid off," she said, making her way around the front of the table.

"Thank you."

"We can get to the material you obviously want to show me after we have our coffee." She pointed with a long, slender finger to the black, ringed album on the sofa next to the pre-need promoter and took a seat alongside it. Janowitz scooped up the tome in one sinewy hand and shifted it to his other side next to the sofa armrest.

When he arrived at the house and rang the bell, Lavina got her first glimpse of him through the front, screen door. What struck her most, after the physique, was the vanilla-colored hair and eyebrows. When she'd gotten closer, she saw the early season sunburn that highlighted his fair brow, nose, and cheekbones. The eyes were pale blue with long lashes, also nearly white.

The voice she found to be rich and probably mid-Western, but she was disappointed when it announced that he was from Evergreen Memorial Park. He wasn't at all the man she expected, the one she had seen in the office doorway the morning before, the man who had shared Elenice Frame's table at the Seventeener. When she'd recovered from her momentary letdown and remembered her manners, she opened the screen door with one hand and invited him in.

"Have you been with the cemetery long, Mr. Janowitz?" she asked as she filled his mug, and then her own.

"Almost three years, Mrs. London."

"You're not from this area originally, certainly." A statement more than a question.

"Not originally, no. I'm from—"

She raised a halting palm. "Let me guess." She lowered the hand to toy with her silver eyelgass-chain and paused, studying his face as if it were there that she would somehow discover the origin of his accent. "Milwaukee," she finally hazarded.

"No." He smiled. "You want to try again?" His lips weren't as sensuous as Jeffrey Marcus's, she noted, but pleasant nonetheless. They were also somewhat chapped.

"Cincinnati?"

The salesman smiled again, broader this time, revealing a slight dimple in his right cheek. No, his left cheek, right as she faced him. He lifted his clearglass mug off the table. "Phoenix," he said, putting an end to her game.

"Oh, my, I'm way off, aren't I?" She could have kicked herself for the careless solecism, but didn't bother to correct herself. "Not that I've made a study of accents or such. I just find it interesting sometimes listening to the way people talk, and I've known a lot of people from all over. With some people, you know, the voice is almost hypnotic, Svengali-like." She laughed again, this time at herself. "Comes from listening to so much radio in my younger days, I suppose." She shook her head. "Something someone your age wouldn't know much about, I'm afraid—and to your disadvantage, I might add." She looked off beyond the man's shoulder. "Radio was a wonderful thing in its day. Left so much to the imagination. Heightened senses other than sight." She looked back again into the man's still-smiling face, a smile of her own on her lips. "The visual is all the thing today, I'm afraid. If a child can't see it, he can't possibly understand it. Even educators have bought the lie. Everything relies on visual aids." She blinked her eyes rapidly as if to chase away a ghost from the past. "You'll have to excuse me, Mr. Janowitz, sometimes I get carried away when I talk about old-time radio."

"Not at all, Mrs. London. You know, in a way, you sound like my mother." The flush that shot across Karl Janowitz's face now was clearly not the result of the sun. "I'm sorry. That must have sounded—"

"Nonsense! I know exactly what you mean. Your mother obviously had a great deal of good taste and common sense, and I'm sure most of it wore off on her handsome son." She was about to add that the woman had probably also spent many an hour listening to the once-famous voice of radio star Lavina London, too, but didn't.

"Thank you, I'd like to think so." He took a swallow of the coffee. "This is very good. I'm used to instant or diner-made, so I can really appreciate a good cup of coffee." She was surprised to see that, like herself, he drank it black and unsweetened. She refilled the mug as soon as he set it back down on the low table.

"Are you married, Mr. Janowitz?" She supposed she should have been embarrassed to be asking such personal questions, but since everyone seemed to expect the unexpected of old ladies, she knew she could get away with it.

"No."

"Haven't found the right girl yet, is that it?"

"Something like that, I guess." Another deep swallow of the coffee.

"Did you come straight to Boulder from Phoenix?"

"Oh, no. I spent a few years knocking around after college—seeing the States, so to speak. My family is fairly well off, so I've never really been without. I was living in New York City before I latched on to this position, which I landed through someone I knew up here."

"Oh?" She was surprised at how open he was being with her. Her harmless, old-lady status, she supposed. That, and maybe the fact that she reminded him of his mother.

"It has certainly been a good move for me—professionally, I mean. And I like the pace up here, too, for that matter. None of the rat race of the big city. I've made some pretty wise investments along the way and I'll probably be branching out on my own in the future. Time will tell. Certainly nothing I'd want to discuss until I was sure." So much for openness in that area, Lavina concluded.

"Are you always on the road in your job, or do you work out of that office up in the cemetery as well?" Lavina asked nonchalantly, steering him back to her immediate area of interest.

"A little of both, really," he said. "Wherever my

leads take me. Which means sometimes even to pleasant lakeside homes with delightful ladies that still bake their own coffee cake." He smiled, once again displaying the dimple.

Lavina laughed. "Someone in your family must have kissed the Blarney stone somewhere along the way."

He ran a finger along the seam of the album at his side, looking down at it, the smile still on his cracked lips. "Of course a lot of my work is in pre-need promotion rather than sales proper."

"One wouldn't think you'd have to promote burial plots," Lavina said with a smile. "I mean we all have to buy one sooner or later, right?"

"Of course, Mrs. London, but my job is seeing to it that people buy them sooner rather than later." He was looking up at her again, trying this time to hold back the smile. He was having a hard time.

Lavina picked up her own mug and held it tightly up in front of her without actually bringing it to her lips. "Who is that sandy-haired gentleman I saw yesterday morning in the doorway of the cemetery office?" she asked, trying again to be as nonchalant as possible.

"Sandy-haired?"

"Yes, I guess that's the best way to describe it. Wavy, too."

"Probably Mr. Creighton. I can't imagine anyone else who'd be at the office that fits that description. Tallish, mid-to-late forties?"

Lavina nodded. "A lot of hair on the backs of his hands and arms."

Janowitz let out a hearty laugh. "Yeah, that's Greg Creighton, all right. The Hairy Ape." He laughed again, as if at some private joke. "He's in charge. Runs the cemetery and crematory. My boss."

"I see."

"Why do you ask?"

"No special reason. Just that I'd seen him the day before at lunch and was wondering who he was and then I saw him again yesterday."

"Where did you see him at lunch?" Another swallow as he watched Lavina over the rim of his mug.

"The Seventeener. He was with Mrs. Frame." Lavina took a sip of her coffee, wondering if she were telling tales out of school. A little chill ran up her spine. When, after a few seconds, the salesman's sunburned face registered no particular emotion, she added. "They had services for her husband at the cemetery yesterday, too, didn't they? I was there for a friend's funeral—Peter Shaw—in case I didn't mention it earlier."

Karl Janowitz stared at her again over the upraised mug, the smile completely gone now from his face. "Yes."

"What a horrible thing to have happen in our own town!" Lavina said, shaking her steely head. "Murder." She paused. "Things like that you expect to read about in the papers happening someplace else, never in your own backyard."

"Did you know him, Mrs. London? Mr. Frame, I mean?"

"Oh, no. Or I should say just by sight. But that's still too close to home."

Karl Janowitz nodded his white-blond head in agreement and grabbed the album at his side, opening it wide on his lap.

"You and your Mr. Creighton must have known him fairly well, though, I imagine," Lavina continued, refilling his mug again. "In a business capacity, I mean."

"Oh, yes, quite well. Leo Frame was hardly the type to remain in the background, if you know what I mean."

"I imagine the police have already spoken to you about his death."

"No, not to me. Or not yet, anyway."

"Do you have any idea who might have wanted him dead? It certainly seems like premeditated murder."

Karl Janowitz smiled again. " 'Wanted,' Mrs. London, sure. Any number of people. Who actually did it, no."

"Difficult to get along with, was he?"

Karl Janowitz paused, looking down at the album in his lap as if it were something he was seeing for the first time. "He was a go-getter, I'll say that much for him. Knew exactly what he wanted and went out and got it." He paused. "And God help anyone who got in his way."

"Much the same type as his killer, wouldn't you say?" Lavina took another quiet sip of coffee, then set the mug down again next to Janowitz's on the cocktail table.

"When you put it like that, Mrs. London, I suppose so."

By the time Karl Janowitz left Hemlock Lake, Lavina had more information on burial vaults than she'd bargained for. What other information she had been able to glean during the course of their conversation, she would have been hard put to say at that point. She also felt an honest twinge of remorse for having deliberately wasted so much of the man's valuable time when she realized that he probably worked on some type of commission basis. Be that as it may, though, she had no intention of disturbing Ken in his present resting place. Purchasing an aboveground vault was probably one of the last things in the world she'd ever consider. Until law stipulated otherwise, what had been good enough for her ancestors would be good enough for her—dust to dust six feet under.

Chapter Eleven

Twenty-four hours.

That's just about how long it took Sheriff Tod Arthur to learn that his good friends Lavina London and Winifred O'Kirk had been seen up at the dead boy's motel. He had to learn it secondhand, at that, from one of the motel maids who'd seen them, one whose day off just had to be yesterday, too. Which was how the twenty-four hours had been wasted. A different maid had discovered the body early Wednesday morning when she let herself into the room to clean up and change the sheets and towels.

"How was I to know the poor boy had been murdered?" Lavina asked in all innocence. She followed the sheriff with her eyes as he stomped up and down in front of the shaded but curtainless windows in his office. She was sorely tempted to remind herself to bring along some Windex the next time she came—if there was a next time. She inched back now on the creaky, straight-backed chair set alongside his dilapidated desk, her white crocheted shoulder bag in her lap. "It didn't make Wednesday morning's *Record*, you know, and I don't get the evening paper. I haven't opened this morning's at all. I was busy with a visitor. If you hadn't phoned, I'd still be in the dark."

"Where did you say Winnie's gone?" This in his deep pseudo-official voice that somehow always amused Lavina. He took his seat again, facing her across a mess of papers on the desk.

"I told you on the phone, Tod. Sean took her down to New York for a few days. Probably be back sometime Sunday. He thought the change would do her good under the circumstances. A Broadway show, maybe, if they can get tickets on such short notice. I don't know what that's like nowadays. I know Winnie would love to see *Forty-second Street* or *Chorus Line*, or maybe even *Phantom of the Opera*. And some window-shopping on Fifth Avenue during the day, I suppose, and—"

"Lavina, for God's sake, will you stop the itinerary already! I get the message." Arthur glowered across the desk at her, a hand massaging his washboard brow. Then he looked down and began shuffling a pile of papers, shifting them from one side of the desk to the other. The balding spot at the crown of his head fairly radiated in the fluorescent-lighted office.

"Am I under arrest or something for concealing information?" Lavina asked when he looked at her. "Should I ask to be allowed to make that telephone call I'm entitled to before you cart me off and lock me up?" She had played a few roles like that, she now recalled. On *Gangbusters* or *Mr. District Attorney*, some such show. It was much too long ago to remember precisely. One thing she would always remember, however, were those famous opening lines, which she voiced now out loud, a smile at the corners of her mouth: "And it shall be my duty as District Attorney not only to prosecute to the limit of the law all persons accused of crime—"

"Cut the melodrama, Lavina! All I want is a little information—and a bit more cooperation."

"The cooperation, you've got, Tod. I'm here aren't I? What information do you want?"

Sheriff Arthur exuded a playful if impatient sneer as he bent his wide shoulders over the desk and folded his large hands on the ink-stained blotter barely visible beneath the mounds of paper. "Guess."

Lavina sighed. "You want to know what Winnie and I were doing in Peter Frame's motel room." She looked down at the bodice of her taffy-yellow, cotton dress and brushed away a nonexistent speck of lint. "Right?"

"Right. That's one up for you." He straightened up again. "Now go on while you still have the ball."

Not one for games, Lavina let the image pass without comment. "Well . . ."—She let her bag slip noiselessly by its long straps to the bare, wood floor, and then folded her hands in her lap—". . . it was Winnie's idea, really," she began. "You know how she worries about stray dogs and homeless kittens and such—well, I suppose I do, too, for that matter—"

"Lavina!"

"All right. All right." Briefly she explained how she, Winnie, and Sean had seen Peter Frame at the restaurant in an advanced state of inebriation, and had made the resultant decision—made over Sean's strenuous objection, she emphasized—to see if they could help the boy in any way.

"Who was having lunch with Mrs. Frame, do you know?" Arthur interrupted before she could go on.

"Gregory Creighton from Evergreen Park." She watched as the sheriff dug a notepad and pen out of his gray uniform's shirt pocket and made a notation. "He runs the place up there, I understand. Might even own it, for all I know." And that just might make a difference, too, she now realized for the first time.

"Go on."

"We got the boy's room number at the motel office and then walked to the room—it was on the upper level. You know what the motel is like, you were there." When Arthur nodded, she went on: "Well, we knocked, or rather Winnie knocked, when we found the room. The door was ajar so it opened in a bit. When there was no answer, Winnie stuck her head in and called him."

"What time was this?"

"Oh, close to two, I'd say. It was just before we went to the funeral home for the wake."

Arthur merely nodded again, his eyes down as he made another notation on the pad.

"Winnie told me later that he was stretched out on the bed; I couldn't see him myself at that point. He must have heard her, though, because he got up and came over to the door. He knocked over the phone in the act, you could hear it. He didn't say anything at first. Just stared at us, sort of disoriented, squinting against the sun outside. When Winnie told him who we were and all, it didn't seem to ring a bell, but, of course, he was pretty far gone by that time, worse than when we'd seen him at the restaurant. There was an open bottle of gin on the bureau. Winnie asked Peter if she could get him something to eat, or if he wanted to come back to the lake with us—I thought that was a little foolish myself, but you know Winnie. He just stared at her bleary-eyed and then started to cry. And I mean bawl! You could hear him out on the balcony, so we edged our way inside and closed the door."

"He was dressed at this time?" The pen was poised over the pad.

Lavina gave a little start. "Dressed! Of course he was dressed! You don't think we'd have gone in otherwise, do you?" When Arthur didn't answer, Lavina gave him the fisheye and went on. "He stumbled back and landed on the bed—fortunately—and Winnie sat down next to him. I remained standing." She paused. "After a while, she finally managed to calm him down. We couldn't make out a word of what he was saying until the blubbering stopped and he said something about being cut out of the will. That's all we could make out, and then only because he repeated it a couple of times, as if he were having trouble trying to understand it. There was no mistaking that part of it, Tod. I—"

"What will was this, his stepfather's?"

"Do you want me to draw conclusions, Tod, or just relay the facts as I know them?" She hadn't cut her teeth on trial procedures with *Mr. District Attorney* and radio's soap opera *Perry Mason* for nothing. "I have no idea."

"Score two for you, Lavina." The sheriff wiped the back of his hand across his mouth, erasing the nascent smile. "Go on."

"Well, there really isn't much more to tell. I told him how sorry I was to hear about his father, how sorry we all were that such a thing should happen, and . . . well, he suddenly started throwing his arms around, shouting, calling his stepfather a bastard. He spiced it with a few more choice expletives, I might add, none of which I'd ever be caught repeating, but I'm sure you get the gist. So if you want to make a connection between this incident and the will bit you can, I guess, but the boy never actually did so, or at least not what I could make out between his crying and shouting."

Arthur was scribbling away again, his eyes lowered. "Anything else," he asked without looking up.

"Just that Winnie started getting a bit more persistent about his having something in his stomach. That's when he began getting nasty with us, so we left."

The sheriff looked up again. "Was the phone that he knocked over off the hook when you left, would you know?"

"Oh, no. Winnie picked it up and set it back on the night table as soon as we got in and closed the door."

"Great!" Lavina would have to be naive or downright stupid to miss the innuendo in his voice.

"How about the door? Did you close it after you when you left?" he asked.

Lavina thought a few seconds, then nodded. "Winnie did, yes."

"You wouldn't know if she—or Peter Frame— locked it?"

"That I wouldn't know. You can call Winnie in New York, I suppose, and ask her, if it's important. They're staying at the Hilton."

Sheriff Arthur tented his fingers in front of him, his shirted elbows on the worm armrests of his wood chair. The pad and pen were back in his breast pocket. "You didn't have any other reason for going to the man's room other than Winnie's concern for his well-being, Lavina?"

Lavina shrugged and started dabbing with slender fingers at her "feather cut." "What reason could I have had, Tod? Besides not wanting Winnie going up there alone, I mean?"

"You wouldn't have been nosing around a little where you didn't belong? Trying to find out something about Leo Frame's death?" He brought the tips of his tented fingers up to his lips.

"What a strange thing to say, Tod."

"Funny you should use that word, Lavina. I had a very *strange* visit here, too, Tuesday morning. Would you care to hazard a guess who popped in out of the blue?"

Lavina started brushing at the bodice of her dress again. "How could I be expected to know anything like that, Tod?" She didn't look up.

"Damn it, Lavina!" Arthur slammed a palm down on the desk, rattling its rickety, plywood panels and sending a pencil rolling off the edge to the floor. "Do you think I was born yesterday?" He leaned down to retrieve the pencil, which he subsequently snapped in two.

Lavina looked up and stared across at him, rubbing at the liver spots on the back of her hands, first the left, then the right, "I don't—"

"Your granddaughter, Lavina. The swimmer, remember?"

"Susanne? Susanne dropped in to see you? How

sweet.'' She examined her nails, turning them in to her palms. ''I don't recall her mentioning the fact.''

''I'm afraid her little tale about wanting information about my swimming secrets was just that, Lavina, my love—a tale. I knew she was up to something as soon as she started, but I let her go on. Really, Lavina, you shouldn't have sent a girl to do a woman's work. Her womanly wiles just aren't as well developed as the rest of her. When she started questioning me about the manner of Leo Frame's death, well, that was just a bit too much to swallow. I didn't let her know I was on to her, of course, though I was sorely tempted to feed her some phoney information just for the fun of it.''

''Tod Arthur, how could you!'' Lavina felt the rush of blood to her face, but it was too late.

''Better to let her think she succeeded in her little mission, don't you? A mission, by the way, that had Lavina London written all over it.'' He shook his head. ''Damn it, Lavina! If you wanted to know something about the man's death, why didn't you just come right out and ask me instead of pussy-footing around, making a Mata Hari out of your own granddaughter, for God's sake?''

''Would you have told me outright anything I wanted to know?''

''Probably not.''

''Well, there!''

Arthur heaved a deep sigh and lowered his arms. ''Then you admit it.''

Lavina shrugged her shoulders and folded her hands in her lap. ''What's the sense of trying to make a bad situation worse? Yes, of course.''

''Why?''

''Why?''

"That's what I said."

"I just thought I might be able to help, that's all. As I told Susanne earlier, it pains me to know there's a murderer here in Boulder. The sooner he's rooted out the better."

"You make it sound like digging for truffles."

"There's no need to be sarcastic, Tod."

"What it comes down to is that you don't think I'm equipped to handle something like this, is that it?"

"That's not it at all, Tod Arthur, and you know it." She drilled him in midair with an accusing finger. "You're a fine sheriff and you run a tight ship. But is it wrong of me to want to help, as long as I don't get in your way? Where's the harm? Maybe in my capacity as a local resident I might become privy to information that would otherwise be difficult for you to obtain. Like the pig or boar that sniffs out those truffles of yours. I might learn something important just by being at the right place at the right time, and maybe innocently asking the right questions."

"And maybe even joining the Frames, father and son."

"If that's part of the Lord's plan, so be it." She paused to let her point sink in. "What about those stains I pointed out downstairs at the funeral home, for example? You never told me the results of your lab tests, by the way, either. Were they blood or not?"

"They were."

"See?"

"I thank you for that, Lavina, of course. Not that we wouldn't have discovered them in the long run, of course—"

"You never know, Tod, you never know. So please

don't start thinking and talking like Inspector Lestrade, will you. My pointing them out certainly must have speeded things up for you, if nothing else."

Sheriff Arthur nodded reluctantly without actually admitting anything outright. "As long as it's come up," he said, "I might as well tell you that we also discovered traces on the carpeted staircase leading down to the Selection Room. They all matched Leo Frame's blood type."

"On the staircase." Lavina was thinking aloud now. "Hmmm. How about upstairs?"

"Nothing on the landing or in the hallway, no, and that's all carpeted up there as well."

"Dark olive, as I recall." She stared past the sheriff through the filthy window beyond.

"Whoever tried to clean up downstairs couldn't have done the same with the carpet, that's for sure."

"What you're saying, then, is that Leo Frame was actually attacked on the staircase, is that it?"

"So it would seem," the sheriff admitted. "And then dragged and dumped into the casket."

"Laid out fairly professionally is more like it," Lavina corrected. Her earlier hypothesis of the existence of some sort of lift had proved to be wrong, at least according to Jeffrey Marcus, for the type used at the Frame Funeral Home. Leo must have been lifted up manually into that fancy casket.

"But his death was not the result of the facial or head injury, right?" she asked by way of clarification.

"No. He died of asphyxia. Undoubtedly smothered by the pillow in the casket."

"Yes. Winnie mentioned that the underside was covered with blood."

"It was stained, yes," Arthur admitted. "How did she know that? It hasn't been let out to the papers yet, to my knowledge." He squinted across at Lavina suspiciously. "I need a veritable Hero of Haarlem to plug up all the leaks around here."

"I think she said she learned it at the post office . . . no, I'm wrong, it was directly from Brad Reeves." She stared off through the window again, then looked back at him. "That's our mailman."

"Amazing! And people complain about the postal service."

Lavina ignored him and went on with the arguments for her case. "Don't forget, Tod Arthur, that because of me you now also know that Mrs. Frame had lunch—or was going to have lunch—with Mr. Creighton the day after her husband was murdered —which may or may not mean something."

"That they were both hungry, maybe?"

"Ha. Ha." She didn't even give him the benefit of a smile. "And don't try to skirt the issue with your weak excuse for levity. But then I suppose you'll tell me that you probably would have found out that bit of information eventually, too."

"And well we might have. We're hardly through with our investigation, you know, Lavina. Hell, we've barely begun!"

"And already you have two murders on your hands."

"What do you expect me to do, Lavina, go out and corral all the possible suspects and bring them back to the Selection Room for a final confrontation? Right now, we're doing the best we can, but we've got to go slow. What we don't need is any amateur interference. Hell, Lavina, don't you realize—"

"Fine!" Lavina concluded, shutting him off,

"then I won't have to bother you with anything I just happened to overhear between a certain young funeral director and an older woman who just happens to run a florist and nursery here in town, will I? I mean, why bother if you'll eventually learn it on your own anyway . . . after another murder, maybe? And Lord knows I wouldn't want to interfere. I'll turn in my Amateur Investigator's card now and go back to my embroidery." Lavina bent down, grabbed the strap of her shoulder bag alongside her chair, and rose to her feet.

"Lavina London, you sit down in that chair and stay put until I'm good and ready to let you go. Otherwise I just might be forced to have you carted off and locked up for concealing information—maybe even without your precious phone call." A grin shot across his face as he reached into his pocket for the notepad and pen. He turned to a clean page and poised the ballpoint. "Okay, let's have it."

Lavina resumed her seat, lowered the bag to the floor, and filled him in on the conversation she overheard in the small rear office of the Frame Funeral Home between Jeffrey Marcus and Annis Barth.

"How do you know he was talking to the Barth woman?" Arthur asked when she was through.

"How many women named Annis do you know in this area?" she said. "Or anywhere else, for that matter."

"Do you know her at all?"

"I've spent more money at Barth Nurseries than I care to recall, so, yes, I guess I can say I know her. Why, don't you?"

"I can't really say that I do, Lavina, except by name, of course. She took the place over after her father passed away several years back, as I recall. I can't even remember when that was."

"Mata Hari and I can drop in any time for more bedding plants and see what we can learn at that end—unless, of course, we're still to butt out."

"Mata Hari?" The corrugated brow again.

"Susanne, remember? My granddaughter, the swimmer?" Lavina smiled now and shook her head. "She has a crush—don't let on I told you, especially using a word like that—she has a crush on the young man that works at the nursery, one of them, anyway. Martin Knappe."

"Well, I can't stop you from buying plants at your local nursery, Lavina, but just remember that you're on your own. You haven't been deputized or anything, so don't think you have. Don't come running to me if you get yourself into some legal jam thinking I'll back you up or anything, because I won't."

"Don't worry, Galahad, I'll go it alone."

"Let me know if you learn anything." He shoved the pad and pen back again into his pocket.

Lavina shook her head, the smile still on her lips. "Your cake and eat it, huh? Okay, I can buy that, I suppose." She grabbed for her bag again. "Is that all? Am I released on my own—what do you call it?—reconnaissance?"

"Recognizance, Lavina, recognizance."

She threw back her head and laughed. "Lord! I'm beginning to sound more like Winnie every day." She rose, lifted the bag strap over her right shoulder, then stepped around behind the chair. "You've ruled out the possibility of Leo Frame having been killed by a stranger, have you, Tod? I mean, the papers said the side door to the home was found unlocked.''

''It seems highly unlikely, Lavina. After all, according to Mrs. Frame, nothing of value was missing. Frame still had his wallet on him with close to three hundred dollars in it. And then, of course, there's the dumping of the man—laying out, if you want—in his highest-priced casket. I hardly think a stranger would have bothered with such an ironic touch, do you?''

''No. And, then too, it's hardly likely the man's stepson would have been killed a few days later, is it?

''Hardly.''

''What is that relationship, anyway?'' Lavina asked, grasping the back of the chair and leaning on it. ''Is the boy Elenice Frame's son or what?''

''No. Frame's stepson by an earlier marriage. From what I can piece together from what the present Mrs. Frame told me, Peter's mother walked out on her second marriage, leaving the boy with Leo. His real father had done the same to her right after Peter was born. She was killed in an auto accident shortly after, and Frame raised the boy as his own. He married the present wife when the lad was in high school, five or six years ago.''

''I see. The boy certainly couldn't have had much of a real family life, could he?''

''I suppose not,'' Tod said. ''Even by today's standards.''

Lavina shook her head. To her, as to many of her generation—and to others, she liked to think—the family was just about sacrosanct. One's character was formed and nurtured in the home, whatever that might be. Her heart continually went out to the single, working parents of today whose numbers seemed to be growing by leaps and bounds. How they managed, she'd never understand; she often wondered if, indeed, she'd had it too easy, what with Ken and all. She just couldn't picture herself a successful single parent no matter how hard she tried.

She ran her tongue over her lips now and a finger over the top slat of the chair back. "Just about everyone who could have been involved seems to have known Peter Frame was at the motel that day," she said, flicking the accumulated dust off her fingers.

"So it appears," Tod said. "And the office remembers getting a call later on in the day inquiring about his room number."

"That's right," Lavina said, her eyes lighting up, "they'd have to know that, wouldn't they? Man or woman?"

Tod Arthur shrugged. "No one seems to recall one way or the other. Not that it would mean much, even if they did. Whoever it was probably disguised his voice anyway."

"Probably." Lavina let out a small sigh. "I suppose you've found nothing helpful in the way of fingerprints or such, either at the motel or down in the Selection Room?"

"Nothing identifiable that's of any help, I'm afraid. I thought we might have something with the phone in the boy's room, but you burst that little bubble."

"Saved you from wasting time, you mean." Lavina shifted her bag to the other shoulder and smiled. "Why, by the way, did you ask if Peter was dressed when Winnie and I got to his room?"

"Because he wasn't when the maid found him yesterday morning, that's all."

"Is that important? I mean, maybe he slept in the nu—the raw. Where was he found? In bed?"

"No, on the bathroom floor."

"Maybe he was going to bathe or shower."

"That's possible, I guess."

Lavina started softly tapping on the slat of the chair with her nails. "There's something you're keeping back, Tod Arthur." If she had to make him feel like a naughty boy, so be it. "You know, I know none of the circumstances surrounding Peter's death at all. I haven't even seen the papers yet."

Arthur heaved a forlorn sigh and shoved back his chair. It screeched across the cracked, dull-brown linoleum.

"The front of his skull was badly crushed in, though not from any of the bathroom fixtures, in case you were going to ask. Judging from the appearance of one of the towels flung up over the shower rod, whoever killed him took time out to wipe off the weapon and take it away with him. From the configurations in the flesh, according to Dr. Errol it could have been something like a heavy tool, a wrench, maybe."

Lavina frowned and leaned against the chair back. "I still don't get the significance you seem to be giving to the nudity."

It was Tod Arthur's turn to display a pale shade of beet, which radiated right up his forehead into his receding hairline. "I don't know why I'm telling you all this, Lavina," he said with a shake of the head, "but there's the possibility—just a possibility, mind you—of a sexual element in this slaying." He paused, biting at the corner of his lower lip. Lavina was sure he was debating with himself whether or not to tell her more. Finally, he added, "Traces of dried semen were found on a second towel on the floor near the door, and the man's trousers and undershorts were in a heap on the rug."

"He was drunk, you know, Tod."

"Of course he was drunk! What difference does that make? It's all the more understandable if he invited someone to his room."

"I thought we ruled out the stranger theory," Lavina said.

"I'm not talking about a stranger."

"You think it might have been the same person who called asking about his room number?"

"It could have been. He didn't make any outgoing calls—not from his room, anyway. Or someone may have called him—maybe that same someone. No one at the office could remember whether or not he'd had any incoming calls."

"And you have no idea who she could have been."

"To be perfectly honest, Lavina, I haven't been thinking along the lines of a *she*. His stepmother seems to think—"

Lavina threw her hands in the air and straightened up again. "I don't want to hear it, Tod, if all it is is that silly woman's conjecture. She also accused him of killing her husband, as I recall."

The sheriff shrugged his wide shoulders. "Okay."

"Is it?"

"She has no proof, if that's what you mean, no."

"The boy's body's been examined, hasn't it?"

"Of course."

"Did your doctor—what's his name, Errol?—find any indication that he'd been sodomized?"

Tod Arthur propelled his six-feet-four frame out of his chair and stood staring across at her, his jaw hanging. "Jeez, Lavina, here I am trying to be as discreet as possible and you come out with a question like that . . . and no, he hadn't been."

"Who's pussyfooting around now? That's called being puritanical, Tod Arthur." She smiled as she turned to leave. "And it went out with Radio."

Chapter Twelve

From where she stood behind the screen door, Annis Barth watched the retreating back as it descended the sturdy, white, wooden staircase leading down from her apartment over the nursery. A crescent moon was bright and clear through the shadow of pines on the rise beyond. In its milky light she followed the figure with her eyes as it crossed the rear yard in the direction of the greenhouse, and without looking up, rounded the building and disappeared from sight. She secured the door latch with a metallic click and remained staring out into the night.

She let an idle hand run down inside the open, mini, lace, wrap coat as far as her thighs, then back again to her breasts. She could feel the cool, night air against the exposed flesh. She closed her eyes briefly and bathed in the coolness.

After a few minutes, she turned to glance at the clock mounted in the stove. One twenty-two. Plenty of time for another drink. There were no pressing jobs in the morning that the boys couldn't handle. She smiled at her use of the term. A few years ago they would have been considered jailbait. Not that Rob was much older. What was he—twenty-two, twenty-three, maybe? But still, when it came to business, she knew she had to draw the line. "Don't touch the merchandise, Annis," she repeated aloud; it was not the first time she had to reprove herself. It would be so easy to slip, and she certainly didn't want to come across as the female equivalent of the boss that chased his secretary around his desk. Or did they still do that sort of thing nowadays? She didn't fool herself, of course. There was really only one thing she feared, and that was the likelihood of being rejected. That was something she'd never learned to handle well. And Lord knows, she'd more than had her share of experience.

She pulled the wrap closed around her slim waist and secured it with the sash, her "boys"—or at least one of them—still very much on her mind. Young George didn't give her any concern; he really wasn't her type. But Marty, well, that was something else again. She'd always been pretty much of a sucker for the blond, Germanic type. She couldn't be sure, of course, but she sometimes wondered about those sidelong glances he'd give her when they were working alone in the shop. She considered the possibility that he might even still have his cherry—did they still use that term?—but somehow couldn't buy it. Maybe she just didn't want to. He didn't talk much about girls—not that she gave him much opportunity. Of course, there was that pretty little blond thing with the athletic arms and legs who usually monopolized his free time whenever she wasn't away at college somewhere. Was he saving himself for her, maybe, or were the two of them already making it together? Just thinking of him now in those terms sent a pleasant chill coursing up her body. For a moment, she considered closing the inside door, but changed her mind. Maybe she shouldn't have taken him on as an apprentice in the first place. But that was foolish. She really needed the muscle and brawn around the place —for practical reasons. She smiled to herself and turned away from the door. She could handle it.

In her bare feet she stepped over to the countertop and opened the bottle of White Label that was already set out. With her free hand she gathered up a rocks glass that stood unwashed in the sink alongside a highball glass. She tossed out the watered remains, washing it down the drain with a quick turn of the faucet. She slid the glass down the counter toward the refrigerator, then twisted off her rings and deposited them in the cheap, ceramic frog on the counter by the sink.

At the refrigerator, she palmed three ice cubes from the storage tray in the freezer compartment and plopped them into her glass, which she then filled with the scotch. She swirled it around until she was sure it was sufficiently chilled, then downed half of the contents. "Ah!" She set the glass down and eased her yellow-dyed hair back over her ears with a finger, securing it on each side with a bobby pin from the pocket of her wrap coat.

In the bedroom, she sat down on the edge of the bed, tossed back the already rumpled sheets, opened the bottom drawer of the night table and lifted out a thin packet of envelopes. She slipped off the rose-colored rubber band and flipped through them twice before replacing it. When she looked up and accidentally caught a glimpse of herself in the mirror above the dresser on the far side of the room, she uttered an obscenity, leapt up, and returned with the packet of envelopes to the kitchen.

From the bottom drawer in the cabinet to the left of the sink she dug out a large box of safety matches, slid open the cover, and took out a match. She struck the red, sulfur head on the side of the box, and as it flared up, briefly inhaled the fumes. Over the sink she brought the pale-peach flame in contact with a corner of the batch of envelopes until they caught and started to burn slowly. After a few seconds, the rubber band snapped and flew onto the countertop. She dropped the spent match and slowly rotated the envelopes until the small bundle was too hot to hold, then let it fall into the sink where she turned and prodded it with the tip of a steak knife she'd taken from the drain rack. She could feel her eyes beginning to tear as the smoke curled up from the sink. She let out a little laugh as, in her discomfort, she recalled the famous Cole Porter lyric, "When a lovely flame dies, smoke gets in your eyes." Corny, maybe, but true. When the flame finally burned itself out, she shoveled up the flaky, black ashes with an egg turner and dumped them into the trash can on the floor alongside the stove, then washed the residue down the drain.

She grabbed her glass again, refilled it, swirled it around, this time with a finger, and brought it over to the kitchen table in the middle of the room. She turned on a well-preserved, old, red, portable radio she kept on the table next to the sugar bowl. They were halfway through an oldie called "Nature Boy." The haunting melody did nothing for her present mood, but she left it on anyway. She took a swig of the Scotch, then made a wry face. Now that she was over a difficult hurdle, it was time to get her life in some kind of order again. Somehow the resolution sounded familiar, but this time, she knew, it would be different, both personally and professionally.

She sat back firmly against the cold vinyl of the swivel chair, bent her head over the upraised glass, and let the tip of her tongue play around in the ice cubes before taking another swallow. Then, she set the glass down in front of her on the table and smiled. With Leo Frame finally out of the way, there'll be no more worry about the threat of P.O.s. The ass had all but controlled local obituaries with an iron hand so that the inclusion of "Please omit flowers" had become almost as common as "nee" and "beloved." He just hadn't wanted the bother the flowers entailed, the extra care and attention, not to mention the frustration he felt with the occasional floral blankets that for all intents and purposes shrouded his precious, overpriced caskets. Annis threw her head back and laughed out loud as she recalled a few of those choice occasions. The man had practically turned livid. Well, with Jeffrey Marcus, things would be different. She had seen to that, too.

Chapter Thirteen

The view from *Moses'* feet came as a complete surprise. Lavina London could see practically the whole configuration of the cemetery. She felt a little silly, though—as if she were hiding behind a man's skirts—concealed as she was now behind the immense, robed statue, her head venturing an occasional, furtive glance around his massive, bent, right leg as he sat pondering with a scowl the horizon off to his left. The immediate object of Lavina's attention was in the opposite direction, down the blacktop road and to the right: the modern, white building housing the cemetery office, or, more specifically, the figure of Karl Janowitz crouched alongside his car tightening the nuts of his left, rear tire that was still off the ground.

Lavina had Susanne drop her off about twenty minutes earlier on the chance that she might get to see Gregory Creighton alone. When she spotted Karl

Janowitz removing his tires from the car, she had signaled to her granddaughter to drive straight through without stopping. As long as she had to bide her time, she might just as well do it paying a visit to Ken's grave. She had sent her granddaughter off on a wild-goose chase to Monticello and walked back to where she now stood, sure that the pre-need promoter and salesman would soon be finished and about his business.

She glanced up at the bearded lawgiver, who must have been a good eight feet or more sitting, and that atop a four-foot pedestal against which she now leaned. Beyond the marble colossus, the blacktop road forked around a surprisingly large, semiformal, English garden at the far end of which towered a Buonarroti replica, this one his dying slave. To Lavina the figure looked somehow oddly obscene with the genitals hidden behind a marble fig leaf. The *maestro* would have turned in his grave. Lavina coughed and brought a hand to her mouth to hold back the fit of giggles she felt coming on.

When she turned back to look down toward the huge, iron gates, the towheaded salesman was still at it. The car—it looked to Lavina like a ten-year-old Chevy— was back again on all fours, the trunk open. She checked her watch impatiently, then looked back to the salesman. She watched as he removed the short, cylindrical iron handle he had used to operate the jack, and shoved it under the spare that was already in the trunk. He slid the chain and jack out from under the bumper and returned them to the floor of the trunk.

Lavina thought he was finished until she saw him lift out a small, blue, plastic box. He snapped open the top, took out an orange-colored gadget, and tossed the box back into the trunk. He took the odd-looking piece with him to the driver's side where he opened the door and leaned in. He then unwound from it a long length of black wire, and turned on the ignition. A grating sound like a buzz saw started up, its strident monotone echoing in the open expanse of countryside. It wasn't until the man unscrewed the tiny cap from the inflation valve in the rear tire and replaced it with the metal tip from a short length of hose from the gadget that she realized he was check-ing the air pressure and filling the tire. He followed the procedure not only for the two tires he had re-placed, but for the two front ones as well. Nothing like being on the safe side, Lavina thought. A man after her own heart.

When he had finished with the last of the tires, Karl Janowitz leaned into the driver's side again and disconnected the little machine—obviously from the cigarette-lighter socket—mercifully putting an end to the racket. He rewrapped the wire tightly around the base of the inflator and placed it snugly back in its lit-tle box, snapping it shut. He then shrugged into a light-green suit jacket he'd lifted out of the trunk, and slammed the lid down. With the car still idling, he went over to the office door. He said something to someone inside, turned, went back and got into the car.

Lavina pulled back behind the statue and waited. When she heard the engine and the crackle of rubber on gravel, she heaved a little sigh. She waited a few more moments until she was sure the salesman was beyond the iron gates. She then looked back up to her biblical protector, patted his sandaled foot, thanked him for his hospitality, and made her way nonchalantly down the wide, winding road to the office, her bag swinging from her shoulder at her side.

"Yoo-hoo! Anyone home?" Temporarily blinded by the sun, she stuck her head through the open office door.

"Just us chickens." That it was a woman's voice that answered temporarily threw her off guard. She entered the office, squinting under a raised hand.

The woman Lavina finally saw, once her vision focused, was in her thirties, with straight, cinnamon-brown hair parted in the middle. Shining, it fell halfway down her back, off her bony shoulders. The low-necked blouse was a definite no-no, Lavina decided when she spotted the woman's prominent collarbone.

"I'm Theresa Francotti, can I help you?" The smile was pleasant, and the teeth, or what Lavina could see of them, white and straight. The woman had undoubtedly spent most of her adolescence with a mouth full of metal and rubber bands.

"I was looking for Mr. Janowitz," Lavina said. "Is he around?"

"You just missed him." Theresa Francotti rose and rushed over to the open door. The lilac culottes stopped a few inches too short above the knobby knees. Too bad orthopedists weren't as successful as orthodontists, Lavina thought. "You must have passed him on your way in," the woman added, peering out the door, first to the right, then to the left. "I'm sorry." She addressed it as if to someone outdoors, then turned and came back to the chair in front of the computer terminal in the corner. She picked up the copy of the magazine she had laid on the chair when she got up and joined Lavina at a pair of upholstered love seats that sat facing each other from opposite sides of an artificial fireplace against the rear wall. She dropped the magazine on top of the glass-topped coffee table that separated the two small sofas, and stood facing her unexpected visitor.

Lavina canted her steel-gray head to look down at the title. *Journal of Creative Ideas for Cemeteries.* How creative? she wondered. Murder even, maybe?

"No problem," Lavina said. "You won't mind if I sit down and catch my breath." She didn't make it a question, and she didn't wait for an answer. "I was just visiting my husband—his grave, I mean—and thought I'd drop in and see Mr. Janowitz while I was waiting for my granddaughter to come back for me." She slid her bag off her shoulder and swung it onto the table in front of her.

"Do you know Karl?" Theresa asked with obvious interest as she poured out a paper cup of cold water from the upturned bottle nearby. She brought it over and handed it to Lavina.

"Oh, thank you, dear, that's very sweet of you," Lavina said, accepting the cone-shaped cup. "Yes"— she took a deep drink, realizing for the first time how thirsty she actually was—"Mr. Janowitz was over to my home a few days ago to discuss the possibility of my purchasing a pair of crypts." It was during the salesman's visit that she learned that she and Sean had been misusing the term vault, when what they should have been talking about were crypts. She still wasn't sure what vaults were.

"Oh, I see." Theresa smoothed the seat of her culottes and sat down on the edge of the sofa facing Lavina. "Well, Mr. Janowitz is gone for the day, I'm afraid. Maybe I can help you . . . if you have any questions, I mean.''

Lavina finished what was left of the water, crumpled the cup and held it in a ball in her fist. "I really don't have any questions. I just thought I'd let Mr. Janowitz know that I still haven't quite made up my mind about the community mausoleum"—another term she'd learned during the course of the salesman's visit. "He's been so kind and helpful, coming all the way over to the lake and what have you.''

"Here, let me take that," Theresa said, extending her hand for the used cup, which Lavina gratefully surrendered. "Aboveground entombment is all the thing nowadays," she said, rising briefly to toss the cup in a metal basket near the cooler. To Lavina, the woman somehow didn't seem quite convinced of her own words.

"I suppose so," she agreed aloud. "It's just the money, really. I mean, I already own a double grave, free and clear. I'm not sure it would be wise—practical—for me to spend the extra money. Being a widow and all." She paused to let the younger woman draw her own erroneous conclusions about the nature of her income, a situation which, fortunately, was far from the truth. Ken had left her more than well provided for, not to mention her own considerable savings and investments amassed over the years in the course of her highly successful professional career.

"Yes, I know what you mean," Theresa Francotti said. "It's certainly not for everybody, I suppose. I know *I*—well, that's neither here nor there." Hardly the makings of a topflight salesman, Lavina concluded, though that probably wasn't the woman's goal anyway, if indeed she had one other than her present position. "You mentioned a lake," Theresa added. "Is that where you live?"

"Yes. I'm over at Hemlock Lake. Do you know it?"

"Oh, yes. I've been to all the lakes in the area. They're all so lovely, especially in the summertime." Theresa sighed, a forlorn look on her long, oval face, like a waif hoping to be adopted by prospective parents. "I've lived up in Monticello all my life." Hardly city living, Lavina thought, recalling her own childhood in the Bronx. That was something she could never understand, all the psychological hogwash nowadays about the underpriviledged having to grow up on city streets. Where the heck did they think people like her had grown up, for heaven's sake? In mansions with private playgrounds? Why, when they weren't eating, sleeping, or in school, she and her friends had practically lived on the streets in the East Bronx. And they were terrific streets, too. They had made them terrific. Roller skating, potsie, jump rope, tag, jacks, ringolevio, statues, I declare war on, hide and seek—always pronounced *hidingoseek*, of course —cutouts; and the boys with their stick ball, stoop ball, orange-crate scooters, rubber-band pistols, baseball cards, stringed-chestnut fights—these and so many others whose names she had long since forgotten, if indeed they all even had names. Then, too, there were the shows they had put on every summer during vacation in the backyard of their Bronx apartment house, with the neighbors throwing down their nickel-and-dime admissions to watch them perform, in front of their clothesline-strung blanket curtains,

songs and dances mainly in handmade, crepe-paper
costumes, but sometimes dramatic or comedy skits,
many of which Lavina remembered having penned
herself in lined, steno pads. That had been her first
exposure to show biz. Little had she realized at the
time where it would all lead. Yes, they had taken
pride in their neigborhood in those days, but pride
now seemed to be a thing of the past. Granted they
hadn't had today's drug problems, but to Lavina's
mind that excuse was an over-simplification. It was
the loss of self-esteem that was the real culprit.

"We've had quite a bit of unusual activity here this
past week," Lavina finally said, changing the subject
and taking the bull by the hornies, as she liked to
express it—for Sean's amusement more than anything
else. "What with two murders and all."

"Yes, isn't it terrible?" Theresa agreed. "We know
the Frame family here very well, being in the same
business, so to speak."

"Yes, of course!" Lavina said, feigning surprise.
"How silly of me. You probably know more about it
than I do." She gave a little laugh, folding her hands
in the lap of her teal-blue skirt. "I suppose they were
even buried here at Evergreen."

"Leo was—that's the father, well, stepfather,
actually—but Peter—his body, I mean—hasn't been
released yet by the police."

"What was the stepfather like?—Theresa, did you
say your name was?"

"Yes. And you're? . . ."

"I'm sorry." Lavina shifted her bag from its position on the table between them to her side on the love
seat. "Mrs. London. Lavina."

"What a lovely name. Lavina London." She let it roll off her tongue as if she were savoring it. "Sounds like an English actress."

Lavina smiled without comment.

"Let's see . . ." Theresa inched back on the couch and extended a rough-skinned, bony elbow to the armrest on her right. "I don't think you'd have cared much for Leo Frame. He was pretty self-centered if you ask me. And he certainly wasn't Mr. Popularity around here."

"Oh? Why's that?" Lavina asked, again feigning innocence.

"I know it's not nice to speak badly of the dead and all, but the man was absolutely impossible. For one thing, he was in the habit of skimming all the gravy and leaving nothing but the measly pickings for the cemetery people, like Mr. Creighton here." Lavina had the impression the woman was mixing her metaphors, but wasn't sure. "In his position at the funeral home, he was naturally the first one to come in contact with the clients. What he'd do was sell them nothing but the best—or try to, anyway—then pick up the phone and call us to put in an order for a cheap grave." Lavina could see the woman was hooked now on what had to be the choicest bit of town gossip since the elementary schools phys. ed. instructor had run off with the high school drum majorette six years ago. She let her talk on. "He had quite a reputation, our Mr. Frame. It didn't surprise me that someone upped and killed him."

"Surely you could have refused phone orders like that," Lavina suggested. "Made your own kind of requirements for sales?"

"Oh, sure, and we did as a matter of fact. But then Leo Frame refused to share the information he had on the family's background and financial situation, sometimes even held back their names until the last minute. Half the time we ended up reading the obituaries on our own. Like bloody ambulance chasers, for God's sakes. Excuse my language, Mrs. London, but the man just refused to work hand-in-hand with us." She was beginning to sound like a shareholder, Lavina thought. Either that or Gregory Creighton had done a good job at indoctrination.

Lavina shook her head in feigned commiseration, not without the appropriate accompanying *t'ch t'ch's*. "Was he unique in what he did?" she asked, sure he wasn't, not from what she'd read about funeral directors in recent news items.

"No, I couldn't say that, but he was certainly the worst in this area. We've never had any major problems with the people up in Monticello like we've had with him."

"Your Mr. Creighton must have done something to protect the cemetery interests," Lavina said, leaving it to Theresa Francotti to fill in exactly what that something had been.

"He had to." She lowered her arm and sat forward again on the couch. "We went into pre-need sales for one thing. That's basically what Karl—Mr. Janowitz—does as our Memorial Counselor." Lavina recalled the somewhat bogus title on the business card he'd given her at the house. "That's one way we have the jump on the funeral director—getting to the client while he's still alive." She smiled as if recalling a gratifying experience. "That and, of course, the crematory." She laughed out loud now. "You should have heard him when that went up a couple of years ago. Since then, the shoe's been on the other foot more often than not." She chuckled. "Leo was furious anytime Mr. Creighton let him have a dose of his own medicine. Like whenever he'd manage to convince a prospect that embalming or a casket were unnecessary wastes of money if they were considering cremation." Even to Lavina the alternative sounded a bit abrupt and grim, so she could well understand the funeral director's reaction. "He'd always try and talk them into putting the extra money into a better urn or a nicer niche location in the columbarium." The new terms were coming fast and furious and Lavina had all she could do to keep with them. She wasn't sure she was succeeding.

"But Leo never quite gave up, even when he was the obvious loser," Theresa continued, almost in the same breath. "In such cases, he usually tried in one way or another to get the prospect interested in scattering the ashes. It really got nasty sometimes. So much so that I hated to pick up the phone if I thought it might be him."

"You mentioned Mr. Frame's ordering cheap graves when he had his funerals lined up. What exactly did you mean by that?"

"Oh, you know. No-Frills, the least desirable of all possible locations, from the point of view of accessibility as well as appearance. He killed any number of big sales for us here—bronze memorials, garden locations, memorial estates—what you're interested in— crypts in the community mausoleum." Lavina recalled Karl Janowitz's sales pitch for bronze memorials.

"He and Mr. Janowitz obviously didn't get along then either," the former actress said.

"Well, Karl was lucky in that respect. Most of Leo's dealings were directly with Mr. Creighton."

"I see. And they certainly don't seem to have gotten on very well at all."

"You can say that again; they argued about practically everything," Theresa agreed, shaking her head. "The latest being who should sell and install the vaults. That's still up in the air. The cemetery hasn't set a firm policy yet, though it shouldn't be long now."

"What do you mean by vaults?" Lavina was finally going to learn the answer to that puzzler.

"That's the outer casing used to protect the casket and the deceased."

From what? Lavina wondered. Certainly not the Final Judgment.

"Actually," Theresa said, "what it does is protect the ground from caving in when the time comes for the casket to begin to disintegrate. It's more for the cemetery's sake than for the family's, if you ask me. Just forestalls a lot of later problems."

"What about grave monuments and markers?" Lavina asked. "I know I was only allowed a small one in the ground here for my husband. They said at the time—this is six years ago we're talking about—that it was the policy in all the new sections of the cemetery."

"That's right. It cuts down on maintenance. But that's a different problem altogether," Theresa said, throwing up her hands. "It has nothing to do with the funeral director at all, so Leo was never involved with that." She paused. "What we're actually doing now, though—or hoping to do, I should say—is set up our own mortuary so people won't need an outside funeral home at all. Everything will be available to them here at Evergreen." The woman spoke as if the idea was the panacea for the whole of Sullivan County, if not for dying Americans everywhere. Talk about monopoly, Lavina thought.

"And I suppose I shouldn't say this, of course," Theresa added, almost as an afterthought, "but Leo Frame was also a dirty old man."

Now there was an expression Lavina would have sworn had gone out sometime back there with the Brooklyn Dodgers. "Oh?" she said.

The woman dismissed the obvious questions with a wave of a fragile hand. "I'd really rather not go into that part of it, Mrs. London, if you don't mind. As I said, I probably shouldn't even have brought it up." No, of course not. With a little more urging, though, Lavina was sure the woman would be gushing away like a geyser. But since she really didn't believe any details of Leo Frame's extra marital activities would add greatly to the basic fact of their existence, she let it pass.

"Does Mr. Creighton own the Park?" she asked matter-of-factly.

"Oh, no!" Theresa was quick to answer, as if coming to her employer's defense. "Evergreen is a tax-free, nonprofit organization." Now there was as obvious a bit of company brainwashing as she'd ever heard, Lavina concluded. "Actually, from the way I understand it," Theresa continued, "the land is owned by a group of promoters or something. It's all rather involved . . . too much so for me, I'm afraid." And all the more convenient if one wanted to conceal any hanky-panky, Lavina thought. She seemed to recall a state investigation along these lines back in the late forties, early fifties.

Just then the phone rang and the younger woman

got up to answer it, picking up the extension on the large, prominently placed desk that obviously belonged to Gregory Creighton.

Lavina turned to glance out the wide, latticed, front window past the dense, pink azaleas. No sign yet of the blue Tempo. Susanne must have taken the chase seriously. Not that she'd find the cheese Ritz anywhere in Monticello, of course. They'd long since ceased making the crackers, a fact to which Lavina could well testify, having written to the company herself by way of inquiry. Although she felt a twinge of guilt, she certainly had no intention of letting her conscience ruin the rest of a beautiful, May morning.

She turned back to look at Theresa Francotti, who was now seated at the desk nodding into the phone and jotting down notations on a sheet of white paper on the blotter in front of her. What a wretched business this whole death business could be. And talk about dog-eat-dog! From what she'd just learned, it sounded to Lavina as if both cemeterian and funeral director had been out to kill each other's business. But what was even stranger was the fact that Leo Frame had as much reason to want Gregory Creighton out of the way as vice versa—if not more so.

Chapter Fourteen

Under the pressure of both hands he squeezed the rinse water out of his hair and lifted his face to meet the fine but forceful spray emitted by the adjustable shower head. His eyes were closed. The water was warm and somehow protective against the cool morning air.

Even as a young boy he had loved lingering in the shower long after the requisite ablutions were done. It was one of the few places that had insured any sort of privacy in a four-room apartment with four older siblings, a mother, and sometimes a father. It was no substitute for his own room, by any means, but at least it periodically gave him a chance to feel like an individual in his own home. He had never been much of a mixer at any time, so it took him pretty much by surprise when the prettiest girl in school invited him to his own prom. And now, at twenty-two, he was actually "involved," as he liked to call it, for the first time in his life—and with an older woman, at that. He wasn't sure if he liked the idea or not; it was still too early to tell.

He turned to face the opposite wall, letting the water beat down on his as yet untanned back. His big toe caught under a loose petal of a faded, floral decal on the tub floor. Someday he'd have his own all-glass, stall shower, one without crappy, mildewed, plastic curtains that always billowed in on you unexpectedly when you were in the middle of something important. With the way things had been going this past week, it might even be sooner than he hoped.

There were the letters, for one thing; they'd been a real surprise. He'd felt a little foolish, of course—not to mention a bit heartless—when he'd finally brought himself to mention them to her, suggesting she might want to buy them from him. But what the hell! A guy had to eat, and that took money, especially if you liked eating out, which he did—and he wasn't talking Burger King, either. Certainly the pittance the county paid him wasn't going to keep him in the style to which he someday hoped to grow accustomed. He laughed aloud at his own play on words, then wiped the water out of his eyes with the palms of his hands.

He hadn't been sure, of course, exactly how she'd take it—he'd even been prepared to say he was joking if she started making a fuss. But she hadn't. She hadn't even seemed all that surprised by the suggestion, not really. Not like he thought she'd be, like a blond tigress or something. She could get like that sometimes in bed, especially with those nails of hers. And those green eyes. He swore he could see them flashing sometimes even in the semidarkness of her bedroom. Like a pair of matching gems. He had been prepared for the possibility that his action might throw a damper on their relationship, kill it even, but it hadn't. Not so far, anyway. The woman obviously needed what he had to offer more than he needed her. He grinned as he let his corded hands run down his wet hairy chest to his stomach. He turned back to face the shower, scooping up handfuls of water and splashing them over his face.

All in all, fifteen hundred wasn't so bad. As far as he could tell, the letters weren't even worth that much. But Annis Barth obviously thought otherwise. She must have. Otherwise why would she have paid? Why not just laugh in his face and send him packing? That would have been as embarrassing as all hell. But no, she hadn't hesitated, not even for a minute, before agreeing to hand over the cash—he'd insisted on cash—for the seven envelopes. Agreed one night, paid the next. As simple as that. The only thing that annoyed him, if he let himself dwell on it, was the thought that he probably could have held out for more. But that was all right. After all—how did the expression go?—he hadn't put all his eggs in one basket. That was just the hors d'oeuvres, so to speak. There was still the matter of the folder. He'd have to handle that with a hell of a lot more care, though. Which was precisely why he was taking his time, figuring out every angle, trying to anticipate every possibility. He'd gone over the papers several times, and while it still wasn't all completely clear to him, he knew it meant big money for a certain somebody whose name was etched now in his mind as clearly as the ones chiseled in those tombstones at the cemetery. He smiled up at the jetting spray, his eyes closed again. From the way he looked at it, there was no reason on God's little earth why that somebody couldn't be Robert Anthony Uberon.

God, what a hick town, he thought as he reached down to turn off the shower. He laughed out loud again as he recalled how supremely simple it had all been. "Candy from a baby" came to mind, and the cliché fit. Better than any he could invent, anyway.

"Go on down to Frame's office there and go through his desk with a fine-tooth comb," the sheriff had told him. "I doubt you'll find anything important, but you never know. And watch your fingers. The boys will want to test there later for prints." Fuckin' asshole. What did he think he was—stupid? Well, he'd shown him who was stupid all right. Too bad he couldn't actually shove it in his nose for him to see. Subordinate "outsheriffs" sheriff.

He'd spotted Annis Barth's fancy curlicue script and purple ink as soon as he dug out the white, linen envelopes that had been shoved in the back of the deep, bottom drawer. They weren't even wrapped; he'd been the one who'd put the rubber band around them before he stuck them in his pants pocket. At the time, he hadn't known what they were. They might have been business for all he knew, though he doubted it, not in envelopes like that. He could tease her with them if nothing else. It wasn't until he opened them at home and read them that he realized he had something that might really interest his superiors—if not Annis herself.

He'd almost missed the thin, accordion folder altogether, filed as it was, unlabeled, under Miscellaneous.

The sheriff had already gone back down to the Selection Room where the lab crew was preparing to dust and vacuum, and the two old biddies he'd been interviewing in the office had taken off in their car after consulting with the funeral director. When he'd sat down on the fancy swivel chair with his back to the bay window and dumped out the contents and scanned them, he knew he was definitely on to something. The fact that it just might have been the key to Leo Frame's murder hadn't seemed important. Or rather, it had, but not in the same way as Sheriff Arthur would have viewed it, and as Officer Uberon should have. He had had no qualms about what he did, none whatsoever. He had joined the force for only one reason, as a possible stepping-stone. To where, he hadn't considered at the time. Maybe somewhere in the storied world of politics. With the materials spread on the mahogany desk in front of him, he knew he'd found his magic staircase sooner, though in a much different way, than he'd expected, even if some prudes might have considered it the back stairs.

The only problem, of course, had been how to get the folder out of the office. Once it was in the car, there'd be no problem. The car was his responsibility, and he usually took it home with him at night and parked it in back of his garden-apartment complex.

After he'd emptied the folder, he returned it to the spot in the file drawer where he'd found it. There was no way he could fit any of the items in his wallet or pockets, and he could hardly walk out of the building with the things in his hands. It would be just his luck to run into Arthur. He looked around, first on the desktop, then around the office. A book from one of the shelves wouldn't help. Too small. And too obvious.

He laughed when the idea finally struck him. "Keep it under your hat, Uberon." And that's exactly what he did, literally. Taking off his wide-brimmed, gray trooper's hat, complete with purple hatband, he folded everything as tightly as he could, and shoved it all up into the crown. He then replaced the hat snugly on his head, making sure it wouldn't fall prey to the morning wind. He remembered now how giddy he felt, like a child imitating 007. Then, in his cockiest and most nonchalant manner, he sauntered out of the funeral director's office, across the expanse of plush, olive carpeting, and out the front door. Once he was back in the car, he looked around outside, lifted off the hat, and dug out his find. Surreptitiously, he shoved the lot under the driver's seat and donned his hat. Then he turned on the radio, tipped the hat down over his eyes, lay back on the headrest, and let the rock beat pour its waves over him.

Chapter Fifteen

"These dwarf dahlias look pretty, Gran," Susanne said, holding up a plastic six-pack of sturdy, young plants. "It says mixed colors, though."

"I already have almost two dozen Rigoletto dahlias I started indoors this winter," Lavina London said as she bent over to inhale the clove-scented dianthus on the display table in front of her.

"You've got such a green thumb, Gran," the girl said with admiration, replacing the pack on the table. "What are we here for, then? Anything special?" We know what you're here for, at least, Lavina thought, a smile betraying her appreciation of the fact. Young Martin Knappe. Unfortunately—for Susanne, at least —the young man was out on a landscaping job at Beaver Lake, or so the proprietress told her when she asked. Not that they hadn't already gotten together since Susanne's arrival, because they had—several times.

"I don't know, dear," Lavina said. "I thought I might like something for the circular bed around the flagpole." She gave way to temptation and fingered the soft, veined, rubbery leaves of the nasturtiums in front of her. "I'm getting tired of having impatiens there every year, but there's really not much choice because the spot doesn't get much more than early-morning sun."

"Did you find anything, Mrs. London?" she heard from behind them. They stood now facing the highway in an aisle between the homemade wood tables in front of the greenhouse of Barth Nurseries, where the first of the season's annuals and perennials had been set out to catch the eye of passing motorists.

"Not yet, Miss Barth," Lavina said, turning her head. "I was just telling my granddaughter here that I was looking for something low-growing for shade besides impatiens."

Annis Barth took a long look at the slim blond girl in white, linen slacks and halter who had turned to face her, and smiled. "So this is your granddaughter." She extended a ringed hand that Susanne accepted in a warm handshake. "I've seen her here several times"—Lavina was sure she gave the girl a conspiratorial wink—"but I had no idea the two of you were related."

"Oh, yes," Lavina said. "Of course she's away at college most of the time. When she's not actually at home in New York with her parents, that is. That's my daughter and her husband, Mr. and Mrs. Halliday." She looked over her shoulder at her granddaughter and caught her eye. "She occasionally makes the supreme sacrifice, though, and comes to visit her old grandmother here in the sticks."

"Oh, Gran, stop. You'll have Miss Barth believing you in a minute." Grandmother and granddaughter exchanged smiles.

"Halliday," Annis Barth repeated, a pensive expression on what to Lavina was an otherwise pale, haggard-looking face. "I don't think I've ever met your daughter, have I?"

"Not that you'd remember, I'm sure," Lavina said. "Tracey doesn't get up this way too often these days, and when she does, it's like pulling teeth to get her out of the house."

"What's your first name, dear?" Miss Barth asked, lifting a long black thread off the waistband of the girl's slacks.

"Susanne."

"Susanne," she repeated, staring now into the girl's face. She ran the tip of her tongue across her dry, metallic-blue lips.

"Do you have any suggestions?" Lavina asked.

"Suggestions?" Annis turned back and looked vacantly at Lavina.

"Shade flowers instead of impatiens," Lavina said, somewhat amused, shaking the woman down from the clouds.

"Oh, yes, of course," Annis said with a faint smile on her cracked lips as she crossed her arms over her substantial breasts. "How about some colorful coleus? I have some dwarf types." She wore an unstarched white blouse open in a *V* at her neck, and a pair of aqua culottes. The skirtlike trousers must be the "in" thing this season, Lavina thought. First the Francotti woman, now Miss Barth. She wondered how she'd look in them, if they'd be too young for her. Her mother, she remembered, had always been a stickler for women dressing their age. Thank God the poor dear had never lived to witness the introduction of women's shorts and pants, not to mention short-shorts. Even Lavina, broad-minded as she liked to consider herself, had been put off by them at the time, though that, too, had changed.

"Coleus?" she repeated. "No, I don't think so."

"Some pretty, blue lobelia, maybe, or wax-leaf begonias?"

Lavina crinkled up her small nose in obvious veto, then turned and moved around the table to the next aisle so that she faced the greenhouse, leaving the four-feet-wide table to separate them. "You've been pretty busy this week," she said, still pretending to search around the table, lifting out one plastic name label after another for bedding plants she didn't recognize.

"No more so than any spring," Annis said. "Most of the annuals are delivered and set up for me here by an outside firm. I couldn't possibly manage to grow all the varieties I need here by myself."

"I wasn't referring to the plants," Lavina said, looking across at the younger woman. "I meant all the deaths we've had."

Lavina couldn't tell whether it had been the injection of the subject or just carelessness, but at that point, Annis knocked over a large flat of marigold seedlings on the edge of the table, sending them hurtling to the hard earth floor.

"Here, let me give you a hand with those," Lavina said, at the same time making no apparent effort to do anything of the kind. "Susanne, help Miss Barth there, will you."

"Thank you," Annis said as the girl, with her

grandmother's unnecessary supervision, helped her gather up the tiny plants and replace them in the flat, firming the soil around their dislodged roots. Together they lifted the flat back onto the table.

When the salvage work had been accomplished, Annis Barth brushed off her hands and looked across at Lavina, her green eyes reflecting the rays of the morning sun. Lavina wondered if the woman wore contact lenses.

"The floral shop, you mean," Annis said, digging soil out from under her long, vermilion nails. "Yes, it was a bit rushed there for a few days. First Judge Cioffi, then Mrs. O'Kirk's father. Even a few unexpected orders for wakes up at Barstow's in Monticello."

"Not to mention Mr. Frame and his stepson," Lavina pinpointed, careful to observe the proprietress's reaction.

"There were no flowers for Mr. Frame," Annis said, looking up from her nails. "He was cremated and had a brief memorial service at the cemetery, that's all. Which is too bad, because a number of people phoned here inquiring, intending to send pieces." She looked down again at her still raised hands, then splayed her fingers, checking the stones in her rings. All told, Lavina could count six of them. "I don't know what they plan on doing about the stepson once his body is released by the police. If it's up to Elen—his stepmother—probably the same thing."

"It's so difficult to believe we've had two murders in town," Lavina said, shaking her head. "Especially when one of them is such a prominent businessman, and obviously well-respected." She paused to let the final, emphasized words sink in, only to be disappointed by the complete lack of visual or oral response. "You must have done a lot of business with Mr. Frame over the years," she added, when it was clear Annis Barth was going to say nothing.

The blond woman shrugged, then tightened the bobby pins that held back the uncombed, dyed hair behind each ear. "More so when my father was alive, I'm afraid," she finally said. "Leo changed a lot over the years. Recently he'd been pretty much against flowers of any kind in the funeral home. Wasn't afraid to voice his opinion, either, I might add." The smile on the thin lips was by far the most pleasant Lavina had seen since the woman joined them. What bothered her, though, was her inability to tell whether the gratuitous admission was an honest, spontaneous one, or whether the woman was just covering herself, figuring they'd probably learn the truth somewhere along the line from young Martin Knappe. At that particular moment she wished Susanne had never met the budding florist.

"That must have hurt your business somewhat, though, didn't it?" she ventured.

"Of course," Annis admitted with a silly-looking grin. She might just as well have added, "you idiot."

"Who do you think could have killed him and his stepson?" While Lavina's lengthy career had for the most part been behind a radio microphone, and therefore unseen by the public at large, she had still managed to develop all the facial expressions that eventually became part of any good actress's natural baggage. The look of disbelief and puzzlement that spread now across her bright, open face could not have failed to fool even the most astute of critics. Actually, she felt downright stupid hearing herself mouth such a banal question.

"I really have no idea," Annis said, obviously accepting the question at face value. She turned and proceeded down the narrow aisle to the adjoining table, Susanne at her heels, and Lavina following suit on the opposite side of the display tables.

"You know his wife, I assume," Lavina said.

"Elenice? Sure." Annis stopped and looked across at her customer, squinting what Lavina could now see were reddened eyes. "Why? Do you think she killed him?"

Lavina adjusted the strap of her bag on her shoulder and shook her head. "Heavens, no. I hardly know the woman. The most I've spoken to her was at Mr. Shaw's wake here this past week. The only reason I mention her is that I understand she actually accused the boy—Peter, wasn't it?—of having killed her husband. That was before he was found murdered himself, of course."

"Did she?" The question was quite sufficient to convince Lavina that Annis Barth had no intention of giving away too much if she didn't have to. She knew, of course, from the phone conversation she'd overheard at the funeral home that the woman was well aware of Elenice Frame's unfounded accusation.

"I thought Mr. Marcus told you." She wasn't sure it was the wisest course of action, but she didn't seem to be getting anywhere otherwise.

Annis gave Lavina the same type of long look now as she had given Susanne earlier. "What is it you're trying to say, Mrs. London? You seem unusually concerned with this whole business if you ask me."

"I should think murder would be everyone's concern," Lavina said. "Especially when it's practically on one's doorstep."

"Lucky for the rest of us everybody doesn't think

the same way." The pleasant smile, fleeting though it was, crossed Annis's face again. "I told Mr. Marcus I thought it was you he described having seen in his office. He couldn't remember your name, only that you were a close friend of the O'Kirks. That, and the physical description—the steel-gray hair, the height, and of course, the glasses on the silver chain"—she pointed now to the culprits in question—"just about clinched it as far as I was concerned." She ran a pointed, red fingernail across her chin. "You wouldn't happen to be spying by any chance?"

"I'm sorry you feel that way, Miss Barth," Lavina said, recovering her composure. It wasn't every day you learned of people talking about you like that behind your back. Not that she'd been doing much differently herself, of course, now that she happened to think about it. "I can't help the fact that I over-heard a phone conversation if that's what you're referring to, now can I? And even though you may associate snooping with elderly women, I can assure you that I have far more important things to do than snoop and gossip."

"I didn't say anything about elderly women."

"You didn't have to." Lavina paused to take a deep breath of cool morning air. "On the other hand, I am very interested in these murders, and intend to do anything and everything I can to help discover who's responsible, regardless of what anyone thinks."

"That's your decision to make, I suppose," Annis said, "if not strictly your prerogative."

Lavina crossed her fingers at her sides. "I've already spoken to Sheriff Arthur and have his blessing."

"I see," Annis said. "And you'd like my cooperation." Again the hint of a smile.

"I'd appreciate it, yes."

"I don't see how I can be of any help, but okay. Shoot. What do you want to know?"

"Tell me about Elenice Frame," Lavina said bluntly, surprising even herself. "What do you think about her accusation?"

Annis looked down and fingered the rings on her left hand. "Well, for one thing, I imagine her intention in shifting the blame for Leo's death onto Peter was quite deliberate," she said, as if no unpleasant words had passed between them. "There's a lot of money at stake there, and as far as I know, everything was up for grabs between her and the boy. Maybe Leo left everything to Peter, and that was the only thing she could think of on the spur of the moment to keep him from getting it."

"If she knew ahead of time that Peter was going to inherit everything, that would sort of rule her out as the murderer in the first place, wouldn't it?" Lavina wished now that she had pressed Tod Arthur for particulars on the man's will. How could she have walked out of the man's office without remembering it? On the other hand, Tod hadn't thought it important enough to mention to her, either. Or had he held it back deliberately? That sounded more like the Tod Arthur she knew, she decided.

"Maybe," Annis said. "Then maybe again she didn't know. Maybe she was under the impression that she was going to inherit everything and found out otherwise too late and had to get rid of Peter as well."

"Now you're suggesting she killed her husband."

"No. I'm just mentioning one possibility, that's all. Who did he leave everything to, by the way?"

"I don't know," Lavina said.

"Then all this hypothesizing doesn't make much sense, does it?"

"It might in the long run."

"Well, one way or another, you can be sure Elenice Frame was on top of things. That cunning little mind of hers is always operating at full speed."

"You sound as if you know her well."

Annis hesitated, then moved out of the aisle. "Let's go inside. It's getting a bit chilly out here with this wind." Her lightweight culottes snapped like little flags now behind her legs, clinging frantically to her thighs and knees. She turned and led Lavina and Susanne past the greenhouse to the white, concrete building adjoining it, where she pushed open the door and preceded them in to the accompaniment of a tinkling bell. The old-time device awakened fleeting memories Lavina had long since put out of her mind.

Once inside with the door closed, Annis looked around the large, open room. Then, obviously spotting whatever it was she was searching for, headed resolutely across to the work table that stretched out unobstructed in the middle of the shop. Lavina halted to inhale the cool, pleasant conglomeration of fragrances that pervaded the room.

Annis picked up a pack of cigarettes from the table and shook out a few, offering them first to one woman, then the other. When both Lavina and Susanne declined, she slid one out, stuck it in the corner of her mouth between thin lips, and lit it from a disposable lighter she'd taken from the pocket of her culottes. "I'm afraid the stools are all I have in here if you'd care to sit down," she said, indicating the tall-backed items in question on either side of the worktable.

"That's all right," Lavina said, "I'd just as soon stand." Actually the small of her back was killing her. Old Peter Pain at work with his trusty pickax again. She'd always enjoyed those old Ben-Gay commercials.

Susanne hoisted her youthful frame onto one of the stools, pushing down on the footrest until the seat turned to face the two other women.

From her own stool, Annis spewed out a stream of smoke high over her head. "You know of course that Jeffrey Marcus and I are . . . well, on good terms. He's been at the funeral home now for over two years, so he's had an opportunity to get to know the two of them—Leo and Elenice, I mean—and see them in action, not to mention Peter, when he was home from school."

"Did the three of them live above the funeral home?" Susanne chimed in for the first time, her hands gripping the seat of her stool as she swung it in a small arc from side to side.

"Yes," Annis said.

Lavina shivered. "That would take some getting used to, I would imagine."

"Not if you have ice in your veins like they do—or did, in Leo's case. Actually, I shouldn't say that about Peter at all. He wasn't a bit like his stepparents. He was much more sensitive. Too much so for his own good, I'm afraid. It's no wonder he went away to board at college. It was probably the first chance he had to get away from the two of them."

"According to the people at the motel, he checked

in there Sunday afternoon, which of course was before his stepfather was killed," Lavina said, trying now to sort things out in her own mind. "When they checked, the police learned that his college had just let out the Friday before. Which meant he must have been in an awful hurry to get back here."

"That does sound odd," Annis said. "Unless he planned to go back again for summer session and had to come home for some reason first. Money, most likely."

"That's just the point, though," Lavina said. "He didn't go home—not back to the house, that is. Why?"

"I see what you mean."

"And if it was just a matter of needing money from his stepfather, I'm sure he could have arranged that just as easily by phone, don't you think?"

Annis shrugged and took another puff on her cigarette. "I suppose so. But under the circumstances, we can hardly believe he came back to kill Leo, now can we? I mean, I suppose it's possible and all, that he killed his stepfather, and then someone else killed him, but it doesn't seem very likely to me."

"No," Lavina said, "I tend to agree. I'm quite sure we're dealing with only one murderer." She certainly had no intention of telling Annis about the boy's strange complaint to her and Winnie at the motel the afternoon of his murder, which, when you came down to it, was probably why he had come home in the first place. It was probably the first chance he had after learning of his stepfather's decision to cut him out of the will, for whatever reason. In that case, stopping at the motel would have made sense. If she only knew the truth behind the will.

Maybe the boy had only been projecting his fears; maybe he'd had nothing to worry about all along. With both Peter and Leo gone, they might never know what was behind it all.

"Did Peter have any close friends here?" she asked, slipping her bag off her shoulder and setting it on the table. "Ones he would have hung out with, confided in maybe?"

"I have no idea," Annis said, flipping through a handful of small, stiff name cards she'd slipped out of the rack attached to the side of the table. "I don't recall ever seeing him with anyone in particular when he lived here. Perhaps Marty or George would know." She darted a questioning glance across at Susanne. "Though, for that matter, I'm not sure either of them even knew him."

Susanne brought the swivel stool to a halt. "According to Marty, Peter Frame was three years ahead of them in high school, and they didn't know him to speak to. This was his last year in college, as a matter of fact."

"You didn't tell me that, dear," Lavina said, scolding her granddaugther with a wicked glance of her pale blues. "That he graduated, I mean." She turned back to face Annis without waiting for the girl's reply. "I wonder if either of the stepparents went to his graduation." She shifted her weight and leaned now against the table, glad for the rubber matting under foot.

"I wouldn't know," Annis said, still toying with the cards.

"That poor boy," Lavina said, shaking her head. "As far as I'm concerned, there's no substitute for parental love and guidance. One's outlook on life starts in the home." When Annis made no reply, she asked, "How well did Elenice and Leo get along, by the way? Do you know?"

"From outward appearances, not well at all," Annis said. "She wanted to run things, and he was just as adamant about staying at the helm. From what little Jeffrey's told me, they battled almost constantly. Upstairs and down." Annis laughed now for the first time. "I just remembered. One of his favorite expressions to Jeffrey whenever he knew he had overheard one of their arguments used to be, 'That woman will be the death of me yet.' Maybe it was more prophetic than one would have thought."

"So it would seem," Lavina said, finally weakening and sliding a stool out from underneath the work table. "Would you have called her a devoted wife?" she asked as she sat down with visible relief.

"If you mean, were there other men, I'd have to answer No. At least none that I've heard of. But then, as I said before, Elenice is very cunning, so anything's possible. Offhand, if I had to make a guess, I'd say yes, but then you might consider that the kettle calling the pot black."

"Nonsense!" Lavina said. "You're a single woman; she's not." Actually, she knew she shouldn't be passing judgments at all. It was one of the things Father Cernac always seemed to have to admonish her for in confession, but it was difficult for her not to when she had been brought up to respect certain values, which, like the dollar, now seemed to be suffering the effects of devaluation.

"Other than that," Annis continued, " 'devoted' is hardly a word I'd use in connection with Elenice Frame, unless, of course, we happened to be talking about money."

"I understand there was a bit of bad blood between Leo and Mr. Creighton over at Evergreen, too," Lavina said.

"You *have* been making the rounds, haven't you?" Annis said. "And yes, they had their disagreements, business ones mainly. But then it would be difficult to find anyone in Boulder or hereabouts that Leo hasn't fought with over one thing or another. You could almost say it was open season on him, which is why pinpointing his killer is going to be so difficult."

"That's not the case with Peter, though, is it? And we're agreed that there is only one murderer."

Annis nodded, squeezing the thin lips close together so as to become invisible. "So we'd be looking for a common denominator, wouldn't we?"

"Which is probably the only way the murders will be solved," Lavina agreed. "There has to be something to connect the two killings. Leo's life reads like an open book, while his stepson's is almost a complete mystery."

"I told you they were unalike."

"What about Mrs. Frame?" Lavina asked, returning to their earlier topic. "How did she get along with Mr. Creighton?"

Annis Barth gave another little laugh. "Now there's an insinuation if I ever heard one. But as I said before, I know nothing more than what I've seen on the surface, which is that they were on good terms—business-wise."

"And Mr. Janowitz?"

"That I don't know. I think Leo did most of his business directly with Gregory Creighton."

"Which brings us to Mr. Marcus," Lavina said, almost voicing the period.

Annis smiled again. It was getting to be a pleasant

habit, Lavina thought. "Leo watched Jeffrey like a hawk," she said. "He didn't trust him with anything. I'm sure he thought he was out to take over the business in some way. He even threatened to let him go a couple of times when Jeffrey spoke his mind."

"Did he have any grounds for his suspicions?"

"Certainly not, he was just being ornery, which with him was just a matter of being himself." Annis's face was more flushed than it should have been. Of that Lavina was positive.

"Maybe he didn't trust him around his wife either," she suggested, displaying now a smile of her own.

"Who knows what was in that man's mind? It wouldn't surprise me in the least, knowing him as I did."

"Did Mr. Marcus tell you all this himself?"

"Yes." She smiled again and took another drag on what Lavina saw from the pack on the table was a Camel. "I know what you're thinking—that's what he told *me*. Well, if there was anything else, I don't know."

"I see."

"I wonder if you do, Mrs. London," Annis said, surprising Lavina with her outspokenness. "Don't get me wrong, I don't mean to question your integrity or anything. I'm sure you're keeping as open a mind as possible under the circumstances, but it's such a damned mixed-up situation that I'm not sure an outsider could possibly appreciate all the ramifications, never mind understand them, what with the whole funeral business and Leo's general attitude of 'Hooray for me and eff you.'

"I'm not one to bend over backwards for anyone,

Mrs. London, let alone Leo Frame, but I went out of my way, if I must say so myself, to try to get him to understand my point of view in the florist business. He wasn't having any part of it; couldn't have cared less. He practically laughed in my face. What really hurt was the fact that he wasn't always like that. Before he married Elenice, he was pretty decent. I remember my father saying as much, too—on several occasions. Well, after that, I'm afraid I just started treating him the same way he treated me. Can you blame me? I mean, a person can only take so much."

"No, not at all," Lavina said. She wondered why the woman had suddenly steered the conversation back to herself, unless she just felt uneasy discussing Jeffrey Marcus. "But getting back to your initial comment, Miss Barth, I *am* trying to understand the whole picture. That's why I'm doing what I'm doing. I certainly hope I don't give the impression that I'm going around half-cocked. I have a feeling that by the time I'm finished I'll know more about Leo Frame than any other person around here, his wife included."

"Well, I just hope you don't end up victim number three, while you're at it." With that, Annis stubbed out the cigarette five or six times in the five-and-dime ashtray on the table, finally pressing it into the glass with her thumb.

"My God!" Susanne said, sitting up straight on her stool, obviously realizing the dire possibility now for the first time. "Gran, I really think you should leave this whole business to Sheriff Arthur, like he suggested."

Annis Barth narrowed her eyes and shot Lavina an accusatory look.

"You don't have to make the rounds with me, Susanne, if you're afraid. I'll understand."

"I'm not afraid—not for me, I mean. But I am afraid for you. And besides, what good would it do to leave you on your own? At least with me around . . . well, maybe whoever might get any ideas about hurting you would think twice."

"Why? Are you into karate now, too, dear?"

The three women broke out laughing at the same time, Lavina the hardest of all.

"Just one more thing, Miss Barth," the actress said as she slid down off her stool and made a grab for her shoulder bag. "What about Leo himself? Was *he* doing any running around, as we used to say?"

Annis Barth looked down between her culotted legs to an indeterminate spot on the rubber matting on the floor, then back up again. "I don't think Leo made any great attempt to keep his philandering a secret— except maybe from his wife, and then, I'm sure, merely to avoid giving her additional fuel to stoke her fire. Whether or not she actually knew—or cared, for that matter—I couldn't say. Leo would never have won any awards for subtlety, I'm afraid."

Even so, he seemed to have been an extraordinarily astute businessman, Lavina thought. "And just how widespread was this philandering, as you call it?" she asked.

Annis shrugged. "Any female on two legs was fair game for Leo Frame, I'd say." She paused. "Come to think of it, I'm not sure he'd even have insisted on the two legs."

"Anyone you'd care to mention?" Lavina asked.

"To be perfectly honest, no one I even know."

"Well, thank you, Miss Barth," Lavina said somewhat abruptly as she hoisted the cloth strap of her bag to her shoulder. "You've really been very helpful, I'm sure."

"I have?" Annis Barth reached for the cigarette pack again and slid it off the table onto her lap.

"Once the pieces are ready to come together, I'm sure I'll find I've picked up several here, thanks to you." She turned to her granddaughter. "Let's go, dear. We'd better pick up something for that flower bed so we won't have completely wasted so much of Miss Barth's valuable time."

"Who are you going to question about me, Mrs. London?" Annis asked without getting off her stool. "Not Elenice Frame, I hope." She gave a little laugh.

At the door with her hand on the knob, Lavina half turned to look back over her left shoulder without actually making eye contact with the other woman. "Catch as catch can, as they say, Miss Barth. Catch as catch can."

Chapter Sixteen

He hated to think that the place was beginning to feel like home.

Besides the obvious black humor in the thought, he was already sick of the plush, seaweed-green carpet that rolled out everywhere underfoot like the polluted waters of the beach he remembered as a kid. Even the rich, highly lemon-polished furniture and the glossy white-sashed bay window of the office in which he now sat had finally gotten to him. Not to mention the perpetual—he winced at the very thought of the word —floral scent that invaded the nostrils from the moment you opened the front door. It was enough to clear up anyone's sinuses.

Tod Arthur had deliberately chosen to sit on the long, brown-leather sofa this time around rather than at the huge, mahogany desk in front of the jungle of plants. His wide-brimmed hat took up the empty cushion that separated him from the not-too-grieving widow at the far end, who sat facing him with one arm on the armrest and the other across the back of the sofa. The assistant funeral director—or had he been kicked upstairs?—sat uncomfortably on one of the armless leather-upholstered chairs he had pulled over from the desk. Arthur had to look up from the couch in order to meet his eyes. It was not a position he generally adopted while interrogating possible suspects.

"Well, it looks like your ideas about your stepson were a bit off base, Mrs. Frame," he said.

"My husband's stepson, if you don't mind, Sheriff."

"As you wish."

"Is that what you came back here to tell me, Sheriff? That I was wrong? Because if it is, I have a lot more important things to do than sit here and listen to you gloat." She brought a hand to her forehead where she smoothed down the already neat bangs. The tight, peacock-blue dress she wore today was as stunning as the dress the sheriff had seen her wear earlier in the week. He was a bit taken aback when he realized that the color nearly matched her eyes, which he was sure he remembered as being green. Probably a trick of artificial lighting.

"I came back to discuss your husband's will more than anything else, Mrs. Frame."

"What about it?"

"Your lawyer showed us a copy, of course. You know how it reads, I suppose?"

"Naturally. Leo and I kept no secrets from each other." Famous last words, Arthur thought. "Everything was to be divided equally between me and Peter. I have Leo's copy upstairs. He also appointed me his executor." One way of saving money.

"That 'everything' includes five funeral homes in the state, I understand."

"That's right."

"Now, you told me the last time I was here—when you made your accusation against young Peter—that your husband had intended changing his will and disinheriting the boy." He didn't think it necessary—or proper, for that matter—to repeat the specific reason she had given him, not in the presence of Jeffrey Marcus. Not only because of the personal nature of the accusation, but more important, because that accusation may well have been a piece of conjecture, if not a downright lie, to begin with. Who the hell knew anything for sure about Peter Frame's sexual preferences anyway? That Elenice Frame told him the boy had admitted as much to his stepfather didn't make it a fact.

"Yes. He intended doing it this week, as I told you, but of course was murdered before he had the chance. That was why I originally suspected Peter of killing him. But I've already told you all this. I don't under—"

"Bear with me, please, Mrs. Frame." Tod Arthur had his notepad and ballpoint out on his knee, but had not yet started writing. "You also told me at that time that your husband had written to Peter informing him of his intentions." He paused, looking down the sofa at Elenice Frame.

"That's correct."

"With the boy dead now too, the whole estate will probably come to you, is that correct?" At least that's what the Frame's lawyer up in Monticello had told him would probably be the case, in accordance with further stipulations in the will that he had outlined briefly over the phone.

"So I understand." Certainly, if she had a copy of the will, she was well aware of the provisions in the event of death of either of the heirs.

"That's quite a tidy sum."

Elenice shrugged and crossed one leg over the other, revealing a bit of knee in the process. "I'll manage to get by, I suppose," she said. She made no attempt to hide the grin.

Arthur coughed into his hand and looked down at the blank page in his notepad. Then he looked up again. "Do you have anything to substantiate your husband's intentions to alter his will? A rough copy in his hand, maybe?" Anything typed would be useless. She could have rigged that up herself.

"No, nothing. Unless you find something in his desk. I haven't been able to go through his personal things yet." Not much you haven't, Tod thought. "I'm still not quite over the shock of it all. And now with Peter too . . . well, even though we weren't close, it's still family, isn't it?" Arthur found it very difficult to feel any sort of pity for the woman.

"We've been through the desk, Mrs. Frame, and his files." Unless Rob Uberon had missed something, there was absolutely nothing to prove what Elenice Frame claimed was true.

"You're sure your husband wrote to him?" They'd found nothing among the boy's scant belongings at the motel. Not that they should have, of course. There was still the boy's room at college. The letter might be there, if he'd kept it—if, indeed, he'd even kept the room. Arthur had already been in touch with the Albany police and was waiting for the results of their investigation.

"I only know what he told me, Sheriff." Hearsay, if that. Maybe Leo Frame had intended changing his will, Arthur thought. Except maybe it was Elenice who was to have been the recipient of the cutting, and not Peter at all. Maybe the whole Peter story was just that, a smoke screen. She'd discovered her husband's intentions, then written to Peter herself with the lie about his being disinherited. All in order to get him back here in time to play the dupe in a perfect setup, while in the meantime she—maybe alone, maybe not —did his stepfather in. But, why was Peter murdered? His death only made things look worse for her. Or was that someone else's intention? It was more than a little confusing, and Arthur was in no position to start making accusations he couldn't back up with hard evidence.

"Did Peter have any friends here in Boulder, Mrs. Frame?" Arthur asked, jotting now for the first time in the little, spiral pad.

"I don't know. I suppose so." The hands to the bangs again. "I mean, all boys have friends, don't they?" If that were only true, Arthur thought, thinking of the numerous runaways and teenaged suicides that crowded police blotters everywhere across the country.

"Not anyone you know in particular though."

"No, I'm afraid not."

"He never brought any friends here to your home?" The wrong choice of words. "Upstairs, I mean?"

"You just about answered that one for yourself, Sheriff," Elenice said, a weak smile on her lips. "Living over a funeral home isn't exactly conducive to entertaining, I'm afraid. Especially for youngsters."

Funny but Arthur would have thought kids would be less bothered by such things than most adults.

"Is that the reason Peter gave for not bringing friends here?" he asked.

"Not in so many words, no, but that's what it came down to, I'm sure." She smiled again. "Unless, of course, he really didn't have any friends."

Not much of a substitute stepmother either, Arthur concluded. "How long have you lived with the boy, Mrs. Frame? How long had you and your husband been married?"

"Peter had just turned seventeen when I married Leo. He would have been twenty-two later on this year."

"Almost five years."

"Well, he was away at college a lot of that time, don't forget."

"Of course." Probably the best years the boy ever had. While he was aware of the fact that he kept thinking of the twenty-one-year-old as an adolescent, he somehow found himself unable to alter the impression. "I gather from your lawyer that Peter didn't have a will of his own," he added.

Elenice froze visibly in her seat as if that possibility had never occurred to her. "Not as far as I know," she finally managed.

On the spur of the moment, Arthur decided that it might not be a bad idea to keep the woman guessing. "He might have had one drawn up with another lawyer, of course," he said quickly. "Maybe up in Albany. His copy may be among his things, if not here, then back at college. Might even have a bank deposit box somewhere. I'll have to have the police up there check that out for us if they haven't already done so on their own." He made a quick notation in the pad.

"You said earlier when you phoned that you wanted to see his room," Elenice said, making a move as if to get up from the sofa.

"In a minute, Mrs. Frame," Arthur said, signaling with a hand for her to stay where she was. The look on her face told him she was not exactly thrilled with the injunction. "We did find the boy's bankbook, by the way, among his belongings at the motel. With Boulder National here in town." He lifted his eyes from the pad and looked across at the woman again. "Over twenty-four thousand in savings in it." If he had expected another surprise reaction, he was disappointed because Elenice merely met his hard gaze with her own. Damn it, the eyes *were* peacock blue.

"Yes," she said with a nod, "Leo opened an account for him when he married his mother. Peter was twelve at the time, I believe. Every dollar he ever received as a gift or earned went into it and was never touched. Leo insisted on it. He turned it over to him just last year when Peter turned twenty-one."

Nice, Arthur thought. Not that it did the boy much good, though. "What did he use for spending money?"

Elenice heaved a sigh of obvious annoyance that matched the sneer on her face. "His father gave him whatever he wanted."

"You didn't approve?"

"I had no say in the matter. Leo made it perfectly clear to me that it was between him and his stepson." She made a sweeping gesture of futility with both hands.

"He must have been very fond of the boy."

"I suppose so."

"Why, then, would he decide, all of a sudden, to cut him off without a cent?"

"I already told you, Sheriff. You can say all you want about Leo, in his own peculiar way he was still a highly upright and moral man. He just couldn't accept the fact that Peter was . . ." The word Arthur was sure she normally would have used never reached her lips; instead she merely completely her sentence with a feeble "homosexual," her eyes at the same time darting across at Jeffrey Marcus in his chair opposite them. The dapper assistant funeral director was staring down at his gray, laced shoes.

"Yes, so you've said." This time the sigh was Sheriff Arthur's.

"I can't help it if you don't believe me, Sheriff. You—"

"I didn't say I didn't believe you, Mrs. Frame."

"Well, if it's proof you're looking for, maybe you'll find that among the things upstairs in his room." She spoke as though she knew exactly what it was he would find to substantiate her accusation. He wasn't entirely surprised.

"The strange thing about his savings account," Arthur continued, returning to the subject, "is that Peter seems to have withdrawn some two thousand dollars over the last two months. Back to early March. Would you know any reason for that?"

Again, no particular reaction from the woman facing him on the long sofa. "I'm afraid not," she said. A slight hesitation and then, "Unless maybe he was keeping someone—some young man, I mean. He'd certainly have to pay for it if he wanted it. He was hardly the most—" It was as if Tod's glare cut her short. She closed her blue-shadowed eyelids and shook her frosted head. "I'm being cruel, I know, and I really don't mean to be. I just can't help it. You've obviously gathered for yourself that there was no love lost between Peter and I"—she paused over the incorrect pronoun as if to flaunt her knowledge of proper usage—"and well, maybe that's the reason. Or maybe I'm just a bit old-fashioned, too. If the boy wanted to come out of the closet, well, I suppose he'd be in good company these days. It's just that I still think that's where family skeletons belong."

You're the one who paraded this one out, sweetie, Arthur wanted to say out loud. From what little he knew, Peter Frame had practiced the height of discretion. He still wasn't convinced the boy had done any broadcasting—to his stepfather or to anyone else. But, then, maybe someone else had. *Fama est*, if his high-school Latin served him correctly . . . Rumor hath it . . . true or not. Whom might it have served besides Elenice Frame? Two thousand dollars over two months. He wondered. Maybe those "foul whisperings" were worth more unwhispered. Had Peter Frame been the victim of blackmail? It was becoming more of a muddle than ever.

What kind of woman was this, anyway, who, in his presence at least, displayed absolutely no emotion over the death of her husband and his stepson? Was it a form of stoicism on her part or was she really totally unmoved? She seemed more like an android than flesh and blood. He'd seen hardened murderers with more visible feelings. When it suddenly dawned on him that he was sitting there staring vacantly across at the woman without so much as a word, he turned to face Jeffrey Marcus.

"What about you, Mr. Marcus?" he asked, looking up into the now raised eyes of the assistant funeral director. He couldn't help but admire the dark-gray suit, white-collared, green-striped shirt and gray-and-green tie. The socks inside the pointed, gray shoes and trousers, he was sure, were equally coordinated.

Just then, as if he had read his mind, Marcus made a grab for his right leg and brought it up across his knee, clutching the green-clad ankle with both hands. "Me, Sheriff?" He was obviously unsure of what was expected of him by way of an answer.

"Yes. What can you tell me about Peter Frame?"

Frame's underling shook his head, every strand of the thick brown hair seemingly in place, yet with absolutely no sign of stiffness. "Nothing at all. I barely knew him, and certainly not on any sort of social level." The man's let-me-set-you-straight tone, Arthur thought, almost smacked of overprotesting, as if fearful of any conclusion that might be drawn from his association with the dead boy.

"Don't get upset, Mr. Marcus. Nobody's accusing you of anything," Arthur said by way of reassurance.

"No, of course not, Sheriff. Nor did I mean to give that impression. I was just sort of surprised that you might think I was even aware of Peter Frame's personal problems." He stuck a couple of fingers under the elastic band in the sock and ran them around inside. "All my dealings at the home here, as I'm sure Mrs. Frame will tell you herself, have always been on a strictly professional basis." He darted a glance in the direction of his hoped-for character witness, who merely nodded by way of corroboration.

"You don't have to be involved personally in any way, Mr. Marcus, to be aware of what's going on around you," Sheriff Arthur said with an exasperated smile. "You don't expect me to believe you work in a place like this day in and day out—nights included—without knowing what's going on with the people around you."

"Well, as far as Peter Frame goes, I'm afraid that was just about the case," Marcus insisted, straightening the top of his sock again.

Sheriff Arthur wasn't buying any of it. "How about Leo Frame?" he said. "You mean he never said anything in your presence about his stepson? Even in passing? Never made any comment in a moment of anger or annoyance? Nothing?"

Marcus shook his head again, grasping more tightly at his thick ankle with strong, nervous fingers. "No. And I don't know how I can make myself any clearer. I honestly don't even remember him ever mentioning his stepson to me."

"How about the boy's drinking problem?" Arthur ventured, remembering Lavina's account of Marcus's supposed telephone conversation with Annis Barth.

"Drinking problem?" Jeffrey Marcus narrowed his eyes without taking them off his inquisitor.

"I was under the impression it was fairly common knowledge," Arthur said, wading out a big farther into the murky waters of his own making. "Even people outside the home here seem to have known about it. You were right on the spot; you must have known what was going on—or at least suspected as much."

"Well, yes, now that you bring it up, I was aware that he drank a bit too much for someone his age—at least from what I could see when he was home from school. But I don't see what that has to do—"

"Jeffrey, for heaven's sake!" Elenice Frame scolded from the sofa in obvious annoyance. "The boy was an alcoholic, or damn close to it. What's to hide, for God's sake? You knew it, I knew it, his father knew it." She looked at Arthur. "And if we can believe the Sheriff here, apparently all of Boulder knew it. It was just another example of his weak character. Don't try to defend him." It was obvious to Tod Arthur that the woman knew little, if anything, about alcoholism.

"What point *are* you trying to make, anyway, Sheriff?" she went on, turning to face Arthur again and forestalling any comeback on the part of the assistant funeral director. "I told you Peter was riproaring drunk when I had the misfortune to run into him at the Seventeener. Ask Mr. Creighton. He saw and heard him; he'll tell you." It was the first time she had actually told him whom she had been lunching with that afternoon. Lavina London hadn't missed a trick.

"No need for that, Mrs. Frame. I don't doubt your story for a minute."

"Then why are you giving Mr. Marcus such a difficult time about the whole ugly situation?"

"Just trying to jog his memory a bit, Mrs. Frame," Arthur said. "And it seems to have worked, hasn't it? If he . . . forgot about that"—he took his time with the phrase—"there's no telling what else he may have forgotten, now is there?"

Sheriff Arthur had no preconceived notions whatsoever of what he would find in Peter Frame's room, so what he found was really no great surprise.

A double bed stood off to the right of the doorway and was covered with a simple, dark-blue, ribbed spread that didn't quite reach to the floor on the side that was visible. The headboard was brass, but not heavy looking. The wall-to-wall carpet was either dark blue or black, he couldn't really tell in the artificial light from the ceiling fixture Elenice had switched on for him before she left him on his own. The little natural light that there was came from a double window that faced north.

Solid wooden floor-to-ceiling bookcases, stained and varnished, met in the opposite far corner behind a catty-cornered, modern, Formica desk with aluminum legs and frame. He moved across the room to stand behind the desk facing them. The lower shelves of the cases within reach of the high-backed swivel chair housed what, from a cursory glance, appeared to be used textbooks and reference works—a surprising number of English and foreign language dictionaries, a set of supermarket encyclopedias, current as well as outdated almanacs, an atlas, a zip code directory, a family legal guide, and a copy of Strunk and White's *Elements of Style*, which Arthur lifted out respectfully and opened. It was dog-eared, annotated, and highlighted in yellow marker on every page. More seemed highlighted than not. He slipped the thin volume back alongside the green paperback thesaurus and tried to picture the now dead lad at work at his desk. It wasn't difficult at all. The image, though, as he turned his head briefly to look at the vacant chair, made it seem more pathetically empty than it was.

Why he didn't know, but he dug out the gold-embossed, mustard-colored legal guide as well, a Time-Life publication that looked every bit the handy yet thorough home reference guide on law that it was obviously intended to be. He noticed the tip of a small, blue, index card sticking out of the top just about in the middle of the book. If it had been in the back section, he might have hazarded a guess that it was marking the discussion of wills. With a finger he opened to the page with the card. He was right; it had nothing to do with wills. The heading on the right-hand page was titled "Going Into Business." He gave the opening paragraph a quick read, just enough to see that it dealt with partnerships. The card had obviously just been stuck in the book randomly. At least that's what he thought as he was about to close the cover and spotted the number in red pen on the face of the index card. 187. The same as the page. He flipped through the pages that followed. Unfortunately for him—if it meant anything, that is—the boy hadn't bothered with the yellow highlight marker here at all. He had no idea what it might mean. He was probably just grasping at straws.

He looked up to scan the upper shelves—an odd mix of hardcovers and paperbacks, fiction mostly, with a heavy emphasis on science fiction, fantasy, and horror, all in alphabetical order by author. Many of them Arthur knew from his own reading—Asimov, Blatty, Bradbury, Garrett, King, Nolan, Pohl, Saberhagen, Thorne Smith, Stoker, Tolkien. He looked for a copy of *A Candle for Liebowitz*. It wasn't there. Nor was *The Uninvited*. He would have liked to spend more time perusing the boy's collection but already felt vaguely conscience-stricken as it was. The thought that he might later feel it necessary to flip through each volume individually in the thorough course of his investigation, however, wasn't altogether displeasing. He was also glad it happened to be Rob Uberon's day off.

Canticle

He turned back to the modest desk and pulled open the single, middle drawer above the kneehole. Nothing out of the ordinary—pencils, paper clips, a ruler, scissors, liquid eraser, a yellow highlight marker. He lifted the latter out of the drawer and uncapped it, then brushed the quarter-inch-wide, felt tip across a sheet of typing paper he took from a three-tiered plastic receptacle on top of the desk. It glided moistly across the page, leaving its yellow wake. He clicked the cap tight again on the marker and dropped it back in the front section of the drawer, which he then yanked out farther. The bulk of the compartment contained the usual pads, index cards, notebooks—all blank. He lifted the drawer out from its track and bent over and peered in, running a hand around inside. Nothing.

The only drawers left were on the right-hand side of the desk, a single one at the top and a deep file below it. He slid out the smaller of the two first. More index cards of various sizes and colors, lined and not, white envelopes in two sizes, USPS pre-stamped post cards, gummed address labels—Peter R. Frame and the Boulder, New York address—clear seal, staples and a Swingline stapler, a boxed black ribbon for a Smith-Corona electric portable, most probably the one on the metal stand off to the left of the desk. He lifted off the brittle and cracking vinyl cover to make sure there was nothing still on the roller. There wasn't.

The file drawer seemed devoted mainly to the boy's college courses, with neatly indexed sections divided into History, Fine Arts, Philosophy, and World Literature, each housing what appeared to be course notes. A separate, bulky folder contained what were obviously term papers on a variety of topics. None of the grades were less than a B+, with many A's and

A + 's. The single file labeled Correspondence was empty. What exactly this might have meant, Arthur wasn't ready to hazard a guess.

It was on the top shelf of the boy's closet that he found them, shoved off in the back corner under a couple of empty shoe boxes, one of which was used to store them. Only the fact that the boy had thought it important enough to hide them lent them by particular significance. They were simply male muscle magazines. Nothing pornographic, and certainly nothing overtly homosexual. Just your typical, newsstand weeklies and monthlies on muscle building. Arthur brought the cardboard box over to the bed where he dumped it out and flipped through the batch hurriedly to be sure. If these were the items Elenice had referred to—and he didn't see what else could be— there was no question that the woman had given the boy's room a thorough search. What exactly she had expected or hoped to find, he didn't know, nor did he particularly care at this point.

He tossed the magazines back into the box, replaced the lid, and returned it to the closet shelf, stacking the empty boxes back on top as he had found them. After a quick examination of the pockets of the jackets, slacks, and shirts hanging on the rack, and the footware neatly lined up on the tiled floor next to an empty, plastic clothes-hamper—four pairs of dress shoes, one black, one beige, one gray, one dark brown, and a pair of shabby New Balance running shoes— he closed the closet door and proceeded over to the bureau where he did the same with the clothes in the four drawers.

When he was back at the door with his hand on the light switch ready to shut it off, he turned and gave the room one final look. Nothing, he was sure, had missed his eye, and nothing is precisely what he left the room with. That, and the sickening feeling of emptiness, loneliness, and waste.

Chapter Seventeen

"I'm sure you'll love it, Lillian. It's nothing like the pathetic television movie they made out of it, that's for sure. I don't know why producers and screenwriters think they have to change books so radically when they make them into films. It seems to me they'd be better off writing their own stories to begin with, and save money."

Lillian Dorchester, her cheeks and throat flushed with a patchy, butterfly-like rash, pulled the multi-colored, knitted Afghan tightly around her legs and laid the library copy of *The Cradle Will Fall,* that Lavina London had handed her, on the table alongside her rented wheelchair.

"I appreciate your picking it up for me. Lavina. And, of course, for doing the shopping again."

"Don't be silly."

"I don't know what I'd do without you. You've been a godsend, believe me."

"It's really the Chaplain's Office, Lillian, that got this visiting-friend service started in the first place. It was an excellent idea, though, I agree. We've all got to help one another in this life if it's to have any meaning."

"I'm sure there are many people worse off than me, though, aren't there, Lavina?"

Lavina looked up from the shopping list she had been scanning and smiled across at the woman. She couldn't have been much more than forty-five, yet she looked twenty years older. Like so many other diseases, lupus was unsparing in the pain and damage it wreaked on the bodies of its unfortunate victims. What in a way was even worse as far as Lavina was concerned were the woman's unpredictable yet insidious periods of remission, at which time she was seemingly once again the picture of health. Then, days, weeks, or months—sometimes even years— later, she was bed- or wheelchair-ridden again, if not back in the hospital for another inevitable round with the wonders of medical technology, none of which could promise anything even approaching a cure. But such was the will of God, and while she didn't presume to try to understand it, she was nevertheless grateful for the little she could do to help the unfortunate woman, and any of the countless others St. Luke's Hospital helped through its volunteer visiting program.

"These are frozen vegetables you want, aren't they, Lillian? Not canned?" she asked, squinting down at the list without recourse to her reading glasses that remained dangling at the end of their chain against her breast.

"Oh, yes. They don't have to be a name brand.

Anything will do. I can't always taste them anyway."
And you have to watch your pocketbook, too, love, I
know, Lavina thought. But she was darned if she was
going to let the woman stuff her already racked body
with No-Frills even if it meant, as it frequently did,
making up the difference out of her own pocketbook.
What the woman didn't know wouldn't hurt her.

"Will your son be over tonight?" she asked,
folding the shopping list and inserting it into the
change purse in her handbag.

"Oh, yes. He or Miriam always stops by to make
sure I'm all right and have everything I need when
there's no nurse or homemaker here. I keep telling
them not to, but of course it's like talking to a stone
wall."

"Well, I shouldn't be long, anyway." Lavina
looked at her wristwatch. "It's only four. The stores
shouldn't be too crowded at this hour."

As if on cue, a ball of white fur unwound from its
stationary position at Lillian's feet and leapt up to
land silently in her woolen lap.

"Don't worry. I've got Leopold here to keep me
company."

"So I see."

"He's such wonderful company, Lavina, you
wouldn't believe. You should get one for yourself."
She looked down lovingly at the small cat curled in
her lap. "He loves to curl up next to me when I go to
bed. Sometimes even on my chest."

How good that was for the woman's touch-and-go
condition Lavina didn't know, but she was sure it was
not for her to say in any case. Besides, the poor soul
had little enough joy left as it was.

"I'm afraid I'm on the go too much to keep an

animal of any kind," Lavina said. "It wouldn't be fair to the poor thing, being alone as he would be most of the time. It would just be selfish on my part."

"That's true, I suppose, Lavina," the invalid said, her eyes lowered again to the animal as she stroked it gently with a lesion-scarred hand. "Are you sure I gave you enough money?" she asked, looking up again.

"Positive, dear. Now you get started on that book while you feel up to it, and see if you don't get hooked right off." With that, Lavina opened the front door, pressed in the button on the inside so it would lock after her, and pulled it until she heard it click shut. Once outside, she opened her bag and deposited the house key in the change purse next to the shopping list. It was then that she realized that there were no store or company coupons, which surprised her. She momentarily considered going back inside to see if Lillian had forgotten them, but decided against it.

She proceeded down the three brick steps leading to the entrance of the garden apartment, then around the side of the one-story building to the parking area where she left the car. It was parked head-on between the newly repainted, white guide-lines under Lillian Dorchester's gated, bedroom window, which was closed. The parking space allotted to the woman was numbered, as were all the others, both those against the building and those by the opposite, low, stone wall that formed the south boundary of the garden-apartment complex. There were something like fifty individual apartments, she remembered Lillian telling her, each with its own parking space and private entrance. They were of varying sizes of course, with Lillian's being a one-bedroom unit. Most of the spaces were empty now with many of the tenants still at work or out shopping for the weekend.

She unlocked the door of the blue Tempo and swung her shoulder bag onto the seat on the right when her ears were suddenly assailed by a blast of rock music approaching fast and furious behind her. She turned just in time to see and hear the screeching tires whip into the reserved area two spaces down from where her car was parked. She was surprised to see that it was a county police car.

It stopped just short of ramming into the strip of concrete block embedded in the pavement at the head of the parking space. The driver cut the motor, and with it the deafening music. Or noise, as Lavina was more prone to call it.

"Half a day, Officer?" she half shouted jokingly over the low hood of the VW Rabbit parked between them.

With his back facing her now, Rob Uberon jerked his head around. The wide eyes and open mouth were enough to tell her that she had taken him by surprise. He tented his eyes against the still bright sun behind her back and squinted.

Lavina walked around the rear of the smaller car over to the police vehicle. "Don't tell me you don't recognize me," she said, a smile on her lips.

The uniformed officer, she noticed, held a large, folded manila envelope clutched tightly under his left arm. He seemed to press it closer to his body as she neared him, much as a child would a stuffed animal he was afraid someone was intent on taking away from him.

"Miss London, isn't it?" he asked, lowering his right hand once she stood facing him.

"Close. Missus," she corrected. Since it appeared

to her that the young man didn't know whether or not to extend his hand, she did so first, which he took in a firm handshake. "I didn't know you lived up here," she said, then quickly added, "Or are you on police business?"

"No, Mrs. London. I live here all right." He motioned with his thumb to the double window beyond and above the hood of the patrol car. "Twenty-seven ten." The apartment in question backed Lillian Dorchester's, which meant that his entrance was around on the other side of the building to the left. "But you don't live in the complex, do you?" he asked, a quizzical look on his lean face.

Lavina shook her head. "No, no. Just visiting a friend here behind you." She nodded in the direction of the apartment she had just left.

"Mrs. Dorchester?"

"That's right."

"Nice lady," Uberon added, shoving the folder farther up into his sweat-stained armpit. "Don't see too much of her though. Sick a lot, I hear."

Not wishing to broadcast the woman's personal business, Lavina merely nodded. "You're in an awful hurry, aren't you?" she asked, changing the subject. "You must have a pretty heavy date on for tonight."

Rob Uberon shook his hatless head and let out a deep breath. "No, nothing like that, Mrs. London." The tone of voice was hard to mistake.

"You seem annoyed." Lavina canted her head to the side awaiting an answer she knew would be forthcoming. Young men, she had learned, found it impossible to resist the kindness and understanding of old ladies, even on those all-too-frequent occasions when they were obviously being just plain nosy.

The young officer looked down now at the envelope under his arm, then up again at the former actress. "You'd be annoyed too, Mrs. London, if you just wasted an hour up at Rainbow's End waiting for someone who never showed."

So that was it, Lavina thought. The young man must have it bad to resort to the local lovers' lane in the middle of the day. Well, maybe not quite the middle of the day, but close to it. Obviously the young lady in question who had apparently stood him up wasn't quite so desperate. Too late, she ran a hand across her forehead, hoping her eyebrows hadn't betrayed her surprise. She was going to say, "A bit early in the day, isn't it?" but caught herself just in time. Instead, she said, "Maybe you got your times crossed." She didn't really think the suggestion would assuage the man's disappointment or annoyance, but it was the only thing that came to mind on the spur of the moment.

With his free hand Uberon raked back the curling strands of damp hair that had fallen down over his forehead. "No chance, Mrs. London," he countered. "Just a case of someone trying to make a fool of me, I'm afraid." He made a weak attempt at a smile that ended up looking more like a smirk. "It will be the last time though, believe me." To Lavina the smirk now looked somehow more deliberate.

"You should at least wait until you've heard the young lady's side of the story, don't you think?" she said. "Don't want to burn your bridges over something that might have a logical explanation."

The enigmatic smile that spread across Uberon's face was a complete transformation, as if he were privy to a private joke Lavina wasn't in on. He finally broke out in a little laugh, adding, "Maybe you're right, Mrs. London, maybe you're right."

"I know I'm right," Lavina said, not at all sure now that she was. Somehow they seemed to be on different wave lengths all of a sudden. She couldn't help wondering who the woman might have been, or even if she knew her for that matter.

"Well, I've got to run," Uberon said, extending his hand again, this time on his own. It, too, was sweaty now. "Still have to get back and write up a few reports before I'm officially off duty for the day. I just wanted to drop something off at home as long as I was in the neighborhood. But I sure as héck don't want the Sheriff on my back for not doing my job." A grin this time, and one that Lavina could well appreciate, knowing Tod Arthur as she did.

"It might be a good idea though," she said, "not to have that . . . that music blasting away on your car radio when you get back to the office."

Rob Uberon laughed again, this time openly. "Yeah, I know what you mean. The Sheriff don't much care for here-and-now music."

If that's what you call it, Lavina thought, I'm readier than I expected for the hereafter, angelic harps or not.

She watched the retreating perspiration-stained back as the young man turned and headed toward the end of the building. For the first time she saw that he was wearing a walkie-talkie on his right hip. She thought he might turn and wave. He didn't. He just disappeared around the corner.

She strolled over and peeked in the open driver's window of the police car. The man's trooper's hat was on the driver's seat, its purple hatband a perfect match for his tie. She stuck her arm in through the opening and picked it up. It was firmer and heavier than she would have suspected. She turned it over. A ring of sweat was clearly visible on the edge of the inner rim. She pressed the double indentation in the high crown, sorely tempted to try it on. She didn't. Instead, she merely dropped it back on the seat and withdrew her arm.

She straightened the rust-colored cardigan around her shoulders and wondered why the trooper had been perspiring so profusely on such a cool, May afternoon. Had he been hotter than she thought over the frustrated tryst? Maybe her own blood was just thinning. She shrugged and went back to her car.

She was turning down the single-car incline toward the exit to the street when she caught sight of the older car out of the corner of her eye. It was parked unobtrusively off to the right by a stand of pines. She thought she recognized it, but couldn't be sure since she was on the alert for any car that might be approaching from the opposite direction. The one thing she was sure of was that there was someone sitting at the wheel.

She found it hard to believe that it was almost twenty past five when she pulled back into the parking space under Lillian's bedroom window. After turning off the ignition and removing the key, she got out and opened the trunk. She lifted out two, double-bagged packages of groceries, set one on the ground, slammed the lid shut, then picked the bag up again, all the while painfully aware of the arhythmic thumping emanating from behind Rob Uberon's closed windows. The patrol car, too, she had noticed, was in its parking space. She just shook her head and continued around the building to her right to Lillian's front door.

When she emerged again about ten minutes later and approached her car, the music was still pounding away. More than five consecutive minutes of it would have given her a headache for sure, and she wasn't one for headaches, thank God.

She was more than somewhat surprised that the policeman had managed to get back to the Sheriff's office, finish up his reports, and return home again before she'd come back with Lillian's shopping. The lowering sun skimmed its late afternoon rays across the shiny car roofs and hoods, glaring brightly in the windowpanes so that she was unable to see through them.

On a hunch she walked around to the far side of the police car. The driver's window was still down, the hat inside on the seat where she had left it. She straightened up and stared off in the direction of the building. None of it necessarily meant anything of course, but then again maybe it did. If the young man had gone inside and maybe dozed off somehow, he might never have gotten back to the office to finish his reports, in which case he'd be in hot water for sure.

Lavina sighed and subconsciously let the Good Samaritan in her take over again. She headed around to Uberon's private entrance on the opposite side of the building where she had watched him disappear earlier.

Lavina mounted the three steps and pushed the little, lighted button under the nameplate. When no one answered, she pressed again, this time holding a spindly, middle finger on the button longer. Two, three, four jabs. She waited. Again nothing. The beat of the rock music continued unabated inside. As a matter of fact, it seemed even louder on this side of the house. She tried once more, this time with one long uninterrupted push of the button, while at the same time stepping back to see if there was any movement beyond the open venetian blinds on the double window to the left. Even with the music she could hear the strident buzzing inside. The ten or so seconds she must have waited seemed like minutes. A subsequent series of raps on the wood paneling of the door produced nothing but sore knuckles.

As a last effort she tried the doorknob, more to rattle it than anything else—or so she told herself. When it turned, she gave a little start. Once she regained her composure she could see where the door had separated from the jamb on the left. As she pushed it farther in, it opened reluctantly over a deep, ale-colored shag carpet. When the opening was wide enough, she stuck her head in to see a small foyer, as in Lillian's apartment, with a closet in the left wall. Lillian's was on the right. What she was sure had to be the living room lay directly ahead. It was in near darkness.

"Yoo-hoo . . . Officer Uberon!"

She waited, her hand still on the knob of the open door.

"Ready or not, here I come." Good ol' hide-and-seek. She entered the foyer and turned to shut the door behind her. Then she proceeded to advance hesitantly across the thick pile toward the living room. The source of the music was straight ahead and off somewhere to the left.

When she reached the living room, she stopped to

get her bearings. The wall facing her backed Lillian Dorchester's apartment. It was bare except for one framed painting she couldn't make out, it was hung so high. Heavy drapes masked the windows in the right-hand wall, the windows that faced the parking area. Off to the left were the kitchen and bath, the former doorless, with a room-darkening shade lowered to the windowsill; the latter windowless, its door opened in. A dying patch of sunlight, blind-slatted, fell obliquely across the floor and wall in the far corner to her left. Obviously from the windows she had seen outside off the entrance.

She stepped across the imaginary threshold that separated foyer from living room. The culprit stereo system in what looked like a fifties, blond hi-fi cabinet stood against the inside living-room wall to her immediate left. She went over and lifted the hinged cover. The up-to-date sound system she found inside was obviously a recent transplant. How, she didn't know, but she managed to find the right button that controlled what turned out to be a reel-to-reel tape, and shut it off.

"Mr. Uberon?" After the music, her voice seemed to echo hollowly in the eerie darkness. She shook her head to chase the buzzing. "It's Mrs. London. Are you asleep?" Silly question.

As she passed what she had correctly suspected was the bedroom on her left, she could see the empty, unmade bed that stood out from the wall backing the foyer. "I'm going to raise the kitchen shade so I can see better in here," she fairly shouted as if someone was listening. Even to herself she sounded foolish.

Once inside the kitchen she kicked something on the floor, she didn't know what. Seaweed! No, that was ridiculous. It was almost getting her foot tangled that brought that to mind. Besides, there was the sound of metal scraping across the linoleum as it slid the short distance toward the kitchen table over to her left. Thank God it hadn't been an animal. She smiled to herself in the semidarkness as the term "Sleeping Dogs" popped into her mind. Susanne would have some clever retort to that one, that's for sure. She squinted down at the floor but couldn't make it out.

She continued over to the sink where she raised the shade to admit a welcome blaze of daylight. Somehow all she could think of was Miss Havisham's gloomy house in *Great Expectations*.

She turned and looked down again toward the legs of the table to see what it was that almost tripped her. Her domestic seaweed turned out to be a heavy leather belt with an equally heavy buckle. No, it was more. She went over to the table and crouched down. The belt was face down and she turned it over, even though she knew exactly what it was. Rob Uberon's gun belt.

The flaps on two smallish leather pouches were open and the pouches themselves about half full of bullets. The swivel holster was empty. Pen holder, keys and whistle, handcuff case and cuffs, all were in order. The tubular-looking leather case she didn't recognize at all until she slid out the canister. Mace. Everything seemed to be there except the gun, maybe some bullets, and the walkie-talkie. And, of course, Officer Rob Uberon.

Chapter Eighteen

Tod Arthur pressed the heels of both hands into obviously tired eyes, then stared down again in seeming disbelief at the now bag-clad body on the ground-hugging gurney before him.

"How long before you know for sure, George?" he asked, turning to face the doctor seated in the arm-chair between the bathroom and kitchen. "About the strangulation, I mean."

Dr. Errol looked up over the top of his glasses from his notes, shrugged his shoulders, then screw-capped his ancient fountain pen and clipped it into his outer jacket pocket. "Difficult to say, Tod. Depends on how well things go." He glanced down at his up-turned wristwatch. "And I haven't even had supper yet, you know." A teasing smile formed on his crusty lips, lingered there a few moments, then disappeared. "But I'll get right on it after that, trust me."

"You mentioned classic signs." Sheriff Arthur remained standing, waiting for an explanation.

"Well, yes, you know—petechial hemorrhages, the cyanosis, the clenched hands, nose and mouth froth. A few other things."

"Sounds pretty definite to me," Arthur said.

"And that's why you're the sheriff, Tod, and I'm the medical examiner," Errol said. "You should know by this time that an apparent cause of death is just that—apparent and nothing more. The autopsy might well turn up something we can't see right now. We'll have to have a closer look at all the internal organs and tissues to be sure."

Tod Arthur sighed and shook his head.

Lavina London sat listening quietly in a corner of the sofa under a large, gaudy painting of a stalking panther, its wary eyes staring down through glossy oil colors at the scene before him.

Of course. She should have remembered. She'd certainly read enough Agatha Christie to know not to trust appearances, to know that everything isn't always what it seems.

But what was it precisely that was gnawing at the back of her mind? Something she had recently taken for granted—and probably shouldn't have. Why, she didn't quite know, but she was somehow sure it involved Rob Uberon. Something he said, or something she had misinterpreted.

Her eyes shifted to follow the body as two, young policemen alternately tugged and pushed in order to maneuver the wheeled stretcher across the pile carpet and out to the waiting mortuary hearse she had seen, through the window, when it pulled up. She gave a little shiver and pulled her cardigan around her shoulders, knowing that the chill wasn't external.

She had found Rob Uberon after all, stretched out on the floor of the bedroom on the far side of the unmade bed under the windows, his face a somewhat paler version of the purple tie that had all but torn the skin around his throat, so tightly was it knotted. She had almost missed it—the body, that is. What had prompted her to go around the far side of the bed after finding the gun belt she couldn't say, but she had. Lavina telephoned the police from Lillian's apartment and then returned.

"Well, I'd better get a move on, I suppose," Dr. Errol said, getting up from the chair and tugging, first at the seat of his pants, then at his crotch. "Don't call me, I'll call you." With a grin on his face, he bent down and grabbed his black bag from the floor beside the chair, then headed off toward the foyer.

"Thanks, George," Arthur said to the retreating back, then turned around to face Lavina. After a brief hesitation during which their eyes met in silence he came over and plopped down at the opposite end of the sofa, his large hands at his eyes. He let out a wide but silent yawn that he didn't bother to stifle.

"Excuse me," he said, reaching for a handkerchief in his hip pocket.

"You should go home and get a good night's sleep," Lavina said, crossing the ankles of her outstretched legs.

"You're sure you haven't forgotten anything?" Arthur said, ignoring the maternal advise and looking directly at her.

"If anything, I'm more likely to embellish than forget." She never had trouble remembering her lines or scenes. "No."

"Hmmm."

"I gather your men didn't have any more luck than

I did finding that manila envelope." She certainly hadn't wasted her time while she was waiting for the police once it dawned on her that the envelope had disappeared. Now that she thought of it again, that something that kept eluding her clawed again at the edge of her memory.

"You're sure there was such an envelope? I mean, that wasn't maybe one of your embellishments?" He smiled.

"Don't be an ass, Tod Arthur! Of course there was an envelope. Just as I described it. Officer Uberon was holding onto it for dear life." It was the thing that had intrigued her most about their meeting.

"But you know nothing about this mysterious lady."

It was then that it hit her. The woman. The woman at Rainbow's End. Or, to be more precise, the woman *not* at Rainbow's End. She hadn't been a woman at all, or rather she might have been a woman, but not in the sense of an assignation. Rob Uberon was supposed to meet someone there all right, someone that had some connection with that envelope, someone who hadn't shown up. At least not at Rainbow's End. But maybe someone who showed up here later to claim whatever it was in that envelope. She had been the one who had assumed there was a mystery woman involved in some sort of a love tryst. Rob Uberon had never said anything of the kind. She could have kicked herself then and there. Appearances.

"What are you thinking about?" Sheriff Arthur asked, snapping her out of her reverie.

"Nothing, Tod, or at least nothing that quite amounts to anything yet."

"I suppose *you* know what you're talking about, Lavina, because *I* sure as heck don't."

Arthur pounded the arm of the sofa with a clenched fist. "Damn it! Things weren't bad enough with the two Frame murders. Now I have some kook running around town killing off one of my own officers."

"You're assuming they're unrelated then," she said.

"I don't know how they could be otherwise, do you?" He stared down at her from the edge of his seat.

Lavina didn't answer, but instead turned and stared through the open bedroom door in the direction of the now stripped bed.

"What was that thing your man found under the bed that you had him put in the plastic bag? I didn't notice it when I looked under there."

"You looked under the bed!" Lavina didn't have to see his face to get the message. "When? And what the hell for?"

"For the envelope, what else? While I was here alone waiting for you all to arrive."

"Jesus!"

"No need for blasphemy, Tod." She turned to give him one of her own scolding glares.

"Sorry."

A smile crossed her lips. "So what was it?"

"I don't know. A metal bar of some kind about fourteen inches long. Thin. Cylindrical and hollow with a notch of some sort at one end. Probably something of Uberon's. Why? Was that the final clue you needed to piece your puzzle together?"

"No need for sarcasm." She grabbed up her shoulder bag from the cushion on the sofa between them. "Why did your man take it, then, if you don't think it's important? Could it have anything to do with Rob Uberon's death?"

"How would I know, Lavina! You heard Errol. I'm only the Sheriff around here. And I'm even beginning to wonder about that ever since you horned in, pussyfooting around."

"That sounds like a mixed metaphor to me."

"Hanging around here alone after a murder," Arthur muttered, more to himself than anything else. Then aloud: "For Christ's sake—"

"Tod! . . ."

"For Pete's sake, Lavina, the point is you could well have put yourself in serious danger. You didn't know if the murderer was still in the apartment and—"

"Unless he was in one of the closets, he wasn't. I checked."

"You checked?" The disbelief again.

"Well, not exactly for the murderer, no. But I was already in the apartment looking for Officer Uberon and I looked every place *but* the closets." Then she lowered both her head and voice as if in so doing he wouldn't hear the remainder of her admission. "Until I came back after the phone call, I mean, and started looking for the manila envelope. Then I checked the two closets." Her confession complete, she raised her head again and looked at him.

Arthur's head just kept shaking in rhythm from side to side like some kind of wind-up toy. *It isn't true. It isn't true*, it seemed to say, the eyes closed tight.

"How well did you know Officer Uberon?" Lavina finally asked.

"What?" He opened his eyes and looked back at her.

"How well did you know Rob Uberon?"

"How well?"

"Yes."

"As well as one can know a subordinate, I guess. Why?"

"You trusted him?"

"Of course I trusted him. He was an officer of the law, wasn't he?" Something seemed to click in his mind because he added, "I mean he seemed like a good officer. What in . . . what are you getting at anyhow, Lavina?"

"If these murders are connected—Officer Uberon's and the two Frames', I mean—that envelope just might be the key."

"How?"

"It just might have contained something incriminating against the murderer of Leo and Peter Frame, something he certainly couldn't let get out. Not if he could help it, that is."

She then explained how her "mysterious woman" might have been someone entirely different, someone Rob Uberon had arranged an appointment with for reasons as yet unsuspected.

"What you're actually saying, Lavina, is that Uberon was planning on blackmailing this guy."

"It wouldn't be the first time, Tod. A crooked law officer, I mean."

"That's pretty hard to swallow, Lavina." Sheriff Arthur looked down at his thick hands now aimlessly kneading his trousered knees. "I mean I've been working with the guy practically every day for almost three years."

"I'm sorry, Tod, but it's the only thing that seems to make any sense."

"If the murders are connected."

"Yes."

Arthur pushed himself up off the sofa and began pacing the living-room floor, his eyes on the pile rug.

"Do you have any evidence like that you haven't mentioned? Something Rob Uberon might have had easy access to in your office?"

"We've got no concrete evidence of any type, Lavina. Nothing you don't already know, anyway."

"Maybe it isn't all that concrete—to you, I mean."

"We don't even have anything circumstantial, for heaven's sake."

"Could he have gotten hold of something on the side then? Something he might have kept to himself? Information someone might have passed on to him, maybe?"

Tod Arthur stopped dead in his tracks, then turned to stare vacantly across at the ex-actress. "It's possible, of course . . . but there's also something else." He bit his lower lip. "No, it can't be."

"What, Tod?"

"Uberon was the one who examined the contents of Leo Frame's desk at the funeral home after the murder."

"That's it! Of course. It's got to be."

Arthur remained standing, shaking his head again from side to side.

"Why not, Tod? It makes perfect sense. He found something in the desk to tie someone in with the murder and foolishly decided to try and make a little profit from it. Don't you see?"

"Of course I do, Lavina. That's the whole problem. Dammit! I was the one who assigned him the job of examining the desk in the first place. If he did find—"

"Don't start blaming yourself, Tod. If he found anything—as I'm sure he did—and decided to withhold it for his own nefarious purposes, it's hardly your fault, and you know it. What you did was strictly a matter of police routine."

"That doesn't make it any easier to accept, if what you suspect is true."

"All the more reason, then, why you should follow through on it."

"Yeah, sure. And just how do you suppose I do that? With Uberon *and* the possible evidence gone, where's the end of the thread?"

"You'll just have to go back and examine the whole fabric again more carefully, that's all. Take a closer look at the warp and the woof."

"What!"

Lavina smiled as she eased herself up from the sofa, guiding the strap of her bag onto her shoulder. "Go back to square one. And don't be taken in by appearances this time—like we both were."

"What's that supposed to mean?"

"Just what it sounds like. In your job, you've got to suspect just about everyone."

"If I were any more suspicious at this point, I'd be downright paranoid."

Lavina was out on the top step of the entrance before she actually stopped to take stock of her position.

She still wasn't sure why she hadn't mentioned anything to Sheriff Arthur about the car. Well, actually she was, in her own mind at least. She just wanted to make sure before she started hurling accusations, or even hinting at them. Its presence there might have had nothing to do with Officer Uberon at all, or maybe she had been totally wrong about it to begin with. After all, she had only seen it out of the corner of her eye in passing, and then too with her attention fixed elsewhere. There was only one way to make sure —not that Susanne or the sheriff would approve, of course. How best to go about it, though, was something else again.

With a firm grip on the wrought-iron handrail she made her way down the porch-lit steps, and then around the building to her own car, her memory digging all the while through the "backfile" in her mind, through the hundreds of scripts that had constituted her long radio career. She was sure there had been several in which she was forced to confront a killer.

She reached her car before anything suitable came to mind.

The lights were on now in Lillian's apartment with the woman undoubtedly still awaiting her return. She had, after all, half promised she'd be back to let her know what was happening. She looked down at her watch, barely able in the twilight to read the hands. Well, her supper could wait, she supposed. After all, the poor woman *was* responsible for her being on the spot when she was. She owed her that much at least. Not to mention the fact that the poor thing was probably dying of curiosity. It was the latter fact that was the deciding factor in her decision.

She turned, walked around the rear of the Tempo and headed toward the opposite side of the building.

As if in repayment for her charitable act, the skeleton of an old, radio story line popped into her mind. She had a vague recollection that it was from *The Crime Club* or *Crime Classics*, but she couldn't be sure. Now I wonder if I could work out something along those lines, she thought as she dug once again in her bag for Lillian Dorchester's key.

Chapter Nineteen

"Rust? Are you sure?"

With a thick finger he pushed the overgrowth of graying hair back over his ear, then repositioned the receiver.

"But just the towel." He paused for confirmation. "Did Errol find anything in the scalp? . . . Well, give him a ring for Pete's sake"—he smiled to himself, recalling Lavina's reprimand—"and find out . . . No, he hasn't released the body. He's got two of them up there now . . . No, Uberon's . . . Yeah, I know . . . O.K. but then get back to see me as soon as you find out . . . And listen, don't let him give you the runaround. Tell him if he hasn't already done so that I want a closer examination of that head wound—pronto . . . Right."

Throughout the phone conversation Sheriff Arthur had been staring with interest at the woman who sat facing him across the ancient, wood desk, her thumbs

twisting the rings on her fingers. After a while he
knew the route her bright green eyes would take as,
almost like clockwork, they darted from his own to
the dirty windows, then down to the bare, wood floor
where dust balls had settled in like prairie tumble-
weed, then up to his cluttered desk, and back again to
meet his stare. The same itinerary over and over. The
gold earrings dangling on either side of her head
looked like a pair of samurai swords and, like her
eyes, sparkled in the morning sunlight that somehow
managed to penetrate the encrusted panes.

"Sorry for the interruption, Miss Barth," he said
as he replaced the receiver and picked up his pencil.
"You were saying that you burned the letters."

"Yes." Annis Barth straightened up with a creak
of the wood chair. "I regret it now, of course,
but then I had no way of knowing Rob would be
murdered."

"Why exactly are you telling me all this? I mean,
with Uberon dead and the letters burned, who'd have
known one way or the other?" He raised a restraining
palm. "Don't get me wrong, Miss Barth, I appreciate
your coming forth and all—it very much confirms
suspicions we've been having of late about Officer
Uberon—but as far as you're concerned, it really
wasn't necessary."

"To be perfectly honest, Sheriff, once I heard that
Rob had been killed, I started to wonder . . . and
worry. I mean, I couldn't be sure he had given me all
the letters. At this point I don't remember how many
I even wrote to Leo. A few early on when we were in
the midst of our misguided affair—my father was still
alive at the time and Leo wasn't married to Elenice
yet—and then the more recent ones. Rob said he only
found the seven he sold me."

"And you believed him." Arthur never quite managed to understand how stupid some grown people could be—even when their own welfare was involved.

"At the time, yes. If there'd only been the earlier ones, of course, I wouldn't have bothered with them. They were just foolish love letters from a foolish woman. But the last two or three—as I say, I can't be sure now how many—were in a completely different vein and were written—even more foolishly, I'm afraid— after Leo had broken things off and turned on me. After he started his Please Omit Flowers campaign. I don't know if you're aware of that nasty business—there was constant friction between the two of us the last few years over the role of the florist in the funeral business. I—"

"I'm aware of the situation, Miss Barth—in general terms, at least."

"Well, as a result, the last few letters were pretty nasty, I'm afraid. I actually threatened him in them. So when he was found murdered in the funeral home and I learned the letters were still in his possession, well, I figured the police would take a pretty dim view of them, to say the least."

"Which was really what Uberon led you to believe after he told you he'd found them, am I right?"

She nodded, looking down at her ringed fingers. "Yes."

"Bastard."

Annis Barth looked up again to meet his eyes. "Well, anyway," she said, "the point is that after Rob was killed I still wasn't sure there weren't more than those seven letters. I was afraid you might have found others equally as incriminating, so I thought it best to come in and get the whole thing off my chest."

"Which, of course, is what you should have done in the first place, Miss Barth, rather than let yourself become prey to that . . . that piece of slime. Which is what anyone should do in the case of blackmail." He forestalled her demurral with the flat of his palm. "Yeah, yeah, I know. Easier said than done. It's the damn fear or shame—if not both—that holds people back. Which is precisely what those bloodsuckers count on. To my way of thinking—and I'm sure I'm not alone in this either—the blackmailer is the scum of the earth—the lowest form of humanity. I honestly think I have more compassion for a murderer." He tried to recollect from his reading where in hell Dante had placed them—or even if he had—but he couldn't. It was something he'd have to go back and check; maybe he'd even get around to rereading the *Divine Comedy* after all these years.

"Did Jeffrey Marcus know any of this?" he asked, leaning back in his chair, the pencil between both hands in front of his face.

The sudden mention of the assistant funeral director's name had the desired effect. Annis Barth gave a little start.

Arthur watched her as she hesitated over her choice of answers. Finally she gave a little smile and tossed her blond hair back off her shoulder with an obviously practiced jerk of her head.

"About my earlier affair with Leo, yes," she said. "About the letters and the whole business with Rob, no." She looked down at her hands again, splaying her fingers, but not touching the rings. "You seem to know—or suspect—more than I thought. And here I thought we'd been so discreet."

"Someone happened to overhear a private phone conversation, I'm afraid."

"Mrs. London."

"Yes."

"That's what Jeffrey thought. Not that it really matters—not at this point anyway. And yes, we're having an affair." She smiled again, this time to herself. "When I talk about this out in the open like I'm doing I suddenly feel like the whore of Babylon." She looked up again, canting her head. "Actually, though, it's different with Jeffrey. He's asked me to marry him, you know—a couple of times, but I couldn't in all decency bring myself to accept his proposal."

"Maybe now you can reconsider." It was Arthur who smiled now, then lowered the pencil.

"I'd have to tell Jeffrey everything if our relationship were to change. I couldn't be dishonest with him."

"Would that be so difficult?"

"I don't know. Maybe not." She smiled again, then stopped to tighten the bobby pins on either side of her head. "Oh, I almost forgot—*were* there any other letters found among Rob's belongings?"

"No, Miss Barth. There he didn't lie; I guess he was that decent at least."

Annis Barth heaved a deep sigh.

"I'll check, by the way," the sheriff said, "to see what Uberon did with the fifteen hundred you gave him. I might be able to get it back for you when this mess is cleared up."

"That's really not important, Sheriff. I deserve to lose it."

"Don't be so hard on yourself. We all make fools of ourselves from time to time. Wouldn't be human if we didn't. The important thing is to learn from our mistakes." With a large hand he swept aside a batch of papers on the desk in front of him, then jotted something in the little notepad. Without looking up he asked, "You wouldn't happen to know if Uberon had gotten any money recently from the younger Frame, would you?"

"Peter?"

"Yes."

Annis shook her head. "Not that he ever mentioned—or hinted. As a matter of fact, the more time I've had to think about it, the more I've come to realize that I know practically nothing at all about Rob Uberon. As a person, I mean. That's a horrible thing to have to admit, considering all the—the time we spent together."

Arthur looked up from his pad and narrowed his eyes, directing them almost vacantly at the woman seated across from him. "You know, Miss Barth, I'd probably have to admit the same thing, and I'd been working with him for almost three years." It's strange, he thought, when the people you think you know turn out to be perfect strangers. Damn Lavina London and her appearances anyway! No, he took that back. It was his own gullibility, if anything, that was at fault.

Annis ran her tongue over chapped lips. "I guess I've been pretty stupid in more ways than one."

Arthur smiled, but said nothing. That makes two of us, he thought.

He still couldn't take his eyes off the woman—not for very long anyway. He felt as if he were seeing Annis for the first time, and maybe in a way he was. And from the way she was talking, maybe she was seeing herself in much the same way. He just hoped she liked what she saw as much as he did.

"You know," she added after a few moments of silence, "I thought Mrs. London might have suspected something about Leo and me. Do you know her really well?"

Arthur merely nodded, a smile on his lips. Boy, do I ever! he thought.

"She seemed pretty astute the other day when she and her granddaughter stopped by the nursery. There were times I felt she could read my mind—even look into my soul. It was pretty eerie, believe me."

"She might well have at that, Miss Barth," Sheriff Arthur finally admitted, only half in jest. "Knowing Lavina London as I do, I wouldn't be in the least surprised. But even if she did surmise anything along those lines, you can be certain she kept it to herself. Inquisitive she might be, but a gossip or scandalmonger she's not. Tends more often than not to think the best of people. She probably would have considered you an innocent victim. Maybe even have wanted to help you."

Annis gave a little laugh, then let a wide smile flash across her face for the first time. It did wonders for her, Arthur thought.

"After this harrowing morning, Sheriff—getting all this off my chest, I mean—I'm sure it will be a lot easier getting back to confession. That will be my first step, whether I follow through on Jeffrey's proposal or not."

"You're Catholic? Episcopal?"

"Catholic."

"Mrs. London could probably help you there, too," he said. "I'm sure she has a direct line to the Creator—not to mention every priest in Monticello, Wurtsboro, Ellenville, and points west."

With that, they both laughed, after which Annis rose from her chair as if to leave.

Sheriff Arthur followed suit on his side of the desk. "Will Mr. Marcus be taking over as director of the funeral home, do you know?" he asked.

"I sincerely hope so—for both our sakes. But of course I can't say for sure. It pretty much depends on what Mrs. Frame intends to do. She may even end up selling out for all I know. She hasn't broached the subject with Jeffrey—nor has he with her."

"Frame has . . . had . . . a few other funeral homes in the state, I understand."

"Four of them, if memory serves me correctly. *Chapels* is the way Elenice likes to refer to them. Sounds more elegant, I guess. Typical *nouveau riche*, if you ask me." She smiled again, then extended a ringed, right hand across the desk. "Well, if that's all, Sheriff, I guess I'll be on my way."

Arthur nodded, taking her hand. Her grip was firm, but unquestionably feminine. "That's it, I suppose," he said.

"You've been a gentleman straight down the line, Sheriff, and I'm very grateful. You could have made this whole difficult business very unpleasant for me, but you didn't. On the contrary, you made me feel decent for the first time in a long while."

Tod Arthur could feel the blood rising to his neck and face. Compliments were one of the few things he had difficulty handling well. He usually found it easiest to turn around and head off in the opposite direction somewhere. Cornered as he was now though behind his desk made retreat impossible. "You can take it off the next bunch of posies I have to buy, Miss Barth," he finally said. "Which reminds me, I have an anniversary coming up this month.''

It was almost one o'clock before he had a chance to reach for his hat and head down to Al's Diner for lunch.

All told though, it had been a fairly productive morning, especially for a Saturday.

The microscopic evidence accumulated by vacuum in the Selection Room at the funeral home and in the motel had yielded nothing because there was just too much of it, and in great variety—especially hair strands. He'd unconsciously rubbed his balding pate when he read the report. Disappointing though it may have been, it wasn't much of a surprise, considering how many people were in and out of the two rooms every day. There was no report yet on the accumulation from Uberon's apartment, not that he expected that to be much different.

Annis Barth's confirmation of Rob Uberon's blackmailing tactics had been the first bright note of the morning. The other had started with the report of the rust found on the bloodied towel at the motel. It matched that scraped off the heavy metal bar located under Uberon's bed, which in turn was found to contain traces of blood that matched Peter Frame's blood type. Once Errol had gotten around to examining the boy's scalp more carefully, he also found evidence of rust in the wound. When the doctor was shown the cylindrical bar, he didn't hesitate to say that it could well have been the weapon that killed the younger Frame. All of which, of course, tied the boy's murder in with Rob Uberon's.

Though far from a solution, Arthur was beginning to feel more comfortable now with the case. At least he was sure for the first time that it *was* only one case he was dealing with. All he needed now was the link, the thing that tied the three murders together. And that, of course, was the one thing the murderer was out to keep a secret.

The possible homosexual angle he had been faced with in Peter's death now seemed very unlikely. It began to look more and more like a deliberate setup than anything else. A maybe-not-so-clever murderer trying his best to throw the police off the track, hoping they'd think the two Frame murders were unrelated.

Why, though, had the Frames been killed? Had Peter known or in some way learned the same thing Uberon must have discovered in Leo's desk? Or was it something else entirely? And what about the two thousand dollars the boy had withdrawn from the bank two months back?

Another interesting development in the case that morning had been the phone call apprising him of the walloping life insurance policy taken out on Leo Frame late last year by his wife. In a way, he had to admit, it seemed a bit too obvious a motive, but he certainly had no intention of dismissing it unless it proved untenable, especially since Elenice Frame had not seen fit to mention it to him. One might almost think she was trying to conceal the fact—and maybe she was—though how she expected to get away with it under the circumstances, he didn't know.

Outside in the parking lot it seemed somehow too quiet. He stood for a few moments looking out toward the highway. If anything, the traffic was heavier than usual. Still, there was something missing.

When the realization came, it gave him a jolt. It was the rock-'n'-roll music—or rather the lack of it. Usually it would be blaring away in the squad car with Uberon waiting for him behind the wheel, his head tilted back against the headrest, the wide brim of his trooper's hat tipped down in rakish fashion shielding his eyes. The picture brought a lump to his throat. He thought back to Peter Frame's room, realizing for the first time that Rob Uberon hadn't been that much older than the other lad. Both of them far too young to be dead as far as he was concerned—even given Uberon's criminal bent. Maybe that was something he should have spotted himself earlier. How, though, he didn't know. After all, he *was* the boy's mentor and superior. If the boy had lived, maybe he could have helped straighten him out, made a decent cop out of him. Spilled milk.

He trod across the gravel lot to his car, opened the door on the driver's side, bent down and slid in. He yanked a clean handkerchief out of his back pants pocket and, without unfolding it, rubbed the morning's road dust out of his eyes—at least that's what he told himself it was—then slipped the key into the ignition.

God's ways are not ours, he remembered having heard somewhere. Probably in the pulpit, but since he hadn't heard a sermon in years he wasn't sure. He had accepted the fact then, as he accepted it now, not that it lessened the pain any.

As he nosed the car out onto the highway he smiled to himself. Maybe he should tear a page out of Annis Barth's book and have a heart-to-heart talk with one of those priests himself.

Chapter Twenty

Gregory Creighton pushed his weight off the desk he had been leaning on and stood back, his deep brown eyes intent on the figure on the opposite side of the wide, mahogany desk.

"What do you mean you're calling it off?" Elenice Frame asked from the high-backed, leather, swivel chair.

Creighton watched her with amusement as she scrambled to work her feet back into the high-heeled, red shoes she had kicked off earlier. "Just what I said." He parted the flaps of his lightweight jacket and shoved his hands into his pants pockets.

"Well, that's a fine how-do-you-do, I must say!" She was out of the chair now and making her way around the desk.

Creighton didn't know which took him more by surprise—the sharp, cracking sound or the fact of the slap itself. By way of reflex, his hand flew up to his cheek. The flesh was warm; the sting nearly numbing. "Now that was real adult, wasn't it?" he said with a wry smile.

"How could you do this to me? Now, of all times."

"Why? What's so special about now? Not because you're a grieving widow, certainly."

She stood staring at him, her eyes hard, her lips quivering. "I don't understand. I thought . . ."

"What?"

"I thought it was you."

"You thought what was me?"

She looked at him in disbelief. "You know—Leo."

"You don't mean to stand there and tell me you honestly thought for one minute that I killed your husband."

"That's exactly what I mean. I didn't know what else *to* think."

"You thought I killed Leo for you?" He gave a little laugh. "Boy, you've gotta be crazy."

"No need to be nasty, Greg."

He turned and walked in the direction of the long, brown-leather sofa against the opposite wall by the door, then stopped and turned to face her. "You thought that, and yet you went ahead and tried to shift the blame onto your stepson."

"Leo's stepson."

"I wish you'd cut that crap, El, I really do. As Leo's wife, you were responsible for the boy, like it or not."

"Just worry about your own responsibilities, and let me worry about mine." She made a half turn as if to go back to the swivel chair, then stopped and turned to stare at him. "Is that why you're breaking things off—because of what I did to Peter?"

"I'm breaking it off because it's run its natural course, that's all. As far as I'm concerned it's been over quite a while."

"And you're just getting around to telling me now, is that it? 'Oh, by the way, El, I meant to tell you, we're through.'"

Creighton shrugged his shoulders, but said nothing.

"I see," Elenice said. "And is that the only reason?"

"As long as you ask," he said, "no. To be perfectly honest—"

"Yes, by all means, let's do be perfectly honest—and adult."

"To be perfectly honest," Creighton repeated, "since Leo's death, I think I'm seeing you for the first time."

"And you don't like what you see, is that it?"

Without removing his hands from his pockets, he came back to stand alongside her. "No," he said when he reached her. "You've become callous, for one thing."

"And I suppose you don't consider what you're doing to me callous? Don't be so goddamn high and mighty! If we're talking about looking into mirrors, take a look at yourself while you're at it, why don't you. Your dealings at Evergreen are far from pure. I could tell the State a thing or two if I had a mind to, believe me."

"Is that supposed to be a threat?"

"Take it any way you want to."

"Then by all means go ahead and have your little talk with the State—and with any one else you care to for that matter—but just make sure you can prove everything you say in a court of law."

Elenice turned again, and made her way to the high-backed chair in front of the window. She remained standing a few seconds, then sat down with what looked to Creighton like a forced air of self-dignity. She was obviously shaken.

"Don't worry," she said at last, gripping the wooden armrests, "your secrets are safe with me."

Creighton smiled and pushed back the wavy lock of sandy hair that had fallen across his forehead. "If you know what's good for you they are."

"Now who's doing the threatening?"

Again Creighton said nothing.

"You know I'm still not convinced you didn't kill poor Leo . . . no matter what you say. Okay, maybe you didn't do it for me . . . still . . . Leo wasn't exactly making things easy for you at the cemetery, that's for sure. Maybe he even threatened to go to the State about you himself." She let out a little laugh, then brought her hands together in front of her in obvious appreciation of her own deduction. "Yes, of course! That's it! How could I have been so blind? You killed him for completely professional reasons, and here I was naive enough to think it was for little ol' me—if only for my money."

"You know if anyone heard you they might get the impression you were passing the buck again, like you did when you tried to blame Peter. As a matter of fact, they might even get the idea that you did your husband in yourself."

"Don't be tiresome, Greg. I already had everything I wanted while Leo was alive. Why on earth would I take the chance of killing him? That's stupid, even coming from you." She fluffed her bangs with long cockscomb-red nails, then reached for a cigarette from the small, Florentine-leather box on the desk.

Creighton smiled and took his hands out of his pockets. He leaned on the desk and bent over again to look her full in the face. "What about that new insurance policy you took out on dear, unsuspecting Leo late last year, sweetie?"

About to insert the unlit filter cigarette between her bright, glossy lips, Elenice stopped and narrowed her peacock-blue eyes, staring up at him. "What insurance policy?"

"Please, El, no games, huh? I have contacts, you know, just about everywhere—including insurance companies."

"Spies, you mean." She lit the cigarette from the heavy, silver, desk lighter and leaned back in the oversized chair. The red blouse inside the white pantsuit betrayed signs of perspiration now along the collarbone. She stuck a hand in at the V-neck and fanned gently. "That's the worst part of living in a hick town like this—everyone and his brother knows your business."

"No one's forcing you to stay."

"Thanks for the compliment. But you're right, there really is nothing to keep me here—not now anyway."

"You haven't told the police about the policy, have you?" Creighton said. "They're sure to find out about it, you know, if they haven't already."

"So what? Since when is it a crime to take out extra insurance on a hard-working husband?" She inhaled deeply, then blew the smoke out across the desk toward his face. "A woman has to plan ahead, you know—especially nowadays."

"That's precisely what I mean," Creighton said, turning his face to avoid the smoke. "That's probably the way the cops are thinking too—that you planned ahead . . . took out a nice, juicy policy on hubby, then did him in.''

"If the police suspected me of Leo's murder they would have said something—done something—arrested me even.''

"Not if they wanted to give you a little more rope . . . along with a little false security.''

Elenice tugged her short white jacket around her. "I don't think that hick sheriff has that much savvy.''

"Don't kid yourself. That's the kind of thinking that puts a person's head in the noose. Arthur is one smart cookie, and don't you forget it. Not if you want to save your hide, anyway.''

"So this is what it finally comes to, huh? Each of us suspicious of the other. Well, I have nothing to worry about, I assure you.''

"You'll have to admit you're pretty much on easy street now with Leo out of the way. Without him here to boss you around, you have five, well-established funeral homes providing a lifetime of security. Not to mention your cash flow.''

"You seem to know an awful lot about my business.''

He smiled. "You're forgetting it could have been mine—if I'd wanted it badly enough, that is.''

'You should live so long.''

"Anyway, you've still got it pretty good.''

"Financially maybe, but operating those homes isn't going to be too easy. For one thing, I'm not the businesswoman type—Leo always took care of everything himself. I had nothing whatsoever to do with the business.''

"Except to spend the profits.''

She ignored him and took another puff on the

cigarette. "The worst thing is that I don't even have any real friends I can count on anymore."

"Cut it out, El, you're making me cry. We were never friends and you know it. We used each other—just as, in our own way, we each used Leo. We're two of a kind. If we had anything at all going between us, it was merely physical."

"Birds of a feather, you mean."

"Something like that. Only we prefer to feather our own nest."

"You sound more like a vulture."

Creighton shrugged again and pushed his weight off the desk. "Why should I deny it? You know me well enough. In this world you have to look out for numero uno. It's the old question of survival of the fittest."

"You *are* a scavenger. Well, you're in the right business for it."

"There's nothing wrong with my business."

"Not in itself, no—just in the way you operate it."

"Your husband wasn't any better, and you know it."

"I never said he was."

"And, of course, you told him as much."

"I never interfered in his business. It was his before I even met him, and I left it that way. It was his baby —just like Peter was. I was just an outsider."

"That's pretty hard to swallow considering how much you think of the almighty dollar."

"I shouldn't have expected you to understand."

"And I don't. As I said, we're too much alike."

"You know," Elenice said, "I think you'd have become a body snatcher if there was more in it for you."

"Why not?"

"In a way, come to think of it, you were probably doing much the same thing with your new crematory business—robbing poor funeral directors of their bread and butter."

"Poor funeral directors! Now that's a good one. Like Leo Frame, I suppose." He turned and sauntered over to the leather armchair alongside the desk. "What's the matter with you anyway? You getting soft or something all of a sudden? Your conscience bothering you, maybe? Somehow you don't sound like the Elenice Frame I know."

"I'm not naive enough to think I've changed, no. I was just trying to sort things out. I seem to remember that you were the one who accused *me* of being callous."

"I was referring to Leo and Peter. Family. I mean, let's face it, El, cremating poor Leo was the lowest blow imaginable. Low even for you. The crematory, as you so aptly put it, was helping to rob him of his livelihood—and yours, too, for that matter—yet you go and pay me to give him a farewell roast. It doesn't make sense.

"The phony, elaborate, no-holds-barred wake was Leo's thing. He thrived on it. And if I knew him as well as I think I did, I'd be willing to wager that he left detailed plans somewhere for his own. And what happens? The only wake the poor slob ends up with is the one his murderer throws for him when he dumps him in that fancy coffin in the Selection Room. Then you go and add insult to injury." He shook his head and eased himself down into the chair. "He'd turn over in his grave if he had anything left to turn over."

"I thought cremation was poetic justice, that's all," Elenice said, fussing again with her bangs.

"So was the way he died. You sure you didn't orchestrate that little mood poem for him as well?"

She stared at him, then took another long drag on the filter cigarette, leaning her head back against the padded leather. "I suppose you think I killed Peter, too."

"It would certainly preclude your having to divvy up the estate," Creighton said. "I mean, you do end up with everything, don't you?"

"Bastard."

"That's certainly more of a motive than I'd have for killing Peter, wouldn't you say? Or have you somehow managed to invent a better one for me?" He smiled.

"Just because I'm not personally aware of a motive doesn't mean you didn't have one. How do I know what might have been going on between you and Peter."

"Ouch! That was a real low one. Now I've been accused of just about everything. I never thought I'd live to see the day."

"I didn't mean *that*, Gregory—although with you I suppose anything's possible if the price is right. You just about admitted as much, didn't you?"

Creighton laughed out loud this time and shook his head. "El . . . El . . ."

"I wonder if that possibility ever entered the mind of that smart-cookie sheriff of yours."

"If it hasn't, I'm sure you'll find a way to remedy the oversight."

Elenice flicked her cigarette ash into the large, circular, green ashtray next to the phone. "I see someone killed one of his men yesterday."

"A cop, you mean?"

"Yes."

"I haven't had a chance to read the paper this morning. Do they think it's connected with Leo's and Peter's deaths?"

"The paper doesn't say. It just mentioned the fact that the guy was strangled with his own tie in his apartment."

"Probably some young punk on drugs."

"Everyone has to get his high on something."

Creighton wasn't sure of her implication, or indeed if she even intended one, so he just let it pass.

"And now what, El?" he asked, changing the direction of the conversation somewhat. "For you, I mean. Are you planning on keeping Pretty Boy around?"

"If by that you mean Jeffrey Marcus"—she shot a quick glance in the direction of the office door—"I don't know. It's something we haven't discussed. It's still too early."

"Anything between you two, by the way?"

She narrowed her heavily mascara-lined eyes. "What's it to you?"

"Just wondering . . ."

"Then keep on wondering."

"Someone told me he had a thing for Annis Barth. Could do worse, I suppose."

"I wouldn't know."

He shrugged his typical, nonchalant shrug. "No skin off my nose one way or the other."

Elenice stared across at him for a long while without saying anything, then finally asked, "Who is she, Greg? Anyone I know?"

"Suspicion, thy name is Woman."

"It isn't a question of suspicion at all. There has to be another woman."

"Why 'has to be?' "

"Now I ask you! Can you picture Gregory Creighton without a woman in tow? If you were so eager to drop me, there had to be a practiced understudy in the wings. You couldn't manage celibacy for twenty-four hours, let alone the interim between affairs. You'd bust at the seams."

"Touché." He threw a long leg over one arm of the chair, leaning his weight back on the other. "No one you know, though. She's from Middletown."

"Putting up at the motel here or dayhopping?"

"What makes you think she's not staying at my place?"

"Because you'd never let anyone get quite that close to you."

He shook his head. "I have to admit you're right on target today, El. That's two in a row."

"Want to try for three?"

"Let's not and say we did." He smiled. "I could keep you wondering, I guess, but I've no reason now to hide anything. Sometimes she stays up this way for a few days at a time—at the motel. Other times she commutes on a daily basis."

"So you've been seeing her a while already."

"A few months, maybe."

Elenice sighed and leaned toward the desk. With two fingers she half stabbed out the cigarette in the ashtray, leaving it smoldering. "Okay. That's all I really wanted to know. It doesn't really concern me one way or the other. I'm not your typical woman scorned."

"That's why you thought fit to slap me, I suppose."

"That was for the lousy way you went about telling me, that's all."

"I see."

"You're really not worth it, Greg, believe me. Life's far too short."

"Elenice the philosopher."

"The realist, Greg, just the realist."

Creighton managed a smirk, then swung his leg to the floor and rose from the chair. "Well, let me know what you decide, El—about staying on or leaving, I mean, and about who'll be in charge here."

"I really don't think that should matter much to you one way or the other, Greg. Whether I stay or leave, I'll still be setting company policy as long as I own Frame Funeral Homes." She nodded over her shoulder to the window behind her. "Is that your car out front?"

"Of course it's my car. You ought to know it by this time."

"Then get out of here, get in it, and get lost. I never want to see your face around here again. Starting Monday, it's 'Fuck Evergreen and its merry acres.' Before I'm through with you, you'll be wishing Leo were still alive. If you think he gave you a hard time, baby, you ain't seen nothin' yet."

Chapter Twenty-one

The blue Ford Tempo screeched to a rubber-burning stop as Susanne jammed on the power brakes.

"I'm glad I'm in the habit of using a seat belt," Lavina grumbled, her composure barely regained. She dropped her palms from the padded dash and cast a sidelong glance at her granddaughter in the driver's seat.

"I don't know why I have to drop you off out here. Why can't I at least pull in to the office?"

"No need for you to know why, dear. Not right now, anyway."

"You're up to something again, Gran, don't tell me you aren't."

"All right, I won't." Lavina opened the passenger door and, with a snap of the button at her hip, released the seat belt.

"You're very exasperating at times, in case you don't know it."

Outside, Lavina bent down and stuck her head back in through the open door. "No need to pick me up. I'll have a ride, one way or another."

"That sounds ominous. How—"

The slam of the car door and the closed window muted the girl's voice and, along with it, the objection she was obviously about to raise.

Lavina proceeded gingerly around the rear of the car and, once on the other side, without turning waved a half-hearted hand as she headed off in the direction of the large, double, iron gates, both of which were now opened. She looked up at the gilded letters that formed the sweeping arch above them: EVERGREEN MEMORIAL PARK.

Without looking behind her, she heard the car accelerating onto the highway. She heard Susanne yell a parting comment but couldn't quite catch the words —which was probably just as well.

Once she reached the gates, she had a clear view of the office building beyond, to the left of the wide driveway. Three cars were nosed up to the foundation plantings. "Shoot!" she said aloud. She hadn't expected that. Not at that hour. She lifted her wrist to check her watch. Five to six.

She jerked the strap of her crocheted bag onto her shoulder and started off down the slight incline toward the office. The pebbles crunched under her feet and she was more than glad she'd thought to change into her canvas oxfords.

As she neared the building, she could see the thick, flat stems of the pale-yellow hyacinths bent now in half, their elongated flower heads kissing the soil. That beauty should often be so short-lived always pained her when she let herself dwell on the fact.

Life's cycle. Death and rebirth. The thought reminded her again, and she offered up a brief but fervent prayer for Kenneth.

As luck would have it, Theresa Francotti was just on her way out of the building when Lavina reached the open door.

"Oh, good evening, Mrs. London," the younger woman said, sidestepping in the doorway to avoid collision. "I didn't hear your car."

"Good evening, Theresa," Lavina said. "My granddaughter had to let me off up on the highway. She was in a hurry. You know how young people are nowadays—especially girls."

Theresa Francotti smiled as if to say, no, she really didn't. Instead, she said, "Yes, I know." She turned her head slightly as if to look back inside the office. "Is anyone expecting you? I mean, no one said anything to me."

"Oh, yes, I have an appointment. But don't worry about me. You just run along on home. You're probably late already as it is, especially for a Saturday." She made a move as if to consult her watch. "Surely you must have a date."

The younger woman seemed taken aback by the remark, but stepping outside beyond the hearing of anyone in the office, merely said, "Well, yes, I am somewhat later than usual. Mr. Creighton was in a terrible—well, a sort of a hurry this afternoon and absolutely determined to get certain things out of the way before Monday, though why, I'll never know." She tossed her long, straight head of chestnut hair with the same expert movement that had intrigued Lavina earlier. "I was on the phone practically all afternoon. I'm exhausted."

"I'm sure you are, dear, but that's why he's such a successful businessman, I suppose," the ex-actress said with a smile, hoisting her shoulder bag again. The words, even as she spoke them, had a hollow ring about them, and she turned her head to look off into the distance, as if afraid of being caught in a horrendous lie.

"I suppose," Theresa said, not quite convinced, or if she was, she was probably not sure it should involve her or her free time. "Well, take care, Mrs. London. See you soon, I hope."

"I haven't forgotten the invitation to have you over to the lake the first really warm weekend," Lavina half shouted to the retreating back. She looked at the culottes as the woman walked away. These were taupe, and worn now with a pale, pea-green blouse. She made a mental note to definitely try on a pair the next time she went to Monticello.

"I haven't either," Theresa said. "Looking forward to it." This over a bony shoulder as she opened the door to her car and got in. She started the motor, and with a final wave of the hand, backed up, turned with a screech of wheels, and headed toward the gates, with Lavina staring after her.

"Come on in, Mrs. London." Coming unexpectedly as it did from behind her inside the cemetery office, it gave her a little start. The voice, though, was unmistakable.

She turned and squinted inside before entering. To her eyes, accustomed as they were to the sun's glare, the interior was dark.

"I hope I'm not too early," she said, finally venturing to cross the threshold, her eyes down, intent on her footing.

"Not at all. I was just sitting here waiting for you."

When Lavina made it to the center of the office, she blinked a few times until her pupils managed to compensate for the change. She found herself facing two men.

"Nice to see you again," Karl Janowitz said, extending his strong hand, which she accepted. In his short-sleeved shirt, his arms, shoulders, and chest were more pronounced than they had been when she'd seen him before. The mushroom-colored jacket he'd worn earlier was draped over the back of the low, swivel chair pushed in to the computer desk. "This is Gregory Creighton—my boss, I should add." This to the accompaniment of his wide, boyish smile and pale blues that seemed to twinkle behind the ash-white lashes.

The hairy arm Lavina had first seen at the restaurant the day of Peter Shaw's funeral shot out to welcome her as well. "A pleasure to meet you, Mrs. London," Creighton said with an honest enough smile of his own. She took the hand. It was damp but firm.

"Mr. Janowitz here tells me you're interested in purchasing one of our crypts for your late husband. You've come to the right place."

And where else would I go, Lavina wanted to say —to the butcher's? Instead, she merely smiled one of her winning smiles. Or at least that's how she liked to think of them. Whatever they were, they usually worked. "Yes," she said, "a pair of them, actually. One for myself as well. From what Mr. Janowitz has been telling me, now seems to be the time to buy. Before, I mean . . . before it's actually needed."

"Yes, indeed," Creighton said.

If she needed anything else to completely turn her off the man, the 'indeed' did the trick. It smacked— no, reeked—of patronization, an attitude she could never stomach.

"Well, I've seen all the brochures, and studied all the prospectuses Mr. Janowitz left with me," she finally managed. "As I told him on the phone, I'd like to see them for myself before making any final decision."

"Of course, of course," Creighton said. "I'll be glad to take you through the grounds and up to our *Pietà* Plains, give you a firsthand tour so to speak."

"*Pietà* Plains?"

"That's the name we gave to our community mausoleum complex, Mrs. London," Janowitz injected, obviously annoyed. There was probably the loss of a commission involved if the cemetery operator closed the deal himself, Lavina realized.

"*Pietà* Plains," she repeated aloud as if savoring the sound of the name. After having seen *Moses* up on the knoll, she had no difficulty understanding the choice of name. The place was beginning to sound more like Forest Lawn every minute.

"I think you'll agree it's really the most tasteful contribution to aboveground emtombment"—she'd heard that phrase often enough by now—"that you're likely to see anywhere."

This side of Disneyland, she thought.

"That's what I want to see for myself," Lavina added. "In the write-ups the whole idea seems somehow—I don't know, cold, I suppose is the best word."

"A not uncommon first reaction, Mrs. London," Creighton conceded. "After studying the brochures,

I mean. But you're absolutely right about wanting to see them for yourself. I'm sure that once you have, you'll feel the warmth you now find lacking. Especially if you're a religious woman, as I somehow feel sure you are."

Religious, maybe; pietistical, no—especially when it came to obviously phony commercial ventures.

"I hope you're right," she said, ignoring the soft-soap. Give me the good, old, blessed earth any day—and I don't mean with a lead-lined vault either, she thought, not swallowing a word of his line.

Gregory Creighton scooped up a set of ringed keys from the top of his expansive desk, and then turned to his subordinate.

"You can call it a day if you want, Karl. I'll see you on Monday. Just make sure you're in before eight so we can get that matter that I mentioned taken care of." He turned back to Lavina with a smile, then motioned with a hand for her to precede him out the door.

The memorial counselor, his handsome, sunburned face growing redder by the second, just stared at the back of his employer's retreating head.

Lavina found it difficult to take her eyes off Karl Janowitz. If, as they say, looks could kill, Gregory Creighton would have been a perfect client for one of his own interment plans—aboveground or otherwise.

As the car wound its way up the blacktop road, she looked over her shoulder through the window at the figure standing in the doorway of the office building. The rays of the evening sun played light games in the panes of the wide, latticed window.

When they neared the top of the knoll and the white-marble *Moses*, she smiled in the direction of her ever-mute, fellow conspirator who continued to scowl off into the distance to his left, ignoring them both. Once they were passing him on the left, she could barely see through the car window the calf of his bent, right leg, set as he was on the massive pedestal.

They continued around the semicircle skirting the English garden that was just coming to life after its long winter's nap. They were moving too fast for her to actually try to identify the emerging greenery other than the telltale iris leaves and new, pink peony shoots.

"I appreciate what you did, Mrs. London," Karl said from the driver's seat next to her, his eyes intent on the curves in the narrow, two-lane road that passed between row upon row of gravestones, markers, and private mausoleums that stretched off into the horizon on either side of them.

"Nonsense," she said, turning her eyes, from the writhing *Dying Slave* atop his high pedestal, to glance at him. "My appointment was with you, wasn't it? As far as I'm concerned, you're the one responsible for any interest I may have in the community mausoleum. And if there's a sale, you're the one who should get the credit—and the commission."

She could see the smile that formed at the corner of his mouth. He still didn't take his eyes from the road.

"You're a corker, you know that, Mrs. London? A real corker."

"I've been around long enough to realize that that louse was trying to do you out of your commission, if that's what you mean."

"That's what I mean."

"Well, I certainly had no intention of letting him get away with it, let me tell you. I just hope I wasn't rude to him."

"Not rude enough to suit me, certainly." This time he gave a quick turn of his head to meet her eyes. They both smiled.

"Actually I was afraid of something like that when I saw all the cars parked outside the office, and I had a chance to figure out what I'd say just in case. Not that I told him anything other than the truth, of course, which was nothing more than I just told you."

"Well, no matter, you certainly know how to plan ahead."

"I try," she said, "I try." Though, this time, she hoped she wouldn't regret it.

"Do we have far to go?" she asked, changing the subject. She could see no large buildings in the offing.

"Not too far," he said. "Just beyond those hawthorns up ahead." He lifted a hand from the wheel to point off in the distance. "The road drops at that point and heads down to the section that's already completed. You'll be able to see it in a few seconds."

"*Pietà* Plains?"

"Yes."

"It sounds more like a valley than a plain," Lavina said, turning again to peer out her window at a cluster of much older tombstones that they were now passing; thin slabs with their engraving all but worn away by time, several of them almost bordering the road.

Karl Janowitz started to laugh. "You're right, you know. And Greg—Mr. Creighton, that is—tried desperately to come up with a name that suited him, using *valley*—"

"Or *vale*."

"You're way ahead of me, Mrs. London. That, too. But he just couldn't think of anything he liked. Especially anything that lent itself to his religious motif."

"Is that what he calls it?"

She caught his smile again. "You think it's over-done?" he asked.

Lavina shrugged her shoulders. When it dawned on her that he wasn't looking in her direction, she added, "I think it leaves something to be desired."

"*Tacky* is what you're thinking, and I tend to agree, though of course it's not my place to say." He shifted uncomfortably in the tight-fitting jacket. "Well, I don't expect to be here forever, so I really don't let it bother me."

Lavina canted her steel-gray head, staring off vacantly in the direction of the hawthorn trees. "I'm surprised he didn't hit on something like Veronica's Vale. Unless he did and didn't particularly care for the pun."

Janowitz let out a hearty laugh. "Oh, Mrs. London, that's terrific! I love it. *Especially* the pun." He laughed again, shaking his head. "But no, I doubt he even thought of it. I'd mention it to him, but I'm sure he'd insist on using it."

"Stealing it, you mean," Lavina said, punctuating it with a *hrump*.

The counselor merely smiled, his eyes on the road in front of him as it began to slope down to the left.

It was then that she was able to see it in all its funereal glory. Gregory Creighton, she realized, would undoubtedly have preferred a word like celestial. It looked to Lavina like a pearly white version of Emerald City, except that it was situated down in a flat hollow. Who knows, she might even see that famed horse of a different color before her tour was through.

"What did you say you do—or did—for a living, Mrs. London? If it wasn't the ad game, you missed your calling." He laughed again.

She was really getting to like Karl Janowitz. So much so that it gave her no little pain to realize that in all probability he had recently murdered three people. Maybe more, for all she knew. She turned again to look at the handsome profile. She wished with all her heart that she was wrong. If only wishing could make it so. Time would tell.

"I was in Radio, Mr. Janowitz," she said, the capital letter clear in her tone of voice. "Back in what we of the older generation like to call the good ol' days."

"Really!"

She carefully scanned the valley below as they slowly made their descent. "Does it sound that improbable?"

"Not at all. It's just that I'm overwhelmed to know someone with such a unique and colorful background. It's not something that happens every day, you know. You were an actress?"

"For over twenty years."

"Whew!" He turned and gave her an appreciative smile. "I'd ask the names of some of the shows you were on except I'd only show my ignorance for sure. I'm afraid the only ones that would mean anything to me—and probably because of television—would be *Amos and Andy* and *Jack Benny*. Were you ever on either of those?"

"I'm afraid not, although I often broadcast from the same studio as Jack Benny, and sometimes even on the same evening. Actually, I did very little in the way of comedy."

"Straight drama, huh?"

"Yes."

"That's great. You should write a book."

"You sound like my agent. Or, I should say, my former agent. He still calls me periodically though to hound me about it."

"Well, why don't you? Sounds like a terrific idea to me. I'd sure as heck read it."

"My fan club of one."

"You're too modest."

By this time they were at the bottom of the hill where the road leveled off. Janowitz turned the car in the direction of the large, polished-marble edifice that dominated a somewhat geometrical landscape with formal plantings that were somehow out of their element in the native-evergreen countryside.

"Modesty, I'm afraid, is not one of my more outstanding virtues," Lavina said offhand, bending her head closer to the windshield to take in the conglomeration known as *Pietà* Plains. "You say there's another one of these in the making?"

"Let me guess," Janowitz said, "you're absolutely overcome by the magnificence of it all."

She turned in appreciation of his tongue-in-cheek humor. "Try nauseated," she said jokingly.

In front of the outsized mausoleum, centered on a wide rectangle of light-green, mosslike grass, the likes of which she had never seen before in her life, stood a reproduction of Michelangelo's famous statue, the sorrowful Virgin with her dead Son, a role model for mourners everywhere.

"Somehow in this setting it's almost blasphemous," Lavina said with an inaudible sigh.

Janowitz slowed the car as they came closer to the figure in question, but said nothing.

"Is that artificial grass?" Lavina asked, squinting to get a better view of the strange lawn.

"No. It's real all right. It's just something not commonly seen in this country," Janowitz said. "It's imported from Scotland."

"It's the strangest thing I've ever seen. It looks real, yet it doesn't."

"Oh, it's real, all right."

"They have to mow it?"

"Every week."

Janowitz pulled the car up to a point just beyond the statue and the entrance to the mausoleum, then cut the ignition.

A series of four deep but low steps led up to a row of glass doors with what looked from the distance like brass fixtures. Six-foot-wide windows on the side facing them were spaced at intervals in the marble wall and stretched up from ground level to a height of about fifteen feet. Six of them in all, with tinted but unstained glass.

"Maybe you'd rather not even bother seeing the inside," Janowitz said, his hand poised now on the door handle.

"Are you kidding! I wouldn't miss it for the world." She opened her door and got out of the car, then looked across the tattered, blue, vinyl roof as he got out of the other side. "What kind of a salesman are you anyway?" She grinned widely. "You'll never be able to afford a new car that way."

Janowitz smiled as he followed her eyes over the rusting body of the two-door Nova. "I just thought the exterior of the place here turned you off once you saw it, that's all. I certainly wouldn't try and sell you something you find repulsive or distasteful."

"Now that sounds more like it," Lavina said. "That's what I call subtle sales-pressure. A sort of subliminal approach."

Janowitz shook his head of vanilla-colored hair and laughed. "As I said, Mrs. London, you're a corker all right."

Lavina slammed her door harder than necessary, then turned to look around, first to the left, then to the right.

"Looking for anything special?" the pre-need promoter asked, shutting his door as well.

"No, no. Just want to make sure I don't miss anything, that's all." She turned back to look up at the imposing edifice. It was really something else, that she had to admit. "Are there windows like these all around?"

"Just on two sides," he said. "The other two have single windows in the center. You'll be able to see why better once we get inside."

"The crematory isn't in here, too, is it?" She winced at the thought.

"Oh no." He smiled. "That has nothing to do with the community mausoleum. This is just for burial purposes."

"The condo, yes," she said to herself, almost in a whisper.

"Excuse me?"

"Nothing. Just remembering something one of my neighbors said, that's all. Thinking out loud, I'm afraid. It happens when you get to be my age."

"I hope I'm half as sharp when I'm your age."

She thought for a minute he was going to ask what precisely that was, but he didn't.

"How many crypts did you say it had?"

"This one has three hundred thirty-six."

"Heavens!" It was Lavina's turn now to be, if not impressed, at least surprised.

"That's not really very many, Mrs. London. After all, you've got to realize they don't take up all that much room. They're not like apartments, you know." He smiled, and she wondered whether he had caught her slip after all.

"I didn't know we had that many people in Boulder all told, for Pete's sake," she said with a laugh.

"Oh, most of these aren't even from town," Janowitz corrected, obviously taking her seriously.

"Well, then, lead on, Macduff."

As he walked to the steps leading up to the community mausoleum, Lavina leisurely wandered over to the green, and, unable to resist the temptation, crouched down and let her hand run through the soft grass as through a pool of cool water.

When she rejoined him at the base of the steps he was smiling. "Well?" he said.

"It's real, all right," she admitted, though still at a loss to account for the strange blades of grass.

He turned and they started up the spacious steps that proved to her continued surprise to be deeper then she'd imagined, a good twenty inches, as a matter of fact, though only about five inches high.

"Can I give you a hand?" Janowitz asked, touching her elbow in token support.

"Thank you, Mr. Janowitz, but I don't think I'm quite that incapacitated yet."

"Sorry, I didn't mean—"

"No need to apologize. On the contrary, I always appreciate honest-to-goodness courtesy when I see it —which isn't too often nowadays, I'm afraid. It's a sign of good upbringing." Where could he have gone wrong? she wondered. Under other circumstances, it might have been an indication that her suspicions were wrong. As it was, though, they were more than mere suspicions at this point. "You really show your age nowadays if you follow Emily Post. Or even know who she was, for that matter. What ever happened to men holding doors, walking on the outside of a woman on the sidewalk, following her upstairs and preceding her down?" She sighed and stopped in her tracks on the step. "I suppose we have all these women libbers to thank, of course. That's what happens when they want to wear the pants and chase after them at the same time. We all suffer. By we I mean women who would once have been called ladies. I'm sure you'll find that meaning listed in the dictionary as obsolete in a few years."

Janowitz had stopped on the steps and just stood looking at her, obviously at a loss for words.

"Don't mind me, Mr. Janowitz," she said, starting up the steps once again. "Just a case of creeping nostalgia."

At the top of the short flight, she turned to look out over the landscape below them, taking in as much as she could with her naked eye. For the first time she was able to fully appreciate the vastness of the wooded area off to her right, evergreens mostly, and probably a spot already targeted for future expansion.

"You don't need your glasses for distance?" Janowitz asked, turning to watch her.

"Oh, no. Just for close reading—and my embroidery." She tapped the glasses hanging on their silver chain against her breast. "Otherwise my sight is excellent. No cataracts yet, thank the Lord. And I hope I'll never live to see the day I'll need transplants. I'm a bit of a chicken when it comes to things like that, I'm afraid."

"Aren't we all."

"What's that water I hear?" she asked, cocking an ear.

"There's nothing wrong with your hearing either," Janowitz said, turning back toward the mausoleum. "That's the fountain and waterfall on the other side of the building."

"A waterfall, no less. Shades of Ausable Chasm."

"Well, hardly that. Shall we go in?"

"By all means." She stepped aside as he unlocked one of the glass doors. "I somehow feel there should be a doorman in uniform—a long, green coat with gold braid and epaulets. And a matching visored cap. That sort of thing, you know?"

He held the door opened out for her and she preceded him inside. "Yes, I know what you mean."

"Chilly in here, isn't it?" Lavina said, tugging her white cardigan around her shoulders. "Good thing I brought this along."

"What they call 'climate controlled'."

"If you're an Eskimo, maybe."

"Would you like me to turn it down?"

"Hardly that. Up, if anything." She laughed. "I'm teasing, of course. No, leave it alone. We won't be here long enough for it to make that much difference.''

Aware now of the slight echo caused by their voices, she looked up to the lofty ceiling of what for lack of a better word she'd have to call a lobby.

"There's an atrium somewhat like this down in the center of the building," the salesman said, watching her, "with a glass dome you couldn't see from outside, and of course the windows at the end of each wing that I mentioned earlier. If you look straight ahead down the central corridor"—he directed her attention to the indicated area—"—what we call Consolation Corridor—you can see part of it.''

Lavina was amused by the name, but at this point hardly surprised. As a matter of fact, she wouldn't have blinked an eyelid if he'd told her it was called the *Via Dolorosa*.

"Yes, so I see," she said, peering off down the length of the broad corridor toward the sunlit, tropical vegetation. "It's not called East of Eden or anything, is it?''

"No," Janowitz said with a smile. "The crypts are located in the corridors leading off on either side of Consolation Corridor. I'll take you into a few of them so you can get a general idea.''

"They have names too, I suppose," she said, barely able to keep a straight face.

Janowitz sighed. "I'm afraid so," he said. "After flowers.''

"Could be worse, I suppose," Lavina said.

"I suppose so," he agreed.

They started down Consolation Corridor with Lavina taking everything in stride. The white marble, she had to admit, was absolutely gorgeous. And obviously real, maybe even imported. The lighting was indirect and tasteful, the polished marble underfoot like glass, and just as slippery. Again she was thankful for her foresight in choosing her canvas oxfords.

"Do you have a night watchman or caretaker on the grounds?" she asked.

"Supposed to, yes," the pre-need salesman said. "Come to think of it, I haven't seen ol'—sorry—I haven't seen Julie this evening. He's usually in the office long before this." He lifted an arm and slid back a linen jacket sleeve to check his watch, then looked back up. "Around somewhere, I suppose. He never misses a day—or night, I guess I should say."

Lavina spotted the ornate plaques mounted on the marble walls as they approached the first of the intersecting corridors. Lilac Corridor. When they finally reached it, they stopped. The wing to the left was marked East, to the right West. She supposed that the pale-lavender marble flooring inside off the main corridor was intentional, with the purpose of conveying the feeling of the floral name.

"I'm glad they didn't decide to install scentorama, or whatever it's called," she said, entering the right wing.

"Oh, they played with the idea all right, but abandoned it when they learned the cost." Janowitz followed her in.

"Thank God for little things."

Lavina craned her neck to take in the walls on either side of her. Structurally, the crypts were cubicles stacked one on top of the other, in this particular case, six high. She didn't bother to count how many ran down the length of the corridor. The veneer facings on each were identical, again lavender-colored, polished marble. Those engraved were uniform in the style and size of their lettering.

"How come they all aren't engraved?" Lavina asked, honestly puzzled. They were all finished with facings.

"Some of them are still unoccupied," the memorial counselor said, as if they were talking again about apartments. She had a vague recollection of the term "tenement housing" in connection with this, to her, still unique burial phenomenon. It must have been a derogatory remark she'd heard or read somewhere along the line years ago when they'd first been introduced.

"I see."

"Not that they aren't sold. As a matter of fact, all of them in this corridor have been purchased."

"Which wouldn't help me if I had a particular relish for lilacs."

"No, afraid not. If you liked this particular mausoleum, you'd have to settle for another corridor."

"And flower."

Janowitz smiled again, then stretched his shoulders under the tight-fitting jacket. "Actually I would have thought that Mr. Creighton—or whoever had the final say—would have chosen names more in keeping with the feature."

"The feature?"

"Yes, the *Pietà* statue outside."

"Oh."

"Given them some sort of religious names is what I mean."

"I'm sure that would have been much worse," Lavina said with a smile, not even daring to imagine the possibilities that Pandora's box presented.

Janowitz shrugged.

"How large are these crypts?" Lavina asked, going over and rubbing the smooth face of one engraved BELLEW, DOMINIQUE.

"About forty-two cubic feet."

Lavina narrowed her eyes as if in reprimand. "I now know about as much as I knew before I asked."

"Sorry, Mrs. London. Ninety inches long, thirty-two wide, and twenty-five high," he clarified.

"Hmmm. Not too much breathing space, is there?" she said in a weak attempt at humor.

Janowitz either didn't catch it, or more likely, just ignored it for the tasteless remark it probably was.

"If you're interested for both yourself and your husband," he said instead, "we have what we like to call Companion Crypts, double crypts with no dividing wall between them."

In case we want to hold hands, I suppose, Lavina thought, becoming giddier and giddier by the minute. In a way she was sorry Winnie wasn't along with her. The woman would have been near scandalized by some of her remarks—or at least would have pretended to be. She loved teasing her just to see her reaction. On the other hand, she wouldn't for the life of her think for a minute of exposing her friend to the possible danger involved in her present little escapade. No more than she had her granddaughter.

She looked down now at her wristwatch, not sure how long she could stall him with her phony interest in aboveground interment. She winced as she heard the phrase form in her mind. Well, maybe she could qualify for a part-time job in perpetual real estate if she ever needed supplementary income. She giggled again to herself at the preposterous thought.

"There must be a difference in the prices," she said, with the idea of money now uppermost in her mind.

"For the Companion Crypts?"

"No, I mean in general." She waved a vague arm above and around her. "They do vary in price, don't they?"

"Well, yes. It depends on location. The higher up you go, the less expensive the crypt." She noted he avoided the term "cheap" at all costs, which was probably to the point.

"Just the opposite of apartments, no?" She adjusted the slipping crocheted strap of her handbag back on her shoulder.

Janowitz grinned. "Just the opposite," he agreed, "with the addition that those closest to heart level are the most expensive of the lot."

"Naturally," Lavina said, a hand pressed to her own bosom, unable to believe the silliness of it all. "The dearest because the dearest."

Janowitz shook his tow head. "I still say you should have been in the advertising business."

He lead her back out to the main corridor where they stopped. "The way this particular mausoleum is laid out," he explained, "we don't have what is usually referred to as garden crypts and corridor crypts, those on the outside wall as opposed to those with walls on the main corridor. These crypt corridors, as you see, are all transverse to Consolation Corridor. Many other cemeteries have them, though, and price them that way as well, the garden ones usually going for a higher price."

"Is it possible to see the inside of one?" she asked.

Janowitz gave a little start, and looked for a

moment as if he'd been asked to open up a closed grave.

"The inside?"

"Yes, you know, just so I can see first hand what I'm getting myself into." She winced at the unintended pun.

"I suppose so, sure," Janowitz said, apparently oblivious to the double *entendre*. "If you come down to Forsythia Corridor, there are a few there still without facings."

"Ready for burials?"

"No, just not quite finished."

She followed him down the wide corridor past the still bright atrium where she stole a quick glance right and left at the huge tinted windows down the bisecting corridor, and then on to the other end of the building, past Rose Corridor, Peony Corridor, Wisteria Corridor, Gardenia Corridor, and others whose names she mercifully forgot. Even before they reached it, she could see the thick, deep-purple braided rope that cordoned off the main passageway just this side of what she assumed was the yet unfinished Forsythia Corridor.

"Are either of the Frames buried here?" she asked the broad, muscular back in front of her. She couldn't miss the twitch that ran across the jacketed shoulders at the mention of the name.

"The Frames?"

"Yes, the funeral director and his son. We spoke about them when you were down at the house."

He kept walking, eyes straight ahead. "I know who you mean, of course. No, neither of them is here. Or at least not Leo—Mr. Frame senior, that is. He was cremated."

"Yes, of course, how stupid of me. I remember the day well. I was at the cemetery myself that day, if you recall."

"Your friend's father."

"Right." She paused a few seconds, then said, "They don't put cremated remains in here, then?"

"Not as a rule, no. It would be a needless waste of money, especially since we now have our own columbarium."

Columbarium. The unusual name sounded to Lavina more like a bird sanctuary for some reason. "And the son?" she asked.

"The stepson. As far as I know, the police haven't released his body yet."

"Oh." She stopped suddenly, and deliberately, behind him. "That's right, too. I recall Tod—that's Sheriff Arthur—I recall Tod's telling me that they had discovered something unusual at his—what do you call it?—his autopsy."

"Something unusual?" Janowitz had stopped as well, and turned now to face her.

"Something about his head wound and particles of rust or something that they found."

"I didn't read anything about that in the paper," the counselor said, his pale-blue eyes meeting her own.

"Well, no, of course you wouldn't have. I don't think they were going to release whatever it was to the public just yet." She had difficulty maintaining eye contact with him, but felt it was important to do so, now more than ever. "I suppose I shouldn't even be talking about it for that matter, but since it's you, I don't see what harm it can do. Tod and I go back a long way and he just happened to mention it in passing the other evening while I was having dinner with him and his wife . . . such a lovely woman.''

"I see.'' Janowitz ran his tongue across his still chapped lips. "And what was so special about this rust, did he say?''

"Not really, no. And, of course, it probably would have been all too technical for me anyway. But if I understood him correctly, it had something to do with the recent death of his young deputy—what's his name?—Rob Uberon.''

"Interesting.'' Janowitz raised his arm again and glanced at his watch. He made a grimace, then looked up again into Lavina's smiling face. "You know, Mrs. London, I have a confession to make . . .''

She shut her eyes in near panic. This wasn't the way she had planned it at all.

". . . and I feel terrible about it, but well, I'm sure you'll understand, being the lady you are and all . . . well, to be perfectly honest, I have a date tonight and I'm running just a little late.''

Whew! Lavina raised a slightly tremulous arm to check her own watch as well. "Of course, of course. You should have said something earlier.'' She turned back to face the atrium. "We've been here quite long enough now as it is. There's really no need my seeing the inside of the crypts, now is there? The important thing is that you not keep your date waiting. That would be the height of discourtesy.''

"I knew you'd understand, Mrs. London.''

She couldn't remember when she had last breathed such a sigh of relief.

Once outside again, the salesman locked the door to the mausoleum, then turned and led her down the deep, shallow steps to the parked Nova. This time she made no objection to the strong arm guiding her elbow.

He opened the passenger door for her, then went around to the other side. Lavina remained standing alongside the open door, watching him across the frayed, vinyl roof.

"Oh, no."

"What's the matter?" she asked, emitting a second sigh of relief.

"I've got a flat."

"A flat? Can you fix it?"

"I can change it. It must be a slow leak, although it seemed all right coming up here." He stripped off his lightweight jacket and tossed it through the open window into the driver's seat, then headed back toward the rear of the car. "You can sit inside if you want, Mrs. London—if you don't mind the tilt, that is, while I jack up the front end. It won't take long."

"That's all right, I can wait." She closed her door and came and joined him at the back of the car where she watched as he inserted the key in the lock, opened and then raised the lid of the trunk. He lifted out the heavy-looking, dark-green, tubular jack she had seen him use earlier, together with a short length of rusty chain with hook-shaped ends. He then returned to the opposite end of the car where he crouched down to set up the jack under the heavy, front bumper. She could hear the chain drop into place, and then watched as he rose again and came back to join her at the open trunk.

He jerked the lug wrench out from under the spare tire screwed in position in its storage rack, then started rummaging around inside, first in the left well, then the right.

He straightened up again and went around to the driver's side of the car. He opened the door and pushed the front seat forward, then bent over to look on the floor in the back of the car, stretching his hand in and under the driver's seat feeling for something. He replaced the seat, closed the door, and came back again to stare down vacantly into the gaping trunk, his hands on his hips. He closed his white-lashed eyes as if trying desperately to remember.

"Is this what you're looking for, Mr. Janowitz?" Lavina asked, taking out a thin, cylindrical-shaped metal bar from her handbag. It was about fourteen inches long, black, pitted with rust, and wrapped now neatly in plastic wrap. "I hope it hasn't ripped my good bag."

Karl Janowitz opened his eyes and turned to look, first at Lavina, then at the metal bar. His corded hands slipped to his sides.

"Where did? . . ." He raised his eyes to look at her again. "Of course! You were there, weren't you? But now—"

"So you did see me. I was pretty sure it was your car. Not too many Chevys around town nowadays. How old is this one anyway? '73? '74?"

Janowitz just remained staring at her, his hands motionless at his sides, like a man who'd just been hypnotized.

"Pretty careless of you to leave it behind, wasn't it?" Lavina said, tapping the bar against her upraised palm.

The salesman let his broad shoulders drop just a little, then gave a self-satisfied little smirk that changed the whole appearance of his handsome face. It had a diabolical force behind it now that frightened Lavina for the first time.

"It probably still has your fingerprints on it," she said, trying to regain her composure, "unless, of course, you were very careful. Not that it matters much. I see it's a bit rusty. That will probably match up with the rust Tod mentioned finding in Peter Frame's scalp, don't you think?"

"What makes you think it's mine?" Janowitz said.

"Oh, come now, Mr. Janowitz, you do give me more credit than that, I'm sure. How many of these things do you think are around Boulder anyway? Especially with yours missing." She shook the metal bar in front of his face. "And I did see you at the scene that day, remember."

"The scene of the crime." He smiled, pleasantly again this time. "And are you telling me, Mrs. London, that you found this yourself somewhere?"

"Of course," she lied. "Under Officer Uberon's bed."

"Under his bed," he repeated, almost to himself.

"Yes. After I found his body."

"What were *you* doing in Uberon's apartment?"

She thought back for a few seconds, trying to recall the excuse she'd given herself for prying. "I wanted to make sure he hadn't dozed off when I knew he had to get back to the Sheriff's office."

"Your good deed for the day, I suppose." It was a tone he hadn't used with her before, a tone that somehow matched the look she'd seen on his face.

She shrugged her shoulders, sliding a thumb up along the shoulder strap of her bag. "I won't bother asking your purpose in being there, Mr. Janowitz; I have that fairly well figured out."

"Do you now?" He narrowed his eyes without pursuing her comment further. "And didn't you turn this bar over to the police?"

"There's plenty of time for that," she said, looking back down at the item in question. "I didn't want to chance looking foolish to the police until I was sure. I thought I recognized it when I recalled seeing you with your jack the other day." She nodded her head in the direction of the front of the blue Nova.

"The other day?"

"Yes. You were removing your snows outside the cemetery office."

"So I was." He nodded his head in recollection.

"I honestly hoped I was wrong. You seemed like such a nice young man." While it was true, saying it out in the open like this to a man she now knew for sure had committed premeditated murder somehow gave her an empty feeling in the pit of her stomach, a feeling she hadn't had since Kenneth died. For the time being, she just hoped it didn't sound too unbelievable. She had to make sure that he took everything she said at face value—for her own sake if nothing else. Her plan—her life—depended on it.

"But you've certainly mentioned its existence to the police since then," he said, "—to Sheriff Arthur, if no one else."

She could read him now like a book. He wanted to be sure just how much the authorities knew. Her web was apparently doing the job for which it was intended. In a way, she felt shamelessly bewitching, like one of the sirens, if not Circe herself.

"Not quite yet, no," she lied again. "But of course now you give me no alternative, Mr. Janowitz."

"Nor you me, Mrs. London." The counselor shook his head. "You know, I really took you for a much more sensible woman—one with both feet on the ground. But here you are acting just like any other old woman."

"And just what, pray tell, do you mean by that?" Lavina asked with as much feigned indignation as she could manage, playing along. His choice of the term "acting" was most apropos. She'd have to try to remember it when she relived it all later for Winnie.

Janowitz turned and looked around, first to his right, then to his left. Except for the continual splash of water from behind the building, and the occasional chirping of a bird, all was silent.

"What you're telling me, Mrs. L, is that you're the only one who knows about this—this presumed weapon of yours—"

"Of yours, you mean," she corrected.

"Would they consider it a blunt weapon, do you think? I don't recall their having used that term in the papers when they described the cause of death." His laugh now was as diabolical as his earlier smile and tone had been. As far as Lavina could recall, it was the first time she had ever actually been face-to-face with evil incarnate. The thought sent a shiver through her whole body. *Holy Mother of God, pray for us.*

"I won't be the only one who knows after I've seen the police," she said, regaining her composure but ignoring the question. She just hoped he continued to swallow the naive act. She had no time to be critic as well to evaluate her one-time, unrehearsed performance. All she knew for sure was that they'd certainly need more than the instrument of death to prove murder, especially if he insisted the bar wasn't even his. She knew perfectly well, of course, that there were no prints on it, a fact he must certainly have known for himself.

"I'm afraid you're not following me, Mrs. L. You won't get that chance, you see."

He reached out and made a quick grab for the bar, his chapped lips pressed tight, his eyes intense. The veins ran up his thick neck like mole furrows on the soil's surface.

Lavina had expected as much and was prepared for it, surrendering the bar with pretended surprise and a little screech to match. In a way, she was half enjoying the opportunity to act again. It was just a shame her audience was so limited.

"You admit it, then," she said, trying not to overdo her cringe.

"To you, Mrs. L—yes. As a special courtesy."

Lavina crossed her hands at her stomach and gave an audible sigh. "That's all I wanted to hear, Mr. Janowitz."

"I don't know why, for all the good it's going to do you, Mrs. London. You know, I really wish you had stayed at home with your embroidery and minded your own business. I was really getting to like you. You were one of the few decent people I'd met in this burg in the three years I've been here. Or so I thought —until now." He shook his head again. "And all this business about being interested in crypts was just so much pretense, wasn't it? To feel me out, and maybe even catch me off guard . . ."

Lavina just smiled, then turned to look around her.

"No one here but us, Mrs. L. Julie never comes out this way, if that's who you're looking for. He stays in the office most of the night. Just occasionally checks the main gate and watches for any strange lights where they shouldn't be, that sort of thing. Pretty boring if you ask me. Don't really need him as far as I can see since we're already attached to the police station in Monticello through our alarm system. That's why you asked about the watchman, isn't it—just in case?"

Lavina swallowed hard but said nothing. She just stared into the pale-blue eyes that she found so handsome, yet so cruel. Somehow it made her think of Lucifer before his fall.

"You've really been quite naughty, you know, following me like you have with your suspicions."

"They paid off, didn't they?" she ventured, almost sorry for the pointed barb.

"Not in the long run, I'm afraid—not for you, at least. I really don't know what you expected from this drummed-up little drama of yours. It must be the actress in you. You can take the actress out of the drama, but you can't take the drama out of the actress, is that it?" He grinned. "I must say, the unexpected flat tire certainly added to your little scenario, didn't it? It couldn't have worked out better if you had planned it yourself."

She was beginning to worry that he might start to put two and two together, which was something she just couldn't allow. After all, he had planned and executed three nearly perfect murders, so he was nobody's fool. She had to get his mind off the dangerous topic of her involvement and back on himself, the subject that obviously interested him most, as it did all egoists.

"Why did you do it, Mr. Janowitz. I mean, three people . . ."

"I thought you said you had it all figured out—or was that just something else in your script?" He narrowed his eyes again and started tapping fast and more nervously on his palm with the metal bar.

"Why Peter?" was all she said. She couldn't admit

that she already knew about Karl's partnership with Leo Frame, and that they jointly owned the out-of-state funeral chapels. And she couldn't admit the suspicion she had as to the papers in Uberon's manila envelope. He'd never believe she hadn't shared that information with the police—or indeed that she had learned everything pretty much by her own initiative, which after all wasn't far from the truth. "Not for the boy's measly two thousand dollars, surely," she added.

"Two thousand dollars?" It was clear from his tone and the expression on his sunburned face that he knew nothing about the money missing from the boy's bank account.

"No, I didn't think so," she said, leaving him in the dark. "So he must have learned something that made him a threat. What was it? Some scheme you had going with his stepfather?" How she would have loved to show him how much she already knew.

"You continue to amaze me, Mrs. London. You *are* sharp. Yes, that's precisely the case. Unfortunately for the boy, Leo just couldn't keep his mouth shut. He felt he had to confide in someone; why, I still don't know. He didn't trust his wife but he blurted out everything to the boy sometime last March when he was home from college on Easter break. Stupid bastard."

"And Peter approached you with it when he returned home and learned his stepfather had been murdered."

"He called me, yes. From the Seventeener lounge. He was pretty high—and cocky. The booze probably gave him the courage to call. He boasted that he knew about our partnership agreement naming each other sole beneficiary of the businesses. You know the type of thing: 'In the event of the demise of one of the partners, his interest shall revert to the surviving principal . . .' ''

"And Leo Frame laid out the initial investment?" Lavina asked, incredulous. It certainly didn't sound like the Leo Frame she'd been hearing about since his death.

"Not all of it, no. I told you I wasn't poor, Mrs. London. I threw in my share—or enough anyway to make me look sincere. It was chicken feed in comparison to what I expected to rake in once it was all mine."

"You had this all planned from the outset?" She *was* learning something after all. And it sickened her even more.

"Of course," he said as matter-of-factly as if owning up to having chopped down the proverbial cherry tree.

Lavina remained looking at him, shaking her head in disbelief.

"My initial investment wasn't the only thing I had going for me, of course," he continued now that he had, if not an appreciative audience, at least a stunned one. "Leo realized that I knew the cemetery business inside out from having been attached to Evergreen. He knew I'd be invaluable in handling these guys in the future. He didn't want to go through the problems he had here with Creighton. Once that guy gets his own chapel going here on the grounds, Elenice will be finished, whether she wants to be or not, believe me."

"And you won't have that kind of problem with your ill-gotten chapels."

"Every step has been anticipated, Mrs. L, every step. I know these cemetery guys like a book. And we chose our locations very, very carefully. Without Leo, there'll be nothing to do but sit back and count the money. As they say, there are people dying now that never died before."

"And all just dying to get into your funeral chapels," she added, not to be outdone.

Janowitz let the remark pass, obviously having heard the old chestnut more often than he'd care to admit. Not that his own had been any fresher. "I have to hand it to him, though," he said, "Leo knew a good thing when he saw it."

"Meaning the knowledgeable Karl Janowitz."

"Precisely." The sardonic smile again. "I'll have to change the name of the establishments, of course. Since Leo had provided the bulk of the cash outlay, I had to agree to keep the Frame moniker." He shrugged the thick shoulders. "Anything to keep him happy and unsuspecting. He was like a kid—you couldn't imagine—all hepped up about a big promotion campaign he had planned. Used to keep talking about making the chapels the McDonalds of the funeral industry. Can you imagine! Like some sort of fast funeral chain. Crazy old coot!"

"How many chapels are we talking about anyway?" Lavina asked, realizing for the first time that she had no idea of the extent of his envisioned mortuary empire.

"Six. In six different states."

"Including Arizona." It wasn't a question.

"You guessed it."

"And Peter? You didn't quite finish the story." It was the boy's murder more than the others that bothered her most, if indeed such a degree of moral indignation had any validity. And then probably only because he seemed like an innocent victim.

"As I said, he called and told me he was in town, at the motel, and that he *knew*—he made it sound as ominous as possible, of course, as if he expected me to break down on the phone and own up to his suspicions or something. As crazy as his old man.

"He'd been drinking, as I said, but he was known in town for that—at least among people who knew him. I told him I'd come over and have a talk with him, explain about the partnership—I didn't deny that much; from the little he said on the phone I knew he wasn't bluffing. He even thought his stepmother was in on the deal. I hinted at the possibility of turning over his stepfather's share to him. For some reason he was also convinced that he'd been cut out of Leo's will, I don't know why. But even in the condition he was in, I could tell he didn't quite swallow the line I was offering him. He said he needed more time to think. Which, of course, was something I couldn't allow, now could I?"

"What else did you offer him besides a possible share in his stepfather's new chain?"

"What else?"

It was a stab in the dark, and a pretty feeble one at that, based on the supposition Tod had offered earlier, but she took it just the same. "You arranged things at the motel to look as if there had been a sexual angle to his murder, didn't you?"

"You mean you were at that crime scene too, Mrs. L? Wow! You do get around, don't you? A regular Jessica Fletcher—give or take twenty or thirty years."

Lavina ignored the deliberate attempt to rile her

and instead just smiled. Her guess had probably been right on target and hit a sore spot, making him strike out like the wild, cornered animal he was. The oh-so-clever murderer unmasked at his own game. It was no wonder he felt the need to be vicious.

"Surely you suspected something about the boy's nature," she said, "other than the fact that he was an alcoholic. You'd met him often enough, probably heard vicious rumors about him—maybe even from his own stepmother." From the flippant remark he had made about the woman earlier, she was now convinced Elenice Frame had not been in on his plan to kill her husband. Until then, she hadn't been quite sure. It was one of the loose ends that had been bothering her.

Janowitz shrugged again, and without taking his eyes off her, slammed the lid of the trunk closed with his left hand. "So I heard he was queer, so what?" he said.

"And a good-looking man like you—a man in a pretty tight spot, I might add—didn't consider making the most of your physical talents at a time like that? To entice the boy? Catch him off guard with your charm? After what you just told me about your well-laid scheme to defraud and kill his stepfather, I find that hard to believe."

"You pain me, Mrs. L, you really do. Don't you give me any credit for having a conscience?"

"None whatsoever."

"Again, my kudos. It's really too bad you weren't working with me. We'd have made one hell of a team." Hell, is right, she thought. He gave a little laugh and looked down at the metal bar still in his hand. "And, as usual, you're right. As far as the scene at the motel goes, I undressed him in the bathroom—that wasn't easy, believe me, the fat slob"—Lavina shut her eyes briefly in pain—"then I just tossed his clothes back outside to give the impression of the compromising situation you mentioned. I'm surprised the cops up here didn't buy it—or maybe they did. Maybe it's just our star who wasn't taken in by my creativity, accustomed as she is to the ease of setting the proper scene." She hadn't thought about it that way, but in a way maybe he was right.

"As for the enticement, yes, there too you've hit it on the head. I did sort of hint on the phone that, if he was interested, maybe we might get something going between us when I came over."

"But he turned you down." Even she was surprised by the fervor she detected in the statement.

"What are you, anyway, some sort of clairvoyant?"

No, nor did she know it was a fact. She was just somehow convinced that such was the case. Faith, trust, call it what you want. She remembered, too, what Winnie had said about the boy's attending church. That in itself said something—to her at least, if no one else.

"Just a good judge of character, I suppose, Mr. Janowitz," she said. "I haven't lived in this little community all these years for nothing. I hear things, too. Unlike you, however—and fortunately, no credit to me—I happen to prefer to believe the goods things I hear about people." Such wasn't always the case, to be sure, but it was a grace she prayed for at least.

"Miss Goody Two-Shoes."

She made no comment.

"Well, if it makes you feel any better, yes, the kid did reject the suggestion. As a matter of fact, he became pretty hostile over the phone. Can you imagine?"

"As hard as it may seem to you, yes, I can. Very easily, as a matter of fact."

"Turning down a body like this!" He looked down at what to him was obviously one of his own personal idols. He was far from the picture of humility he had presented back at the lake on their first encounter. "I guess what I thought and heard was wrong, that's all," he said. "The guy was probably straight after all. Just square."

"Or maybe he just had more guts and self-esteem than you'll ever have, Mr. Janowitz."

"More . . ." The memorial counselor left the unthinkable to fend for itself in midair. Either because he honestly considered it such, or was too afraid to face the possibility that what Lavina said might be true. Instead, he merely gave a weak, little self-satisfied laugh at some private notion that only he could appreciate.

"You phoned the motel office later on for his room number," Lavina said, to substantiate another of her suppositions. So far she was batting a hundred. She was bound to strike out somewhere along the line.

"Right again."

"Elenice Frame knew nothing about the new chapels at all then." This, just to make doubly sure.

"Not from me she didn't, no. The kid told me his old man confided in him—said he was the only one he was telling—because he had to share it with someone." Janowitz uttered a little noise of surprise as if discovering something new for the first time. "Old Leo must have thought more of him than the kid realized.

"I'm not in the regular will or anything, so there's

no way anyone else around here can tie me in with Leo's death—and even less with the other two. That was the beauty of the whole plan, which was all drawn up nice and legal-like.''

"What about out of town?" Lavina asked. "You still have to prove Leo's dead in order to get his share of the partnership, don't you?"

Janowitz's head was nodding even before she had completed the question. "Already taken care of, dear lady. That was the least of my worries; it was no problem at all for me to get the necessary copies of his death certificate—not in my position. I'll be forwarding them on to my lawyer in Phoenix in order to have the survivor clause put into effect."

"That's all there is to it?"

"Just about. Who's to know Leo died from anything more than asphyxiation—which is how the certificate reads. Happens every day. No one out there is going to care about the death of some old guy in Dullsville, USA, much less ask questions. And the murder is hardly likely to show up in any of their newspapers. I've been having a friend in New York send me copies of the six major dailies just to be on the safe side. Started it almost two weeks before I . . . before Leo's untimely death. So far, nothing. I'll keep them coming a while longer just to be sure. Maybe another week."

Besides her annoyance at his continual disparaging remarks about Boulder, Lavina somehow didn't believe it could all be quite that simple. Surely there'd be someone "out there" who'd want to know more about the sudden death of a man so soon after entering into partnership with his surviving beneficiary— even if the chapels were in six different states. Either

Karl Janowitz was too naive for his own good, or there was something wrong with a legal system that could allow such a thing to happen.

"Elenice Frame will retain the Frame name and the five homes here in New York State; I have nothing to do with them at all. I'd be foolish if I did. Of course I'll probably have to stay on here another couple of months to make it look good. After that, I'll just suddenly become restless or homesick, quit Evergreen, and head back west. With no one the wiser. Karl Janowitz will be home free."

"Meanwhile, what about Lavina London?" She asked, squinting as the lowering sun grazed the tops of the evergreens, its orange intensity blinding the human eye.

"Ah, yes, the ex-radio actress. I'm afraid the 'ex' will just become more definitive."

"I'm next, is that it? A fourth victim?"

Janowitz showed one upturned palm, the other still grasping the metal bar. "Is that my fault, Mrs. London? You were the one who wouldn't let well enough alone."

It was funny, but hearing the trite phrase now rang the proverbial bell, sending her memory back Lord knows how many years. It was after hearing just such a comment that one of her dearest friends had named her new cat Well Enough. She smiled now, though more at the idea that the silly fact should pop into her head at a time like this than at the fact itself.

"What do you find so amusing?" the salesman asked.

"Just a personal recollection," she said. "I'm at least entitled to that much, I suppose? The condemned man and all that?"

Janowitz shrugged. "I'm glad you're taking it all so lightly. I continue to admire you, for one reason if not another."

"You can't possibly get away with it, you know. They're bound to put two and two together when they find me."

"But that's just it, Mrs. London; they won't find you. Oh, they'll send out a search party and all, no question about it. It will go on for a while, but pretty soon they'll be forced to give it up as a lost cause. Just too many unexplored woods still in these parts, for one thing. And then, too, they can't be expected to waste too much of the taxpayers' money, even on a favorite, longtime, local daughter."

"What exactly is it you're not telling me, Mr. Janowitz?"

Janowitz looked down again at the metal bar, then back up, the smile reforming on his dry lips. "You did say you were eager to have a look at the inside of one of our crypts, didn't you? Well, while your Emily Post might not quite approve, I think I can accommodate you after all."

"You're not planning on burying me alive, surely?" she said, a shiver running down her spine, not sure just how far he would actually go, given the chance.

"Mrs. L . . . now really! Again you disappoint me. How heartless do you think I am? I'm ashamed of you." He gave another one of his self-satisfied little laughs. "Poe I'm not—more's the pity. I do love his morbid imagination, though, don't you?"

Between the pages of a book, yes. Man's strange attraction for primal fear. "What if I scream?"

"Be my guest." He swept the air with his free hand, outlining a wide arc. "Who exactly do you think will hear you way out here? The dearly departed?" He let his muscular arm drop again, the white hairs glistening in the setting sun. "Scream, by all means."

Lavina said nothing, her firm grip tightening on the crocheted strap of her shoulder bag. This was the dangerous part. If things didn't go right now, it could well mean curtains. Her finale of finales, so to speak.

"Now if you'll just turn and head back up the stairs like a good girl, I promise I'll make it as painless as possible for you. I'm afraid you'll have to settle for Peony Corridor though; I have a nice single ready and waiting that should suit you just fine once you get settled in—and this one's even on the house." The murderer laughed, enjoying the whole thing. Where evil ended and dementia began, Lavina didn't know, and the laugh that rang in her ears now gave her no clue either.

"Surely you can't just wall me up in one of the crypts?" she said, finally speaking up.

"Why not?" The smile hadn't disappeared.

"They'll know back in the office, for one thing. Mr. Creighton. Theresa." To her it sounded perfectly obvious.

The pre-need promoter laughed again, this time apparently in appreciation of her own naiveté. "Oh, Mrs. London, if you only knew how funny that was. The last ones to know anything about the everyday running of this operation are those two. Once I slide you in"—Lavina didn't particularly care for the sound of that one—"add the facing and seal it up, I'll go back down to the office, enter a phony sale, and bury you in my friendly, little computer, to be dug out only at my beck and call. All under a false name, of course."

"Are they that stupid down there? Surely they know what's going on."

"You'd be surprised. And even if it ever dawned on them to ask questions about your crypt, why would they doubt the computer? As far as they're concerned, the computer is the final authority. Like so many other stupid people nowadays, they just don't take into account the real movers behind these golden calves. Do you honestly think either one of those two pay any attention whatsoever to the work details around this place? How do you think I got where I am? I'll be able to wrap their ilk around my little finger once I'm in control of my new chapels. Wise up, Mrs. London; I'm the only one around here who gives a damn about concrete details, keeps all the records. That's one of the reasons I insisted they get a computer. To help me—not the damn cemetery. As it turns out, it's paying off even better than I expected.

"As for Theresa, she couldn't care less about what goes on around here. She puts in her forty hours and takes home her little pay check—and very little it is, I might add. Outside of that, she doesn't want to know from nothing. I should know—I recommended her to Creighton for the job."

"Laying your plans even back then," Lavina said.

"You better believe it."

"And what about Mr. Creighton? He's the boss or owner, isn't he?"

"Two-bit con artist is more like it," Janowitz said with a smirk. "Thinks he's clever. He may pull the wool over the eyes of his partners, or whatever they are—probably does. But when you come down to it, it's pretty much penny-ante stuff. Probably get caught before he's finished. He's out for himself, all right, but he has a very short reach. And God forbid he should get his hands dirty—which is the reason he couldn't be bothered with the day-to-day workings of a place like this. Leave that to the minions, like Karl Janowitz. That's the one thing that bugs me about all this secrecy; I'll never be able to shove it in his face.

"You ask him, and I bet he couldn't even tell you how many people are buried in this mausoleum, not within fifty of the actual count. So I ask you, do you seriously think he's interested in who's buried where? You think a hotel owner gives a damn who's in what room—or what he's doing there? Creighton is just here to make sure he's the one to skim all the cream from this operation."

"And you're not, I suppose?" Lavina said.

"Sure, I am; that's the name of the game. Only with me, I don't let the milk go sour waiting."

He made a little motion with the plastic-wrapped metal bar. "Well, enough of this chitchat, Mrs. L. It may be your cup of tea, but it's not mine. Besides, I don't want to hang around here too long. Ol' Julie might start wondering. So if you'll just move"—he pointed with the bar—"up the steps."

Lavina remained standing, staring at him, doubting now for the first time her seemingly well-contrived plan. Maybe it hadn't really been working as well as she thought. Maybe—

"I said turn and get a move on." The tone of voice this time was sharp, sharp and bitter, the chapped lips tight and curled in.

Lavina turned, and in so doing, let her bag slip off her shoulder and down her arm to the ground. Janowitz swept it up and handed it back to her before she had a chance to do much else, motioning her attention back to the steps.

She lifted a foot to the first of the deep, low,

marble steps, then closed her eyes, half expecting to feel the impact of the metal bar on the back of her skull. Was she going to witness firsthand those stars writers like to summon up so often in the course of their descriptions of hard-boiled heroes who become victims of the butt end of a .38? It was incredible to think she could be in such a predicament, but there she was. She took a deep breath and offered up a quick prayer to the Blessed Mother and the Sacred Heart, then swallowed hard.

Without opening her eyes, she raised her other foot to join the first. This had to be it.

When nothing happened, she opened her eyes again, looked up at the sky above the mausoleum, and made a hesitant move to the next step.

A weakness like muscular atrophy seized her legs. The glass doors at the top of the steps began to melt one into the other. She was going to throw up.

A muffled shout and then, when it came, it jolted her whole taut body with two spasmodic jerks . . . first one shot . . . then a second.

Chapter Twenty-two

"You were a plant, Lavina?"

"That's right, Sean." Lavina set the can of Ballantine in front of him on top of the long picnic table that was set out under a white, canvas awning on the side of the house. She went around to sit facing him on the attached wooden bench on the opposite side, next to Tod Arthur.

"What do you mean, a plant?" Winnie asked, adjusting for the umpteenth time the rubber band at the back of her walnut-red head.

"A decoy, dear," Sean clarified.

Winnie, at his side, hesitated, then said, "Oh, a sitting duck."

Tod Arthur laughed. "Just about, Winnie." He reached across the table and patted her hand. "And you should have seen her."

"If you say a duck out of water, Tod Arthur, I'm going to let you have it for sure." They all joined in laughing this time, all, that is, except Winnie.

"That could have been dangerous, though, couldn't it?" she asked, obviously concerned. She paused, then proceeded to pour her beer into a pilsner glass.

"Well, hardly that, dear," Lavina reassured her, deliberately minimizing the danger for her friend. "It was all very safe, really, what with Tod and his men on the sidelines ready to pounce once I gave the signal."

"I'll have to see that *Pietà* for myself," Father Cernac added from his seat on the other side of the sheriff. "Must be pretty big to screen the three of you from sight."

"Oh, it's that, all right," Arthur said. "I didn't believe it either when Lavina first proposed her original plan to me back at the office. She had seen a picture of it in a brochure and had already seen some of the others."

Father Cernac—Paul to his pastor, fellow priests, and close friends—just sat shaking his grizzled, wiry head back and forth in disbelief. "I wish you had let me know what you were up to, Lavina," he said, looking around Tod Arthur's massive chest to the actress beyond him.

Lavina knew she was being scolded by her confessor, but smiled just the same. "Now, Father, you know that if I told you anything of the sort you would have forbidden me to go ahead with it." Like many of her generation, Lavina could never quite bring herself to address a religious—and especially a priest —by his first name.

"Forbidden, no, but I certainly would have advised very strongly against it." Thirty years as a priest had taught him many things, not the least of which was to expect the unexpected at all times. Lavina, as he never hesitated to let her know, had more than once substantiated the truth of this conviction.

"Well, there you are," she said, pouring herself a Diet Cherry Coke from a three-liter plastic bottle. When she failed to cut the flow in time, the foam surged quickly to the top of the glass and spilled over onto the oilcloth that covered the crude, wooden tabletop. She reached for the Handi Wipe in the circular, metal bar tray she used to carry out the glasses and soaked up the spill. When she cast an eye in the priest's direction, she saw that he was smiling at her.

"You mean you figured everything out by yourself, Lavina?" Sean asked, stubbing out his cigarette in an aluminum coaster and then reaching into his skirt pocket for his pack. Winnie's stubby hand was across his chest without a word to halt the chain reaction in progress. He withdrew his hand and, without argument, reached instead for his can of beer.

"No, of course not, Sean," Lavina said. "Tod did most of the actual investigative work." This with an unconcealed wink in Winnie's direction.

"How did Tod and his men happen to be in the cemetery at the time, Lavina?" Winnie asked, honestly puzzled.

"We didn't 'happen to be,' as you put it, Winnie," Tod said, jumping in. "That was the whole point; it was all planned in advance. Julie, the watchman, had let us in through the rear gate earlier. We left the patrol car on the far side of the valley and made our way to the mausoleum by foot."

"That's why Julie wasn't in the office when he normally would have been," Lavina added.

"You had this all timed out then," Sean said.

"We had to," Lavina said. "We couldn't chance Karl Janowitz seeing the police before the trap was actually sprung."

"Right," Arthur said. "The boys and I stayed behind the mausoleum out of sight until Lavina and Janowitz went inside, then, after deflating Janowitz's tire, the three of us stationed ourselves out front behind that huge statue I was telling you about."

"Anyway," the sheriff continued, "I had arranged with Lavina to let the air out of the tire so he'd have to use his jack—and, of course, the missing pump bar we'd put in Lavina's bag to confront him with."

"We were lucky he didn't just try to inflate it with that inflator thing of his," Lavina said. "I thought of that later."

"That's not the only thing you were lucky in," Father Cernac said. "You could have been killed."

"Now, Father, you more than anyone else should know that wasn't luck," Lavina said, thoroughly enjoying the chance to rib her friend on his own turf.

"Touché," the priest said with a smile, at the same time turning an unenviable shade of red.

"I guess we were at that," Arthur added, ignoring the private interplay between the two on either side of him.

"And this cemetery salesman, this Janowitz fellow, didn't realize his jack bar was missing?" Sean asked.

Tod Arthur took a long swallow of his beer, then wiped the foam from his upper lip with the back of his hand. "From what he told us at the hospital after we took him in," he said, "no. According to him, he had taken it with him into Uberon's apartment to use as a weapon—as he had on young Frame earlier—but when the opportunity to kill him presented itself,

Rob's necktie just seemed better. He was in such a hurry to check for Leo's copies of their partnership papers in the manila envelope—which, after all, was what he was really after—that he just forgot all about the metal bar. It never even entered his mind, he said, until last night when he needed it to operate the jack. That's when he realized he'd left it behind at the apartment. On the bed, he thought, so it must have rolled off onto the rug and got knocked under the bed without him knowing it."

"Unfortunately—for him," Sean said, shaking his white-fringed head.

"And fortunately for us that Lavina here had seen him using it earlier so that she was fairly sure what it was when I showed it to her yesterday."

"It was hard to believe that Rob Uberon was black-mailing anyone," Lavina said, thinking back, "but it was the only thing that made any sense after a while. When Tod told me Friday that Rob was the one who had examined Leo Frame's desk at the funeral home, and I remembered that manila envelope he was holding on to after returning from what I thought was a failed love tryst, I was pretty sure he was out to blackmail somebody, and that it was in some way connected to Leo Frame."

"But you didn't know it was this Janowitz," Sean said.

"Not right then, no. Not until I had time to think things out. Even after I'd spotted what I thought was his car at Uberon's garden apartments, I had difficulty believing he was the killer. I couldn't see any motive for the killing of the two Frames. Still, it seemed to fit. When I figured things out as best I could on my own, I went back to Tod with my suspicions, and we put our heads together. That's when he showed me the metal bar which pretty well clinched it as far as I was concerned.''

''This was Saturday?'' Sean asked.

''Yesterday afternoon, yes.''

''Didn't I read something in the paper yesterday,'' Father Cernac asked, ''about possible robbery in the death of your deputy?''

''That's what we thought at first,'' Arthur admitted. ''As a matter of fact, that's why Janowitz took Uberon's walkie-talkie and revolver. He wanted us to think just that.''

''Just like he tried to make Peter's death look like something else,'' Lavina added. She looked toward the sheriff and smiled.

''Was the bar the only evidence you had?'' Winnie asked.

''At first, yes,'' Arthur said. ''At least the only concrete evidence. When Lavina finally got around to telling me about his car being at the apartment complex''—this with a friendly glare in the direction of the actress next to him—''and after I showed her the bar, we still didn't have a motive.''

''Right,'' Lavina added. ''It all came down to what was in the manila envelope, what precisely Uberon had found in Leo Frame's desk that day. To all intents and purposes, Karl Janowitz looked like a highly unlikely suspect. After all, he was—from all outward appearances, at least—only a salaried employee at the cemetery. Gregory Creighton was actually the one Leo Frame dealt with all the time. Theresa Francotti told me as much.

''The possibility entered my mind that he might have been a partner at Evergreen, after all. Since we didn't want to approach Mr. Creighton himself on the matter—we probably would have gotten a run-around anyway if we had—Tod phoned a judge friend of his up in Monticello to check into the background of the cemetery. When he finally got back to us, it was with the disappointing information that Karl Janowitz's name was nowhere in evidence. Which was pretty much the point he made with me at the mausoleum, that he had no connection here with anything at all, nothing whatsoever to tie him in with Leo Frame. It was all part of his long-range plan. And well thought out it was, too, for the most part.''

"So how did you proceed from there?'' Sean asked, leaning closer to them over the tabletop, his hand reaching to his shirt pocket. This time the move was unimpeded and he dug out a cigarette, which he lit, tossing the paper match into the aluminum ashtray between them.

"Tod actually had the whole answer all along without realizing it,'' Lavina said, happy now to share the glory of their joint success. "It was all in black and white in a legal guide he had seen in young Peter's room. The boy had marked off a chapter on partnerships with an index card. At the time he first saw it, of course, it didn't mean anything to him. When he mentioned it to me yesterday and asked what I thought, I had a few more facts to work with than he did.

"I got to thinking about what Karl Janowitz had told me the first day I met him here at the house—his past, the irons he had in the fire that he was reluctant to talk about, investments and branching out, things like that. That's what gave me the idea that he might have been in secret partnership, not with Gregory

Creighton, but with Leo Frame. From there I started thinking about Phoenix, where Karl told me he was born."

"And a good thing, too," Sheriff Arthur said. "Or we might still be over a barrel." It was obviously a mutual-admiration Sunday afternoon.

"Tod placed a call to the police there and within an hour they were back to him with the information. They can really get a move on when they want to, can't they?" This with a smile at Tod. "As it turned out, there *was* a new funeral home about to open there under the Frame name. Well, if there was one, why not more? After all, Leo had five of them already in New York State alone. The man thought big, and if he had a partner, he was bound to think twice as big."

"The Phoenix police were very cooperative," Arthur said as if basking in some sort of fraternal benevolence. "It took a little while but they finally tracked down the right insurance company out there. Don't forget they had to check out a number of them before they hit on the right one. That, plus the fact that it was Saturday. Lucky for us the one company covered all six of the new homes in the six different states. It had nothing to do with the partnership, just the basic coverage of the homes, but it was the perfect way of verifying our suspicions of their actual existence and learning their locations." He hoisted his beer can and took another long swallow.

"That was all Tod's idea, you understand," Lavina said, still in her generous mood. "And when it panned out, we were off and running. The insurance was in both their names, of course, which helped.

"It was at that point that I proposed my plan to

trap Mr. Janowitz—my feigned interest in crypts, the phony flat, and what have you. Fortunately, I had already laid the groundwork for the mausolem bit, so that worked out very nicely indeed."

"Trap is right," Arthur said, shaking his head. "I almost didn't buy it; it sounded so far out. I mean, I believed everything she said and all, but it just sounded . . . I don't know . . . unprofessional, I guess . . . not to mention highly dangerous."

"You can say that again," Father Cernac added, and took a slug from his own can of beer.

"Nonsense!" Lavina said.

"That's what she said then, too, Father. That's why I went along. I mean, who can argue with logic like that?" He gave a little chuckle.

"Whatever made you think about that flat-tire business anyway, Lavina?" Sean asked.

"Actually," Lavina said, "it was a variation on an old radio script I'd played in way back when."

"You remembered something like that after all these years?" Winnie said in obvious amazement. "I swear, Lavina, sometimes I think you have a pornographic memory."

Father Cernac turned away from the table just in time before he spewed out the mouthful of beer he had just taken. "Excuse me," he finally managed between alternate bouts of coughing and laughing as he reached for the handkerchief in his pants pocket.

The others at the table seemed to enjoy the priest's humorous reaction even more than the actual "Bunkerism" Winnie had inadvertently come out with.

"Sounds like a euphemism for a dirty mind to me, Red," Sean said before the laughter had completely died down.

"Photographic, Winnie, photographic," Lavina corrected her between spasmodic bursts of laughter. "And no, my memory is far from that, I assure you."

Winnie dismissed the lot of them with an annoyed wave of her small, chubby hand. "You all know what I mean, so don't be so funny."

"By the way, Lavina," Arthur injected, wiping the corners of his eyes with a finger. "I think I forgot to tell you that the Albany police phoned early this morning. It seems that the two thousand dollars missing from Peter Frame's bank account went toward opening up an IRA."

"Nice of them to finally get around to discovering it," Lavina said. "They could take a few lessons from the Phoenix police, if you ask me."

"Now, now, Lavina. Rome wasn't built in a day, as they say." Tod Arthur, the ever-indulgent policeman.

"What was that signal you mentioned before, Lavina?" Father Cernac asked. "The one you said you and Tod had arranged between you?"

"My handbag," Lavina said. "We'd agreed that I'd drop it when I felt I was in any real danger, and that the next move would be up to Tod. Until that point, I held on to it for dear life lest I let it slip too early and spoil everything. My thumb is still sore." She looked down now at the finger in question, exercising it back and forth.

"Weren't you nervous?" Winnie asked, fingering the condensation on her tall glass.

"Not really," Lavina lied. "I knew Tod had everything under control." How she had kept herself from throwing up or passing out, she'd never know. But after the two shots the sheriff had fired at Karl Janowitz, the thing that had frightened her most, she was fine. They must somehow have triggered off some kind of reverse action in her brain, overriding all other motor functions. She'd have to remember to ask Hamilton for a medical explanation, if indeed there was one.

"He's all right though, isn't he?" Father Cernac asked. "Mr. Janowitz, I mean?" There hadn't been enough time for the story to hit the Sunday edition of the *Record* that morning, so this was the first time they were hearing the complete story, and firsthand at that.

"Physically, Father, he's fine. I only hit him in the shoulder, and then only because I had no choice. The other bullet went high. We didn't want to hit him at all, naturally, but after Lavina had dropped her bag and turned her back, he suddenly raised the bar. I gave the shout to halt, but I guess he didn't hear it; we were probably too far away. I couldn't take the chance on his lowering that bar. Maybe that wasn't his intention, I don't know, but it sure as heck looked like it. Why, though, before they got inside the mausoleum, I don't know, I didn't think to ask him when we questioned him. Maybe he just wanted to catch her off guard, figuring she wouldn't be expecting anything at that point. As Lavina says, he really didn't want her to suffer if he could help it."

"Nice of him," Sean said with a sarcastic sneer.

"There's still something I don't quite understand though," the priest added.

"What's that, Father?" Arthur asked.

"Didn't Karl Janowitz think about Leo Frame's copy of the partnership papers before your deputy came up with them? Surely he must have; he seemed so thorough about everything else."

"Sure he did, Father. And he planned on getting it,

too, the night he killed Leo. I won't go into those grisly details now, if you don't mind. He said he went to the office and started going through the file, but heard someone coming down from upstairs. Probably Elenice Frame. Naturally, he didn't want to be caught on the premises with the body still warm downstairs, so he made a hasty retreat out through the open, side door, the same way he had come in, planning to come back when he could the next day on some pretext of business and pick it up. Unfortunately for him, he never got the chance. If you recall, Winnie and Lavina were at the home bright and early the next morning.''

"He probably figured no one would find the body until much later, is that it?" Sean said.

"Exactly.''

"But that couldn't have been his reason for stuffing Frame's body in the casket,'' Sean said. "I mean, he wouldn't have known that he'd need more time to retrieve the partnership papers.''

"No, that just turned out to be a lucky fluke,'' Arthur said.

"Why *did* he put poor Leo in the coffin, did he say?'' Winnie asked, sliding the base of her glass over the little puddle it had made on the oilcloth.

"Casket, Winnie,'' Sean corrected, smiling across at Lavina.

"Precisely for the reason we had originally surmised,'' the sheriff said. "He just thought it would be—to quote him—the crowning ironic touch.''

"Sick, if you ask me,'' Sean said.

"All the more reason to keep him in your prayers, Sean,'' Father Cernac said.

"As it turned out, Elenice went him one better with

the cremation,'' Lavina said. ''But going back to Officer Uberon for a second, I imagine his attempt at blackmail must have come as a godsend as far as Karl Janowitz was concerned. If *you* had found those papers, Tod, this whole affair would have been wrapped up long ago.''

''And Rob would still be alive.''

''Don't start again, Tod.''

The sheriff passed over the original compliment, but did agree with her on the promoter's reaction. ''You're right on both counts, Lavina. Janowitz did say that Uberon's call came as a relief, knowing that the papers were in the hands of an unscrupulous cop —his words, not mine. He said he made the appointment to meet him up at Rainbow's End, but fearing that Uberon might not have the papers with him, went instead directly to the apartment where he tried to let himself in. When he couldn't manage it, he just waited in his car for Rob to return. After the kid left you, Lavina, and went on inside, Janowitz went over and rang the bell. Naturally, the kid let him in as soon as he saw who it was.''

''How did he know where Uberon lived?'' Winnie asked.

''Rob hadn't lied to him on the phone. I guess he told him who he was so Janowitz'd have no doubt he had access to the papers. After that, Janowitz had no trouble getting his address. Good old telephone directory.''

''It's all so sordid, isn't it?'' Winnie said.

''Show me a murder that isn't, Winnie,'' Arthur said.

''And Leo intended to keep his new chapels and partnership a secret from his wife?'' Sean asked.

"How long did he figure he could keep that up, I wonder? If Elenice Frame was any kind of a wife at all, she'd have wormed that out of him in no time."

Winnie shot an elbow into his ribs without so much as a word or a glance, temporarily knocking the wind out of him.

"The secret wasn't intended to be permanent, Sean," Arthur explained, smiling at the antics across from him. "According to Janowitz—and I'd heard the same thing earlier from some of the people who knew them—Elenice Frame was constantly picking on Leo for not making enough money. The new chapels were intended as a surprise. He was waiting until they were completed—or so Janowitz says—before breaking the happy news."

"It will be a surprise all right," Lavina said. "With her luck, she'll probably end up with the lot of them, don't you think?"

Arthur drained what was left of his can of beer, then turned and tossed it in the black, plastic bag that lined the plastic barrel behind them. "With Leo's share, maybe," he said, "though it will probably end up in the courts before it's all sorted out. I guess Karl Janowitz still legally owns his own share, though what good it will be to him now, I have no idea."

"Probably be able to afford one of those big-time shyster lawyers to get him off scot-free, that's what," Sean said in obvious disgust at the thought.

"It will take more than a lawyer, I think, Sean . . . much more." Arthur thought back again to young Peter Frame who had been unwittingly caught in the middle of the whole stinking mess, the boy who, as it turned out, had unknowingly left them the key they needed to solve the series of murders. "I wonder what that whole business of Peter's being left out of his stepfather's will was all about," he finally asked aloud, not really expecting an answer.

"Karl Janowitz didn't know?" Lavina asked.

"He had no idea, as I think he said he told you."

"I thought he might have been holding something back."

"No."

"Maybe this Peter chap was gay after all," Sean suggested, "and admitted it to his stepfather when he was home at Easter. With the type of guy Leo was, he might have taken it as a personal insult to his manhood or something. Maybe he really did threaten to cut the boy off."

"It would have had to be long after Easter, I think," Lavina said, "if that's what really happened. If Peter told him back in March and Leo decided to disown him, he'd hardly have waited all this time to have his will changed, do you think? I mean, the boy was still in the will when Leo died. If he did admit anything of the sort, it would have been much more recently, I think, maybe by phone or in a letter. Otherwise it makes no sense."

"Or maybe Leo just cooled off and changed his mind," Winnie said, punctuating her contribution with a sip from her glass.

"And aren't all you gentle people being just a little bit uncharitable?" Father Cernac said, not without a hint of annoyance in his voice. "In the first place, you're pretty close to accusing Peter Frame of something you have no proof of. And even if you had proof, you'd still be out of line."

"Father's right, of course," Lavina said, not quite looking at anyone in particular. "We're casting stones."

"And here it is Sunday, too," Winnie said with a shake of her head.

"Monday through Saturday wouldn't make it any better, I'm afraid, Red," Sean said.

"Now don't start donning sackcloth and ashes on me either," the priest said with a smile. "Just be a little more careful, that's all."

"Why do you think Leo Frame made someone like this Janowitz fellow his sole beneficiary to the new chapels?" Sean asked, changing the direction of the conversation. "I mean, once he let his wife in on the surprise and she found out about the partnership, there'd have been all hell to pay, I'm sure. If his original intention was to satisfy the missus, he would have defeated his whole purpose."

"Maybe so, Sean, but he had no choice," the sheriff said. "Janowitz told him that was the way it had to be, take it or leave it. If Leo wanted a partner with Janowitz's kind of know-how in the funeral and cemetery business, he had to agree to the mutual survivor clause. As it turns out, he also had a lot of connections in real estate out his way. I doubt that Leo made much of a fuss over it; the 'mutual' part probably made it look pretty kosher to him. And he had no reason to suspect anything . . . least of all from someone as seemingly pleasant as Karl Janowitz. I mean, who did? Janowitz was a pretty smooth character straight down the line. Had us all fooled." He turned and smiled at Lavina sitting next to him. "Even our senior Nancy Drew here—for a while, anyway."

"For a long while, I'm afraid," Lavina admitted.

Arthur looked down at his watch. It was almost two o'clock. "Well, I guess I'd better start heading home," he said. "Pol gave me strict orders when I left not to be late for dinner. Sauerbraten."

"I wish you had brought her here like I asked you to, Tod," Lavina said, sliding off the wooden bench to enable him to swing his long legs out the side. "I've got plenty, what with the baked ham and barbecued ribs—not to mention all the salads. I'll be eating left-overs for a week."

"I would have, Lavina, honest, but by the time you asked me this morning, Pol had already marinated the meat and started her ritual. You don't know her when she starts cooking German; her whole personality changes. Reminds me of Kraus on *Benson*." He made an exaggerated, militant face that set everyone laughing. "I'll take a rain check, if that's okay with you."

It had been after the eight o'clock Mass at St. Michael's in Monticello when she invited him and Polly, though he was alone at the time. As a matter of fact, she had been so surprised to see him at church that for a while she almost convinced herself it was someone else she had spotted on their way out after the liturgy. When he showed up later at the lake with Father Cernac in tow, she was downright flabber-gasted. She had invited them both, of course, but she never in a million years would have expected them to arrive together, aware as she was that Tod had drifted away from his church over the past several years. She was dying to know the story behind it, but just couldn't bring herself to pry. Not directly anyway, and certainly not in front of the priest. She didn't fool herself, of course; she was well aware that her curiosity was often misguided. It was one of her more "regular" sins in her monthly confession. But she was working on it.

She trudged with Tod up the sloping, bright, spring-green lawn to the narrow road that encircled the lake and passed her house, separating it from the parcel of land she owned on the other side where Kenneth had built their two-car garage and workshop. The sheriff had turned his car around earlier and it was now facing the direction from which he had come. He got in on the far side, and Lavina leaned in the open window on the passenger side, her arms heavy on the door.

"I hope this means I'll be seeing more of you and Polly again, Tod," she said. Their drifting apart over the years had been as much her fault as theirs. "It's been a long time since you've been here on a social visit. I enjoyed it, I really did."

"So did I, Lavina." He slid up his adjustable seat and attached the belt across his broad, now un-uniformed chest.

"How about two weeks from today for that rain check?" she suggested.

"Sounds fine to me. I should be free—unless we have another rash of murders, that is."

"God forbid."

"Tell you what, let me have Pol give you a ring during the week and you can arrange things between the two of you, okay?"

"Fine. I'll be waiting for her call."

"But tell that granddaughter of yours that I won't be giving any free swimming tips." With a wide grin, he turned the ignition key.

"The subject won't even come up, I promise," Lavina said, returning the smile and crossing her heart at the same time. She pushed herself back away from the car and waved as it started off down the road. After she stood looking at it for a few moments, she turned and headed back down to her other guests on the lawn.

"Where did you get those culottes?" Winnie asked, reaching out to finger the item in question as Lavina passed behind her at the picnic table. "Not quite your thing, are they?"

"You don't think so?" Lavina said, looking down appreciatively at her bright, turquoise culottes. "I kind of like them myself." And all the more so after Winnie's remark; she made up her mind on the spot to treat herself to another half dozen pairs—at least.

"I never saw them before. When did you get them?"

"After they took Karl Janowitz into custody yesterday evening, I went up to Monticello to unwind. I stopped in Maude's when I saw them in the window. I didn't even bother to try them on. You know, they make me feel ten years younger."

"More like thirty, if you ask me," Winnie said.

The two friends caught each other's eye, held it a moment, then broke out laughing.

"Can you picture me in a pair of those?" Winnie said.

"I think you might be too short, Winnie."

"Too short on thin is what you mean." The comment set them off laughing again, this time with Father Cernac and Sean joining in.

When they settled down, Lavina rejoined them at the table, sitting down alongside the priest.

"Tell me, Lavina—I meant to ask Tod—how did Mr. Janowitz know Leo Frame would keep mum about their plans?"

"He didn't," Winnie said off the top of her head. "He told his stepson."

"Outside of that, I mean."

"Karl Janowitz told Tod that it was Leo's idea from the start," Lavina said. "He's the one who approached Janowitz, not vice versa. Maybe he had other reasons besides Elenice for wanting to keep it all hush-hush, who knows? Janowitz, alert cookie that he is, saw it as a golden opportunity."

"Speaking of opportunities, Lavina," Winnie said, sitting up as straight as she could manage on the backless, wooden bench, "now that I have it, you and Sean mentioned last week when this whole thing began something to the effect that a person couldn't bleed after he was dead, you remember?"

"Oh, oh! Here we go," Sean mumbled under his breath, eyes heavenward.

"Yes," Lavina admitted, looking from the wife to the husband, then back again. "Why?"

"Well, we met a doctor at the hotel down in New York. He was from Virginia or someplace like that . . . lovely man. We got to talking one day in the lobby while I was waiting for Sean here, and I remembered what you said and I asked him about it." Good, ol', ever-trusting Winnie. "And a good thing, too. He said you were probably misinterpreting, meaning, of course, that you had it bass ackwards." She paused and narrowed her eyes as if trying to remember, then went on: "If there is no blood in a wound, that means that death was earlier and by some other means; but there *can* be blood from a wound caused after death, depending on the amount of time that has elapsed.'' The explanation complete, she let out a deep breath, grabbed up her glass and took a deep swallow. It sounded suspiciously to Lavina as though she had memorized the whole thing verbatim.

"Interesting," she said. "I stand corrected then." But I'll double check with Hamilton, thank you, just to be sure when I go for my next checkup, she thought. "And as long as we're on the subject, dear, I should tell you that Dr. Errol found fibers from that bloodstained casket pillow in Leo's nasal passages." Hard as she tried, she just couldn't resist the opportunity to go her friend one better. Another one of her little vices that needed working on. "So he undoubtedly already received the facial injuries before he was smothered."

Winnie played in the little puddle again with the base of her glass. "Maybe," she said without looking up.

"And if Doctors Kildare and Gillespie can put an end to their palavering long enough," Sean said, "maybe we can get to those ribs I keep hearing about."

"Hear, hear!" Father Cernac seconded with a rap of his fist on the tabletop.

"No sooner said than done." Lavina rose from the table to go inside and spotted the blue Tempo pulling into the open garage across the road. She was happy to see that Susanne had young Marty Knappe in tow —had him driving as a matter of fact. Nothing like a healthy young man to make short work of good food.

At the rear door to the house, she looked back over her shoulder to watch the two youngsters, their arms around each other's waists. For a brief moment it was herself she saw there with Kenneth. She smiled and went inside to the kitchen. While she hoped and prayed they would one day be united again, she had to admit she wasn't in all that much of a hurry. For one thing, she wanted to be around for her granddaughter's wedding. And after that, the first great-grandchild. Maybe even more.

As her hands washed the ribs in the sink, her mind was with the wonderful people she watched through the open window in front of her. It gave her a warm feeling to see them enjoying themselves, to know that they were an important part of her life. She was relieved, too, at the thought that the community was safe again. In a way, it was too bad she hadn't thought in time to invite Theresa Francotti. And Annis Barth and her young man from the funeral home. To Lavina nowadays they were all "young" men, no matter what their ages. Well, it was only May and the long summer still lay ahead. Plenty of time for a few more get-togethers.

She bent over to the screen in the window. "Now if one of you young men out there doesn't get that barbecue started, we ain't never gonna get this show on the road."

* * * *